ONE WOMAN AND FOUR OTHERS

Mireya Robles

Translated by Susan Griffin in

collaboration with the author

Order this book online at www.trafford.com
or email orders@trafford.com

Most Trafford titles are also available at major online book retailers.

Note for Librarians: A cataloguing record for this book is available from Library
and Archives Canada at www.collectionscanada.ca/amicus/index-e.html

Printed in Victoria, BC, Canada.

ISBN: 978-1-4269-0995-5 (Soft)

*We at Trafford believe that it is the responsibility of us all, as both individuals
and corporations, to make choices that are environmentally and socially sound.
You, in turn, are supporting this responsible conduct each time you purchase a
Trafford book, or make use of our publishing services. To find out how you are
helping, please visit www.trafford.com/responsiblepublishing.html*

*Our mission is to efficiently provide the world's finest, most comprehensive
book publishing service, enabling every author to experience success.
To find out how to publish your book, your way, and have it available
worldwide, visit us online at www.trafford.com*

Trafford rev. 10/292009

 www.trafford.com

North America & international
toll-free: 1 888 232 4444 (USA & Canada)
phone: 250 383 6864 ♦ fax: 812 355 4082 ♦ email: info@trafford.com

and I came here to talk about when I was very small and they dressed me in my little sailor shirt and little white shorts and it occurred to me to be scared by the fact that I liked shorts more than skirts and that my father, always playing with me, should say, laughing, look, my child, if I win the lottery I will buy you a pair of gold and mother-of-pearl revolvers and the best hammer and the best hooks so that you can catch blowfish and scratch their bellies so that they inflate themselves until they want to burst and we will buy you a horse and you will be the best cowboy of all, better than the ones in the movies, and me thinking that I already have hooks and lots of blowfish that I catch and I already have some revolvers with chambers that turn and I have cartridge belts and holsters and everything, and I'm always doing carpentry with my dad's tools and I like this whole conversation about the lottery because it's like dreaming, but I always get scared when we get to the part about you're going to be the best cowboy, because even if I wanted to, I know that I will never be a cowboy, and if he wins the lottery I'll learn to ride the horse that he buys me, and so many times I imagine myself crossing something like a forest at full speed, and my mom tells the old Arab woman and the old Biscayan woman that I don't like dolls and look how she says it again and again with so much pride as if she were referring to something special about me, about everything that I am and I don't say anything, but the truth is that I do like dolls, but not very many, well, very few, but the girls' games are very boring, and if the babies were real, well, that I really like and it even makes me want to cry and something almost as if I were going to urinate because a baby is something very tender; but I also like to run a lot, really a lot, with my little white shorts and sailor shirt, and if I meet up with some boy that pesters me, I like to beat him with my fists and for me to win and to feel strong and to run a lot until I go home and I worry because I like

1

my shorts so much and a few months ago I wanted to find out and I sat down on the ground without any panties on and I opened my legs and bent my head to look and nobody is going to catch me hidden here behind the bed and I looked for quite a bit and saw nothing surprising but I am going to see what's inside there and I'm open and thinking and I see clearly all the floorboards and there, resting quietly, as if thrown on the ground, is a little silvery nail, and this is it, and I took the little nail and I open myself well up and I start to put it into me to see what would happen because if the little hole becomes bigger I can see better and I'm going to find out about everything that is inside there and now I make a decision and I push the head of the nail with my finger and the nail went in and won't come out, and I want it to come out, and what a fright, the fear in my very heart that is beating so fast, and I get up from my hiding place and put on my panties and I go to the bathroom and I take off my panties and I try to urinate standing up and I try to urinate sitting down and a little stream comes out but the other thing is still there and I'm left with that worry the whole morning, and all midday and now in the afternoon they give me a bath and that thing inside there and me quiet and without speaking with anyone at all, and the fright, and we're all out on the front porch and some are sitting on the green swing and others on the big rocking chair and the small rocking chair and me thinking that when I need to urinate, I'm going to look for the little chamber pot because then I can see if it comes out because on the toilet it will come out and I won't see it, and while I'm thinking all this, a burning down there, all around, that's the little nail and now it is going to come out of me and as I'm about to get off the rawhide chair Raglán comes running up, a dark, dark black, Gwendolina's brother, and they're all Jamaicans and they talk like Jamaicans and Raglán is about fifteen years old and is a grown man and really thin and tall, and Raglán is desperate and he speaks to my mom really quickly, and look, I have to go right now, and my mom, but Raglán, what's wrong, and Raglán, well, to the bathroom, right now, and Raglán was already shouting, I have to go, I have to go! and my mom, go in, son, run, the bathroom, at the end of the hall, and I'm going to protest because I know that the little nail is about to come out and I continue protesting, Mamá, Raglán mustn't go to the bathroom, and my mom, don't be like that, child, we all have the right, and me, but I also have the right because I can't wait any longer, and I went in and I almost couldn't run down the hallway because that thing was starting to hurt me and I pushed the bathroom door open and Raglán was crouching, perched on top of the wooden box that has a hole in the center through which you see the sea, and I grab the blue chamber pot with tiny white spots and I was going to take it out of there, but Raglán gets up and wait, I've already finished, and he leaves the bathroom and I sat down on the chamber pot, and the hot stream, and the pain, and pling, the sound against the metal, and I got up to look to be really certain and there was the little nail and now I do go calmly back to the front porch because the sea breeze is really pleasant although sometimes it brings a stink, and the months pass by and I continue in the same little school belonging to the Calderón sisters, and people always say that the two sisters are very proper and they are elegant, tall, mulatto women, wearing powder, and I don't like the school because it is difficult to be amongst so many people, and the best part is reading time but reading time almost never arrives and when it does, it is always the same, Christ, A, B, C, and they sit us down for ages on these benches that are so long, and I think that the best part is to come to school to find things out, but I already asked the little old woman who is the Calderón sisters' mother, excuse me, what is that large earthenware jar for, the one that's so huge and sits on the patio? and the little old woman says, well, that's for water, and I say, and doesn't the water get dirty? and the little old woman says no, because it's filtered, and I say, what is it filtered with, but I didn't understand the answer because I think the little old woman said with a stone, and I, every afternoon I took myself to the patio to watch the little old woman, but she didn't even move from her wicker rocking chair, and I'm thinking that the bit about the stone is not going to happen, and I think it would be better to go and investigate Fermina, the Chinese woman, she and her husband have a store on the corner, a few houses down from the Calderón sisters, and the other day I go to the store to buy a small notebook and my heart is jumping quite a bit and I want to speak to Fermina, and right now I talk to her and I almost speak and nothing comes out and I want to talk to her because she always wears a hat like the Chinese do and a long robe like the Chinese, and if she would tell about the place where she came from, but Fermina always speaks Chinese with her Chinese husband and her Chinese children and is always distant, as if in another world, and I want Fermina to tell me, but I think that if she were to start talking like me, she would break something, she would break the mystery, and I keep quiet and I point to a small notebook on the shelf and Fermina's husband holds it out to me and I pay him one *real* and I return to the Calderón sisters' house and that afternoon once again Christ, A, B, C, until they dismiss us at three in the afternoon, and I walk along all the sidewalks to my house, thinking that the vacations are on their way and that in this school you can't confirm even that bit about the stone and Fermina is never going to tell me anything about her hometown, and the other little school that I attended before, it was so boring, and thank goodness they took me out of there, but it was because a dog bit me on the bum when Lourdes was taking me to school, and Lourdes told my mom that she thought the dog had rabies and my mom took me in a taxi to Guantánamo and the taxi cost her quite a bit, and we head for the house that's in Calixto García Street and they call the doctor and the doctor looks like a skull, and he looks at my buttock and says that no, no need for injections or anything, that I'll soon be well, but everyone kept on taking care of me, and I liked that, but I hope the dog doesn't bite me again, and they take me to Caimanera again and now I don't know what I'm going to investigate, but I escaped to the salt works because maybe I'll find something there and I climbed another small hill of salt and I'm about to start running down it and I fell and I'm rolling and my thighs are scratched and this definitely burns quite a bit and I decide to return to my house and I don't say anything about the scratches because you can't see them under my skirt and imagine not finding anything in the salt works, but first thing tomorrow I'm going to look for some treasure underneath the houses, because here the houses are on posts sunk in the sea and beneath the houses I'm going to find some treasure and I spend the day watching to see how I could get away, but there's no way and the afternoon arrives and they give me a bath and they powder me, and the cologne, and my white socks, and the blue pique dress that they asked Teresita the embroiderer to embroider, and now with all this on I definitely won't be able to get myself under the house, but it's the best opportunity, now while everyone is on the front porch, good, I can always take care not to get my clothes wet and I pull my skirt up to my waist and I enter the water and I start walking down there and there's nothing but trash and some white balloons that they told me I should never pick up because they're called condoms and are dirty and I start feeling desperate because I can't see any treasure and I bend over to see the bottom better and I forget my skirt and everything gets wet and now I've definitely done it, what a good hiding they're going to give me now, and I get out of there really quickly and I go running across the backyard to the merry-go-round that is really close by and with the *peseta* that I have I can ride four times and now I'm feeling dizzy from going around so many times, but the air is drying my dress and now to run around the wooden street until it has finished drying and now I'm certain no-one will notice, but where could the treasure be and I suspect that it will be in the gap that separates the two houses, the one that is next to the front porch, where I throw the hook to fish for blowfish, and that's where I'm going to go when the tide is low and there isn't anyone around there until one day no-one's around and the tide is out and I throw myself into the gap and I fall on a plank that has a rusty nail sticking out and the nail buries itself in my right leg and I start to bleed out of the wound, but even like that, dripping blood and everything I carry on looking for the treasure but I can't find it and it makes me scared to be here on my own and I start piling up stones so that I can climb up and get out, and now on the front porch, every time someone comes near I put my hands on my leg so that they can't see the wound and I'm going to cure this but I can only find medicine for a sore throat and nose and I apply a little of each one on my own wound and every day I apply the medicine and I had already started to believe that it wasn't going to get better but it started improving, and now mom is talking to her friend about a thing that gives you lock-jaw and which is called tetanus and which is caused by rusty nails and I spend my days touching my jaw to see if it is locking and the worry and fear all the time until listen, Mamá, well, I fell on a rusty nail, the kind that gives you lock-jaw, and she says, but why didn't you say something before, and I say, that, well, it was an unimportant accident, but when I heard you the other day talking about that tetanus business, well, tell me, do you think that my jaw is going to lock? and she examines my wound carefully and well, no, because this has already healed but listen, imagine you not telling me about your fall, and I pretended not to hear and I left there quickly; across the street is

5

Miramar, the restaurant that belongs to the Chinese and they make pies out of puff pastry with guava filling and lemon filling, pineapple and coconut, and everyday I head for their restaurant because I want to learn to speak like Fermina and every day I tell the Chinese to teach me a word and sometimes the Chinese are in the restaurant in their t-shirts and, at the beginning, the Chinese didn't pay any attention to me and I used to tell them that I wanted the owner of the restaurant to teach me to speak Chinese, but that it had to be the owner because surely he's the one who knows best and I say, every day, where is the owner and the Chinese don't tell me, but one day I see this Chinese man who's well dressed and who is not sweating in his t-shirt and I ask him and he says, yes, he is the owner, and I say to him my few words in Chinese that the Chinese wearing t-shirts taught me, and he laughs, and I say that for a long time I have come every day to look for him so that he can teach me and he laughs and says yes, that he will teach me, but at night, after the workers on the base who arrive on the six o'clock launch have eaten, and I say yes, and my mom lets me go across to the restaurant every night, and he teaches me to count and to greet people, and words and words, but one day I went to New Orleans, the restaurant of the other Chinese people, that's about three houses down from where I live and I said the words to them and they didn't understand me because they speak a different class of Chinese and I was left wishing that they would indeed understand me, and they told me that the Chinese from the restaurant across the street sleep in the very same restaurant and I want to investigate whether they sleep on the tables, but I can't find out because at night the Chinese close the restaurant with those corrugated doors that look like those sheets of zinc on the roofs and the back part of the restaurant juts out over the sea and one can't climb it, but right now I'm going to the backyard of the restaurant of the other Chinese people, to see if I can see any beds and find out how the Chinese sleep, and I go from my backyard to the next door backyard and I see this backwoods woman breast-feeding a little girl about a year old and I stay there, watching through the trellis, because it would be great if I were the little girl, and while I'm thinking this, Rafaelito, who's already about four years old, appears, and he starts crying for the teat and the woman puts the little girl on the ground and picks Rafaelito up and it makes me really mad to see him stuck to her breast, and I leave and I cross another backyard, and now I'm in the restaurant's backyard, and the back door is open and the Chinese are seated on the ground, smoking some long reeds like bamboo, and I watch them for quite a long time and now every afternoon I go to spy on the Chinese who always seem to be sleepy, seated on the ground, and the reeds and the smoke, until one day, listen, Mamá, why do the Chinese sit on the ground to smoke reeds? and she asks me, how do I know, and I say, that, well, one day I ended up by mistake in the backyard of the restaurant and she shouts that, if she ever catches me doing that, she is going to beat me, and I say, it was a mistake, and she says, she has ways of finding out and if she found out that I had even gone near the restaurant's backyard, get ready for the hiding I'm going to give you, and I imagined the whole town discovering me spying on the Chinese and afterwards, the hiding, and I didn't go back, and now sometimes I go to speak to the backwoods woman, she's always sitting on a little bench in the backyard and she has light eyes, like hazelnuts and like a statue, and she sits there as if far away and she's always disheveled but in her hair she has some blonde streaks like maize and she tells me to play with Rafaelito and I play with him, but one day I yanked his arm for sucking at her breast, and afterwards I felt sorry for him because I know that Rafaelito doesn't even know that it made me mad seeing him sucking at her breast, and now, I don't know what is happening to me because everyday I head for the house next door, where Emma the Arab lives and I sit myself in a corner, in the wicker chair, and in the beginning I set myself to watch, to see if it is true that the furniture has bugs, but I never saw them on the chair; Emma always wears white dresses, long ones, of linen, and her aunt Flora, who is really old, also wears long dresses and smokes a pipe with a decanter of water and also puts some little coals in a little thing that I think is like a little bronze plate and she also has a little tube in her mouth and the liter of water starts to make bubbles, and aunt Flora greets me in Arabic and I answer her, but that's all I know now, because my mom told me that when I started to speak, I didn't say anything in Spanish, because I started saying some strange things and making sounds that she didn't understand, and she went in a fright to Emma, look, Emma, I think that this child is going to have speech problems because she says everything strangely and no-one understands her, and Emma starts to laugh and explains, no, it isn't a problem, everyday, when you leave her with us for a little while, Flora talks to her in Arabic and she already understands and can say a few words, and my mom all amused and happy that this wasn't anything, and she still tells the story to me and some guests, although I don't know any Arabic anymore, and I come and visit Emma everyday because I really like the shop and the glass counters contain bottles of perfume and scarves and blouses and when it is time for shore leave, she goes out to the wooden street and speaks to the American sailors in English and she brings them to the shop and she shows them the merchandise and one day I was in the shop and an American gave me a coin with the figure of a buffalo on it, and I'm always with Emma, saying how's business, and Emma says, so-so, it's a struggle, but people say that Emma has quite a bit of money hidden in the house, and before, I spoke to Emma more often, but now I sit in the wicker chair and there I am, quietly, quietly, and one day the shop disappears before me and all the counters and the perfume bottles disappear before me and I'm standing at the helm of a small yacht, captaining it, I'm the yacht's captain, and behind me is this woman wearing neither a blouse nor a bra and her breasts begin to grow and grow so that they can store more milk, but Rafaelito isn't allowed to have any, and the woman standing behind the captain and her breasts grow to store the milk, until at times they reach the ground and at other times she throws them over her shoulders like a stole and there I am, every afternoon in the chair, captaining, and the woman standing behind increasing her store, but not for Rafaelito, and one day, a trip to Guantánamo, and my cousin's friends will surely be there, and I want to be really strong and I'm not going to allow this business of being with so many people to frighten me because that thing that my mom talks about has already passed, that since I was born, I've always been stuck to her, and that she couldn't even go to the bathroom without me because I'd start screaming, and afterwards I started to become attached to Mercedes, who was the one who looked after me, but I don't remember her, and when I wasn't even a year old, Mercedes got it into her head to take me out into the street to feed me because I was refusing to eat, and Mercedes who was desperate took me, with food and everything, to the grocery store of a little Spaniard because the store was really close to our house, at the end of the wooden street, and Mercedes went and sat me on the counter and began to speak to the little Spaniard about how impossible I was, and look, Serafín, this child doesn't want to eat, and to demonstrate this to him, she gives me a spoonful of food, and I ate it, and I carried on eating until I finished everything Mercedes fed me, but when Mercedes stopped speaking to Serafín, then I refused to eat, and everyday she had to take me to the store and Mercedes and Serafín had to talk so that I would eat, and I don't remember any of this, because now in that corner of the wooden street there isn't any store, nor have I ever seen that store, but I do remember that long ago, if they didn't tell me stories I used to refuse to eat and to sleep and at midday, a story and at night, another, and my mom would say, I'm already tired of telling stories because I don't know what to invent anymore, and I, I would push my plate away and not sleep at night, and my mom started to tell me the story of a bear in the forest, and later, the same thing, with a bear of another color, and I let it go a few times until one day I threw a tantrum and protested because it was always the same bear and it was boring even if it was a different color, and my mom started to laugh at my tantrum, but child, it's just that I don't know what to do about these stories anymore, until one day Lucas, who's fat and has a mustache and laughs like an idiot, arrived and brought with him a walking stick made of segments that looked like pieces of ox horn, and one piece was a sort of charcoal color, and another piece was a sort of bone color, and I immediately start walking with the stick, and listen, Lucas, what is this walking stick made of? and Lucas says, he doesn't know, and I say, yes he does, that he must tell me what it's made of, and he says, probably of ox horn, and that bit about ox horn seems really boring to me, and no, not that, it has to be made of something else, and you must tell me, and Lucas starts to scratch his head, which is sweating, and to laugh, and he throws out that it's made of shark's spine, and I ask if it is only one shark, and he says, that it's made of hundreds of sharks because each piece comes from a different spine, and then I did get excited because I'm scared of sharks and each time we go fishing in the skiff and my dad throws out the spinner to start fishing while the skiff is running, me, I'm quiet, and I don't speak to anyone because of this fear, and they already told me that if you fall into the sea and the sharks come, that behind them come the dolphins to save you, and that when the sharks see the dolphins, they run away and then the dolphins give you a piggy-back ride to the very shore, without being bitten by one shark, but when I'm in the skiff, even though they tell me that bit about the dolphins, I'm filled with fear and I start praying to the Guardian Angel, because I believe that he is even faster than the dolphins, because I think that when you fall into the sea, the first ones to come are the sharks, and behind them come the dolphins to save you, but if the dolphins swim slowly and they don't have enough time to get there before the sharks start to bite, then they can't carry you on their backs to the very shores of Caimanera, and that's why I know that it's better to pray to the Angel, because in case of danger, he gets there faster than the dolphins, and now I'm going to enjoy myself quite a bit with this walking stick because I have the sharks by the spine and each time I go out for a walk along the wooden street, I take the walking stick, and that's how I get control over all the sharks and now at lunch time they don't have to tell me stories because I place the walking stick beside me, and at bedtime they have to hang the walking stick from one of the cords of the mosquito net so that I can see it from my bed, but before, when I used to sleep in the cot on wheels that my dad made out of wire mesh around a frame, I remember that one night I tried to call my mom, but I didn't know how to say Mamá yet and not being able to say Mamá made me so scared that I wasn't even able to cry, and once I knew how to speak, I told this to my mom and she said to me that it wasn't possible, because no-one can remember things from when they are a baby, but I do remember, and I was already almost not a baby because I wanted to talk and I also remember when I was about two and my dad, playing, asked me if I wanted to go to Guantánamo with him, and I say, of course, and everyone was amazed because I was always so stuck to my mom, even in the bathroom, and now, yes, that yes, I'll go, and my dad was saying to my mom that there weren't going to be any problems, and my mom told him that I was going to throw a tantrum in the train because I always threw tantrums and I started throwing myself about in the living room and rolled as far as the kitchen, and I continued throwing tantrums until I was about five years old, when I'm sitting on the floor screaming away, and my dad, without saying a word, gets up from his chair and gets a jar of iced water from the icebox and pours it over my head, and my mom's shouting, what did you do that for, she'll get pneumonia, and he says, no, you'll see how she gets over her tantrums, and I was cured, but when I was two years old, my dad, as always, the optimist, no, she's not going to throw a tantrum on the train, and I knew that I wasn't going to because I did want to go to Guantánamo with my dad, but on the seat in front of us, on the train, there was a man with a bag of bread, and there was a baguette of bread, and I said I wanted the bread, and my dad said, that bread isn't ours, and I said, I want the bread, I want the bread, and now I am losing my temper, and my dad's embarrassed, and the man with the bread hears all this and without knowing us, he gives me a baguette, and my dad's a little shame-faced, and the man says, not to worry, I know what it's like because I have one just like that at home, and my dad ends up so grateful and so pleased, and I never threw another tantrum during the whole trip, but now that I'm seven years old, I'm going to spend a lot of time in Guantánamo because they're taking me out of the Calderón sisters' little school and now, when classes start they're sending me to the *Colegio Teresiano* and this makes me a little afraid because there are going to be a lot of people but my cousin's been there for one year now and she says that one learns a lot of nice things with the nuns and they have a little baby Jesus in a crib and she's already known how to pray for a while now and she has lots of friends, and I have to be strong so that so many people don't make me scared, and when I go to the nuns I'm not going to see the Chinese anymore and I'm not going to learn anymore words in Chinese, and now I'm in Guantánamo and my cousin tells me that her friends are in the house across the street, and if you want, come, so that you can meet them, and I'm a little frightened but I'm going to meet them and I'm going to be strong, and we're all in the backyard at Inesita's house and the girls talk and talk and I keep quiet, and there's a really pretty girl that they call Nelly and she has olive skin and really black hair and really pretty teeth and everyone is talking and I say nothing, but I'm thinking that in order to marry Nelly, first I have to be big and earn money, but also, but then they all start talking about what they are going to be when they are big and one says that she is going to be a rich woman, and another says that she doesn't know, but that she thinks that the best thing would be to be a mom, and Nelly says that she's only eight years old but that she also thinks that she wants to be a mom, and me all quiet, but then each of them starts to ask me, and you, what are you going to be? and I don't say anything and I don't say anything and I start to feel that I can't breathe, but then Nelly asks and I can breathe even less until I stop and I point to her with my index finger moving my hand perpendicularly, and my voice comes out hoarse: what I want is to grow up and be a man and to marry you, and some of them start to laugh and Nelly started to run and my cousin gets up and really angry: right now I'm going to my house to tell my mom, and when she runs out I follow her, but I cross the street slowly and I feel a kind of exhaustion because I don't know what I'm going to say when they're scolding me, and when I get to the house my cousin had already got her mom out of the bathroom, where she was going to take a bath, and she had told her everything, and now I'm on the porch in the backyard where there are quite a few hanging flowerpots and plants and some flowers and a parakeet and a cement washtub, she looks at me with fear and with an intense desire to scold me and she squints and continues looking at me as if I were something ugly and suddenly, listen to me, that thing that Marianita told me you did, that is something very bad and very ugly, what you did only boys do, and when she said boys I thought that she was going to throw up and it made me very frightened that she would want to vomit because of what I had done, and I try to change all of that, now she is not going to squint anymore nor will she see me as something so ugly and then, listen, Marianita, all I was doing was playing, and that isn't anything because you know well, Marianita, that you told me that you used to play at being dads and boyfriends with Inesita, but Marianita shouted furiously, no, no and no, what you did wasn't that, you even went hoarse when you said that you wanted to marry Nelly, and once more Marianita's mom says with a nauseated expression, and that is a boy thing, and I don't know why it should make me so afraid that she should tell me that it's a boy thing, if in Caimanera I was going to be the chief of a group of boys and I proposed this to the son of Chinese Antonio, who's name is Emilito, and he said yes, that he wanted me to be his chief, and we were going to tell this to Tuto, who is the son of the postman and we were going to tell this to some more boys and then I was going to direct the excavations and the plans to find treasure, and it makes me even more frightened when she says to Marianita, listen, tell the girls that it was just a game, tell them again that it was a game, and Marianita agrees, and then her mom comes over to me and tries to convince me, it was all a game, isn't that so? and a few days later my mom comes to fetch me and I don't know if they are going to tell her about that thing with Nelly and if they do tell her it would make me really scared if it made my mom want to vomit, but the days go by and my mom doesn't say anything, and in the days that I have in Caimanera before classes start, every afternoon I go over to the corner in Emma's shop, and there no-one bothers me and I can be the captain with a white captain's cap; I know how to handle the wheel better than anyone, I sail the sea, and I'm never scared because I know the way and I always turn the wheel where it has to be, here I have never felt alone because the woman is always standing behind me and there are the milk stores, that always start out small and then grow, the woman never speaks to me, but she knows that I am the captain and she admires me because I am at the wheel, I know that her stores are there for me and when my mom calls me for my bath I tell her not yet, Emma laughs and tells her that it's because I like looking after the shop, and no-one knows that I'm captaining the yacht, and I feel sad when I leave the wheel and the sea and the silent woman who stands behind me; the day arrives when I have to go to school and they take me to the train and they ask Víctor, the ticket collector, to keep an eye on me, because Víctor is an older man and very respectable, he married a little late and his wife had twins and one died, I didn't suffer when the twin died because I hardly knew him but I did suffer because the mom was sad and when she walks along the wooden street that is the street in front of our house, she comes up to the swing and speaks to my mom, and my mom says, well, dear, one must just accept, you have to live for your other son and for poor Víctor who is always so sad, and I always stop to listen to see if they say anything about the dead boy because I want to know how people die and what they say before they die, but she never said anything, and I, I want to know this about death, and that's why, when René's little brother died, I went to René's house because they said that they were holding a wake for the boy and he was only months old and I couldn't see him because they already had the little white coffin high up, in a kind of corner unit on the wall, and I wasn't able to see anything, and immediately they told me to leave because my mom might not like it, but that's because they think that I've never seen a dead person, but they don't know that on the little hill that's near here I saw a dead baby, wrapped in bloody cotton, laying on the little hill and I ran away and

I told my mom about it and my mom became sad, and how awful, that must surely be an abortion, and I ask and nobody wants to tell me what an abortion is, and now, with René's little brother, who's a few months or a year old, I want to ask if he died of an abortion, but I don't dare, Lourdes, who washes the dishes and takes me to school, is René's girlfriend, she's sad because of the baby and I ask her why he died and she doesn't tell me, and I don't mention anything about abortion because people get insulted when I say that on the little hill there was a baby that died of abortion and that I saw the cotton full of blood because that's how babies who die of abortion are, but very soon I'm going to find out what children who are going to die say and what they do when they are going to die because my mom told me that Elenita is going to die soon from typhoid, Elenita is already big, about fourteen years old and now she only has a few more days before she dies and my mom told me that if she sees me appear even on the porch of Elenita's house, that I should get ready for a hiding, because typhoid is contagious, and people die from that, like Elenita is going to die; and Elenita and her brothers and sisters and her dad and her mom are really respectable mulatto people like the Calderóns, I play a little with Elenita's sister, who is little like me, but I never play with Elenita, but I'm going to see her before she dies, and I spend all afternoon near the porch of her house until I can no longer see anyone I know on the wooden street, there is no-one on the porch of my house and I run onto the porch of Elenita's house, knock on the door and her mom comes out, and I say, without greeting her or anything, I've come to see Elenita, now we're in the living room and after the living room there is a little room and in the left-hand corner of the little room is Elenita, her mom receives me very well, come, come in, so that you can see Elenita, and I draw nearer and Elenita is seated on a wicker chair and she's wrapped in some very fine blankets and she's really thin and almost as if she couldn't move, and I'm standing before her and I don't know what to say to her because I hardly know her and I'm scared of what they say about typhoid, until finally, listen, Elenita, if you want I'll bring you a packet of candy, and Elenita like this, almost fainting, shakes her head and says no, thank you, but I think that she liked the fact that I wanted to bring her candy, and now it would be better for me to run around and to ride my bike on the wooden street, but I stay thinking that Elenita is going to die and a few days later she died but no-one told me anything until after the funeral and when they told me I thought that, in the long run, I already knew that she was going to die because I saw her wrapped up in blankets and she didn't want even a packet of candy, all this happened a long time ago and already people say that Víctor has learned to accept the death of the twin, and my mom takes me almost to the train rails and the train is ready to leave, and look, Víctor, keep an eye on her for me until she gets to Guantánamo, because Marianita's mom is waiting for her there, and Víctor says yes, of course, and my mom buys me a packet of plantain chips and another with little cookie drops of vanilla and lemon so that I can eat them on the way and when the train pulls away my mom is standing there, and goodbye and goodbye with my hand, and when I can't see her anymore I start crying and continue crying until after Novaliche and then I open the packets and I quite like the chips and the cookie drops, but now I know that I will never again be able to learn Chinese; the first day in the Sisters' school I'm a little frightened, all Marianita's friends are there and they all put on quite a few airs because the one's father is a coffee grower and the other one's father is a doctor and they only ever talk about buying all their clothes at *El Encanto* and *Fin de Siglo* and they are always showing the tags on the clothes so that people can see where they were bought, but my uniform is definitely good because Marianita's mom made it for me with the linen that my mom bought for me, and our uniform for going to school is white and has a brown leather belt and a brown hat with a little brown ribbon hanging down the back of the hat and the uniform for attending mass on Sundays, which is the formal uniform, is made of silk with a wide band of taffeta at the waist that falls to the right and looks like a machete, and the cap is like the one worn by the Canadian sailors, the one that looks like a fried egg but white on the inside with a brown brim, and as my mom says, this business with the nuns costs major but really major money each time the nuns take up a collection, because they take up a collection nearly every day, the Sisters announce the names of the rich girls that have given the most money in class; in first grade we have Sister Elvira who teaches English and has false teeth and Sister Tomasa who is the one who listens to us recite Catechism and on the first day she assigned me a paragraph of sacred history that I have to learn by heart and when I went home I didn't understand what I was reading because the Calderón sisters never did more than Christ, A, B, C, and I had to ask Marianita to read it to me a few times until I learned it but it made me quite frightened because Adam and Eve committed original sin and were exiled from the earthly paradise that was their first abode and I say to Marianita's mom, what's this bit about the abode, and she says, that's like their house, and I say, then exiled must be something like thunder getting inside you because original sin must be very big because it is original, and Carmen, Marianita's mom says, no, exiled means that they have to leave the paradise that is their home, and that it is a very pretty garden and I didn't understand, because it wasn't that Adam and Eve moved, instead they had to go because of everything that was original and the next day Sister Tomasa starts to call on each girl one by one and each girl has to go up to the platform where the Sister's desk is and recite the lesson from memory and when my turn comes my heart is jumping and I feel like I'm asphyxiating but I say everything about the abode and Sister Tomasa is as still as a statue and I had to say to her, that's all, Sister, and the Sister says, very well, next; the Sister I like best is Sister Lupe who is really thin and has a long face and she's olive skinned but a little yellowish and she's Mexican and when she wants us to understand things, she tells us about miracles because these are things that almost aren't going to happen but they do happen and one miracle had to do with the Guardian Angel, that the little girl loved her Guardian Angel very much and the little girl died and not being perfect she couldn't go to heaven and they sent her to purgatory and she said that she was prepared to accept her punishment but that she had never been anywhere without her Guardian Angel and she wasn't going to enter purgatory without him now, and the Guardian Angel liked this quite a bit and said to the little girl, look, child, wait here outside purgatory until I return and the little girl waited for him there because without her angel she wasn't going anywhere and a little while later she saw the angel who was heading her way very cheerfully and he told her that, since he wasn't able to enter purgatory, he had got permission for the little girl to enter heaven and the little girl went up to heaven full of happiness; Carmita has already bought me a book for learning how to read that is called *Upa!* and when I get home from school she teaches me to read and afterwards I practice every night until ten and in a few weeks I am going to learn to read but in the beginning

I suffered a lot with one lesson that said that the rabbit was going to shine his shoes but I already learned by heart what it says beneath the book's drawings and I recite it as if I were reading; everyday at around 10 in the morning, Carmita sends Marianita and I a *bistí*, our name for the beef tea which Toya, the black woman, brings in the thermos and which is the juice from the meat because meat is what prevents anemia which is what Marianita has and they give it to me so that I don't get it; now I am seated at my desk which is at the back where there is a window that looks out onto the patio and in the classroom there is a big girl who must already wear bras because her bodice is all lumpy and she is dark but with blonde kinky hair and very ugly and her name is Fortunata and the girls say that she is really poor but she's really good because she's always quiet and she doesn't bother anyone but when her father, who sells eggs, passes by the school, he always shouts his cry, eggs, eggs, eggs, frrrreeeeeeeesh eeeeeeeeggs, very cheap by the dozen; and the girls start laughing and lift the lid of their desks so that the Sister doesn't see them and they call Fortunata very softly, listen, Fortunata, there goes your dad with his *huevos*, and when Fortunata's dad doesn't go past, the same thing, listen, Fortunata, and where are your dad's eggs? and when the cry is heard, listen, Fortunata, your dad's eggs are already on the sidewalk, and Fortunata keeps quiet because she loves the egg seller and his wife because they were the ones who took her in when she was a baby because her real mom didn't want her and gave her away, and the one who abuses Fortunata most is Sara who is large and fat and is about nine years old and I don't like this abuse until one day, listen, Sara, if you mention the eggs once more to Fortunata, I'm going to beat you up, and I wished that Sara wouldn't mention the eggs again because if she does, I'm going to have to fight her and she's very big, but the next day, the egg seller with his eggs and his cry, and Sara, listen Fortunata, there go your father's eggs and I lift the lid of my desk and duck my head so that Sister won't see me, and listen, Sara, at the ten o'clock break I'll wait for you in the patio, and I lower the lid and I stay really serious for the rest of the class thinking that Sara is very big for me, but at 10, in the patio, I laid into Sara and we punch each other and Marianita sees the size of Sara and comes running to defend me and in one swipe she rips the ribbon from her uniform and punches her so that she falls on her bum and Sara calls her friend and her friend lays into me and the other girls start shouting and the Sisters come running and they get between us until they separate us and when they complained to Carmita I told her about the eggs and she didn't scold me; on June 23, 1942, they give me the little diploma that says that in the first grade I got a B for conduct and an A for application and before that, on March 19th, I took my first communion along with Marianita and our dresses were of fine linen and they sent them to Teresita to have them embroidered; during the vacation in Caimanera I go to fat Vigil's movie house, they say that in the two o'clock show the whores from the Red Light district go to see a movie and I want to know how you recognize whores and I started to ask and a girl who lives on the wooden street told me that you can recognize them because they carry a key in their right hand and wear a little chain on their right ankle and from that day on I started to keep watch from behind the window that looks out onto the front street which is the wooden street and I watched all the women that passed by and I saw two with a key and a little chain and I asked Bodí, who is very dark because she's Raglán's sister and she's the one who washes the dishes now, I asked who is that blonde woman with quite a lot of hair, so thin and a little ugly, kind of wrinkled, and Bodí says, oh, that's Blacamán, she works in Big María's café, she was pretty before but she's started to lose her looks, and I ask, again, who is that really pretty dark woman who also carries a key and wears a chain around her ankle and that often walks along the wooden street, and Bodí says, oh, they call her María Félix and she's the one who does the most business in Big María's café, some man wants to take her away from the Red Light district and set her up on her own, and I don't understand this bit about setting her up and Bodí, who worked as a servant in the Red Light district and knows all the stories, and well, he has his own room and she works for him because he's a pimp; it worries me that the women have to work so much and I ask Bodí what they have to do, and Bodí laughs like a silly girl and she starts walking slowly while she tells me: whores' work, they do whores' work; and I want to see Big María's café and to see what it is that whores do because I know that the Red Light district is behind the white hill but I'm too scared to go because they say it's all really bad but I did go to the matinee and I felt a tickling on my foot and I touched myself and a bug bit my hand and I wanted to scream because it really hurt, but I held back for quite some time because if I scream my mom will haul me out of the cinema and I want to see the movie and when it was over I told my mom, and oh, child, that must surely have been a scorpion bite, and she got quite frightened because she always gets frightened when something happens to me and she took me to the pharmacy that's near the cinema and the pharmacist put arnica on my hand and said that it wouldn't give any more trouble and that's how it turned out, and another day I went with my dad to Vigil's theater but I got scared because it was *The Werewolf* and when the moon came out the man turned into a wolf and I sat on the arm of my dad's chair and when we left he had to carry me on his shoulders and he used to tell me that the werewolf couldn't do anything to me but I saw in the movie that he was really mean and now every night I sleep with a pillow on my back to protect me from the werewolf; what I still really like doing is riding my bike on the wooden street and going at night to the hamburger stand and eating a hamburger or a tiny fried steak sandwich, and the man who has the hamburger stand is Spanish and he cooks delicious hamburgers and he chops the onion very fine and then in tiny pieces and starts frying the hamburger or the small steak and he seasons it all with a liquid that he has already prepared and then he makes the sandwich with water biscuits that have the same dough as really tasty bread and you break them in two and between them goes the hamburger or the small steak and if not, sometimes, at night, which is when mom doesn't cook, we go and buy roast pork because the roast pig stand is near the hamburger stand and they roast the piglet on a revolving spit and the skin gets all crisp and delicious and we almost always buy ribs and we go and eat them at the swing and if you want, nearby there is a place where they make milk shakes that I like to drink more than anything else because they're made with mango or papaya or sapote or *níspero* or anona and so many other things that I don't know what to ask for and they have a glass counter with chocolate bars and chocolate kisses but that I definitely can't have because one day I started to expel some little green jelly beans and my mom thought that Francisca, the black girl from Emma the Arab's house was giving me gum drops and she scolded her and Francisca says, no way, I don't give her anything to eat without permission, and when the green jelly beans kept coming the doctor in Santiago de Cuba, which is where Mamá took me, said that it was my liver and my mom had to apologize to

Francisca who has a bum that sticks out and short hair like little raisins and everyone says that under her bum she has a huge tail; because of my liver I have to drink hepatic salts which Santiaga gives to me because otherwise I won't drink them because she's the one who always comes to bless me with basil and to pray when I'm sick and also she massages my stomach when I have indigestion and once when she massaged my stomach she said that what I had was indigestion from water and when she gives me the salty drink, my head moves all by itself and a neighing like a horse comes out of me and then I have to lie down on my right side which is where my liver is and now I like Santiaga more than Emma the Arab because Santiaga comes every afternoon and she sits on the swing and talks to my mom and I think she loves me, she's Biscayan and is a little old lady who holds herself erect and she seems really serious but she's really nice and sometimes we go for a walk, Santiaga, my mom and I, to the El Deseo salt works and they say that once they were grinding salt and a man fell into the machinery and if I ever see salt a little pink I'll know it's the man who was ground up, when we're resting at El Deseo, my mom sees a gadget near us and, what could that be for, Santiaga? and Santiaga shrugs her shoulders because she doesn't know and I do know and I tell her, that, well, it's a pluviometer which is a device for measuring rainfall, and my mom gets really proud, and I know to say pluviometer because I saw the drawing in the dictionary but I liked it when they told me that I'm intelligent; Santiaga's husband is called Andrés and he's also Biscayan and he's quite short and has a nose like a tomato, round and really red because they say he's always drunk but he walks quite straight and without reeling and I never hear him talk and I want to know why he doesn't talk and my mom tells me that he does talk to my dad and I want to know what Andrés talks about because when I greet him he moves his head a little but never says anything and with such a big moustache he looks really serious and I want to know what Andrés does and my mom tells me that he's a fisherman and he goes out in the boat to fish with the casting nets which I really like because they're really big nets and they have weights all along the edges and the fishermen cast them into the sea and when they pull them out the fish are in the nets and I want to know if Andrés fishes with lobster pots because my father knows how to fish with lobster pots which are little wire cages that you throw into the sea and they trap the fish and I don't remember whether we caught lobsters with them the night we went fishing with my dad but he lit up the sea with some really powerful lights that we brought in the boat and when we were going to catch crabs we had to catch them carefully with our hands so that they wouldn't bite because their teeth are like pincers, the crabs are big with a grey shell and they throw them in sacks like the ones that the coal comes in and when we take the crabs home my dad cleans them with a brush and takes out this ugly thing that they have inside them and he boils them in order to make crab stew which is absolutely delicious, you cook it with tomato, onion, garlic, olive oil, olives and beer and with the stew we drink some beers with Coca Cola and it's the best meal; they told me that many years ago Andrés used to go to Boquerón in his boat to sell things to the merchant ships and Emma used to go along to sell to the ships, but now they are not allowed to go because only those who have permission can go; this Summer my mom met Isabel who lives in the Maison Bernard which looks like a Swiss chalet and she's married to an American who has an important job at the base and she has two children and one is very blonde with almost white hair and is really adorable and is called Billy and is three years old and often we go to El Cayo to swim with Isabel and her two children and some people laugh at Isabel because sometimes she disappears into another world with her mouth open but she's always reading and she knows a lot and she speaks English and French and German and also Italian and she's very tall and I want to know things the way Isabel knows and every day I draw pictures so that Isabel can tell me in English how you say house and dog and inkwell and bell and other things and I write the names in English on the drawings; and one day I'm sitting on the swing with my mom and people start telling us the news, excuse me, did you know that Maggie died last night? and my mom, is that so, and how did that happen? and every time someone goes past they tell us the news and now a woman with a big stomach tells us that Maggie died of a heart attack, and everyone says, and now what will become of Cristina, and I want to know everything about the death, and I know that Maggie owns the café that's in the next block and my mom tells me that Maggie took Cristina in when she was very little and she's about fifteen now, and the old mulatto woman, the one who has attacks of epilepsy, walks along the street and says, all excited and waving her arms in the air, it's at four, the funeral is at four o'clock and the announcer of the radio station that's next door and which isn't a real radio station because it only has a microphone with loudspeakers and the announcer is always reciting, you will pass through my life without knowing you've done so, you will pass silently through my love, and as you go by I will feign a smile and it always ends with you will never know it, and the announcer was also a boxer and works on the base and now he's here, next to the swing, saying that the funeral is this afternoon at four, and as soon as my mom goes inside to stir the beans and to check on all the lunch which is already on the stove, I immediately head for the next block to walk past the café and I look inside and I can't see anything, and I remember when Maggie, who was really fat, with rolls and everything, and who had a perm and was American with light hair, was always behind the counter at the bar and my mom used to tell me to be careful not to so much as stick my nose into the café and every chance I got I walked past there during liberty and the café was full of American sailors and I always suspected that the women with the little chains were hidden in all corners of the café and one day in the morning there was a man in the bar arranging bottles and I lent in at the door and I told him that I'd come to see the café and the man told me very angrily that there is nothing to see here and that little girls aren't allowed in the café and I had to leave; today I already know that my mom isn't going to the funeral and I spend all day watching the clock and a little before four I head for the café and the hearse pulled by horses is already in front of the door, and they definitely had to bring it from Guantánamo because in Caimanera there aren't any hearses nor funeral parlors, and I'm watching everything and some men open the back of the hearse and other men bring the coffin out through the door of the café and they put it in the hearse and Cristina leaves the café behind the coffin and she's crying like I've never seen anyone cry before because she's weeping so loudly and with such loneliness and I start to cry too because I know that Cristina is with her mom for the last time and now who's going to look after her, and she's such a beautiful girl, tall, with long, straight, light brown hair and eyes like honey, the people hold her because she has her arms stretched out towards the coffin and all she says through her sobs is, Mamá, I'm all alone, I'm so alone, the hearse starts moving and the people stay behind, holding Cristina and I head home with a sadness that I had never felt before and I know that this is something I am never going to forget; now in second grade they've put me on the top floor and each time a group of girls climbs the stairs, Sacred Heart of Jesus in You I trust, which is what you have to say on the landing as you pass the picture that's on the wall, for second grade I got Sister Venancia who's always furious and I don't understand what she says because her lips are all sunken as if she were eating them; one of the girls who sometimes comes to talk to me asked me if I know how babies are made, and I say, yes, I know because at home they've already told me the bit about the stork, and she starts to laugh and, look, you're so big and so stupid because babies are made when the man sticks his weenie in the woman's wee-wee and before she can have babies the woman has to start having her period, which is when she bleeds through her wee-wee every month, and what the man does to the woman is called this, and she told me a word so ugly that I never want to hear it again and I tell her that she's a liar, and she says, and what you are is a silly fool and what I told you, you can ask anyone about because it's true, and when I see her so sure I get really scared and I already suffered enough when a girl told me that Santa Claus and the Three Kings are our moms and dads and I didn't say anything at home because I thought it was bad to know that, but one day Marianita said it, we've known for months about the Kings, and we weren't scolded, and now I don't know if they'll scold me but I'm going to tell Carmita and as soon as I get home I make up my mind and, listen, Carmita, I have to ask you something but I don't want you to get cross with me, and Carmita says, well, why should I get cross with you? and I, just promise me, and Carmita, well, I won't get cross, and I say, I, well a girl told me that women have a period which means bleeding through their wee-wee every month and this happens before having babies and I want to know if men have a period every month before having children, and if not, when do they have it; we're both seated at the table where Carmita makes her sewing patterns and her eyes are lowered as if staring at the table, until, well, I won't get cross with you because I promised, but never ever mention these things again, you'll know all about them when you're big, and I say, but if no-one ever tells me, how will I know when I'm big, and Carmita raised an eyebrow and made a long-suffering face, and, well, these are things for adults, and I knew she wasn't going to talk about that anymore; on June 21, 1943, my little diploma, a B for conduct and a B for application and immediately it's Summer in Caimanera and I don't want war to come to the base and maybe it won't come because I never go to bed without praying for the war to end because otherwise the Japanese and the Germans are going to appear here, on the wooden street and they've already said that there was a German submarine near, but really near the base and they also said that Errol Flynn was on his yacht at the base and everyone in Caimanera can only talk about Errol Flynn's yacht and I spend all my time on the swing waiting for Errol Flynn because if he comes along the wooden street I'm already here and I'll see him, and one night I'm sitting on the swing and here comes a group of Americans in civilian clothes and they all go into Emma's shop and I'm looking really carefully at all of them and there is one who has a very handsome face and that one must be Errol Flynn and I want to talk and the jumping of my heart won't let me but I look at him a lot and I stand in front of him until he says hello and I say hello to him but very quietly because I can't breathe and I want to ask him if he is Errol Flynn but my breathlessness won't let my voice come out and before I can ask anything, they all leave; now every afternoon I sit on the swing, but the little room where Emma's shop was, Emma has rented it out to the harbor pilots and they have an office there and Emma's shop is now in Emma's living room, she lives alone with Francisca because Flora died, and the pilots are always talking about the merchant ships that come to Boquerón and there's a tall mulatto man whose face is really elegant and really handsome and really friendly and who's always on the office's little porch and me on my porch and I really like talking to him because when he was young he was a telegraphist on a merchant ship and he traveled the whole world, and I mean the whole world and when he says that there is no country like Brazil he gets really cute dimples in his face and I like how he smokes and I tell him that I also want to be a telegraphist and the next day he brought me a little apparatus to practice telegraphy and now he shows me Morse Code and we spend the afternoons wrapped up in the emotion of transmissions but sometimes I don't get a lesson because my mom and I go to Santiaga's house and what I like best is the huge tree that's planted in front of the house and has a wonderful smell, like linen sheets kept in a trunk and each time I go there I get very close to the tree and nobody knows that I love it so and the leaves are green and have a white edge and sometimes I take a leaf with me and it keeps me company, Santiaga's house is white, wooden and really, really clean and next to her house there are two more houses that belong to her and across the street there are some little houses that also belong to her and which are wooden, yellow, and are on posts sunk in the sea and next to Santiaga's houses is the church and Santiaga has the key to the church and sometimes she lets us go in when no-one's there, I like the church a lot because it has a really pretty Virgin Mary whom I think is the Miraculous Virgin but there's a strong smell of staleness in the church and people say that it's the smell of bat and when I go to church I pray that bats won't come; last year Marianita and I had a private tutor who taught us at home all of third grade so that we could skip from second to fourth grade and now I have Sister Virginia who is oh-so fat and very scary because she's always furious and she has toad eyes and you can clearly see her beard stubble and she's Mexican but she's not nice like Sister Lupe and when she walks she lurches and now I'm on the first floor again and I want the nun to talk about baby Jesus and the Guardian Angel, like the miracle that Sister Lupe told, but the miracle that Sister Virginia tells is a little frightening because it's about a girl who is very good and almost perfect and who wanted to see her soul but the angels didn't want to show it to her but she kept asking them to show it to her and the angels said to her, well, look, this afternoon you'll see it pass through your house and the girl spent the afternoon waiting and the only thing she saw was a leprous woman with her whole body rotten and with pieces of herself falling off and the girl was very frightened but she asked the woman who she was and the woman said to her: I've come here for you to see me, I'm your soul; and I got frightened too because with all the bad words I say, the woman who is my soul must be really ugly; Sister Virginia always begins the hour of religion with how life is like a little stick being carried by the water and I see how my life is like the little stick being carried by the water and I want to reach the little stick and to save it from the river's current but the river carries it away in whirlpools, and after the bit about the little stick, Sister Virginia talks about hell where there are enormous cauldrons with boiling oil and slicing machines through which they send everyone who is in hell every day and as the machines have oh-so many blades, the bodies come out in slices and I hear all of this until one day I get up enough courage and I ask her if there are little girls in hell and she tells me that I can be certain of this, that quite a few girls go to hell; when the nun talks about the devils neither Marianita nor I can sleep at night because devils live forever in the fire but they also go everywhere and now, at night, I look carefully to see if there is anything under the big bed where Marianita and I sleep because one of the little devils could get into the room and hide in a corner; apart from religion we also have calligraphy which consists of drawing vertical lines without pause and circles without pause until you form a tunnel with the circles so that we can produce the letter like the nuns write it which is the Palmer Method and we follow this method until June 26, 1944 when they give me the little diploma which has on the bottom the name M. Aurora Calvillo who is the Mother Superior and who is Mexican and white like milk and almost pretty but she never talks to the girls because she is the Mother Superior, her office is at the entrance, to the right and then you get to the hallway where you'll find the painting of Christ's face which was imprinted on Veronica's cloth and they say that if you look at it some time the eyes move and even the face and I look at it quite a bit but it never moves; the diploma says that I got an A for conduct and an A+ for application and in the upper middle part there is a photo of Santa Teresita de Jesús and on the other diplomas there was a shield that said homeland, God, family and then, in the lower middle part, a globe of the world, a lyre, a book, an artist's palette with paint brushes and everything, three roses and a sign that says education, teaching; now I'm in Caimanera and every Saturday a little Sister of Charity called Sister Virtudes comes here and she's from the San José shelter in Guantánamo and the shelter is for children and old people and ever since I was very small we went to the shelter on Three Kings day and we took toys that my dad made because he can do carpentry and he made little tables and little rocking chairs and other things and they also bought toys a few at a time during the year and my mom kept making clothes and we took it all on January 6th and my mom knows a lot of nuns but especially Sister Virtudes and Sister Pilar who are really nice and come to Caimanera to take up the Saturday collection because wages are paid at the base on Friday and the two of them always have lunch at my house and one day Sister Virtudes came by herself because

Sister Pilar was transferred to another town and Sister Virtudes is quite old but she's always happy and laughing and she eats all the chicken and rice that my mom makes for her and she drinks Hatuey beer and eats the crème caramel with crystallized sugar and toasted meringue on top, we close the door and she takes off her black clothes because they make her very warm and she rests a little and talks quite a lot and laughs until, well, now it's time to do my round through the Red Light district, and my mom, dear Lord, Sister Virtudes, aren't you scared to go there? and she says, no, dear, there are some women there who grew up in the shelter, because what can a poor woman do? marry, become a nun, or become a prostitute, you, who always asks me, but Sister Virtudes, how is it possible that such a happy person as yourself became a nun? well look, I wasn't destined for marriage and I know that I could never have been a prostitute, so here you have me, a nun, and don't worry about me in the Red Light district, nothing has happened to me nor will happen to me, just think of it, when I arrive, the girls are waiting for me and they go with me to all the cafes to take up the collection and sometimes it pains me to see there the little girls I watched grow, but when I say to them, oh, girls, if you could only get out of here, at the same time I wonder where they could go; and my mom, thank goodness the Americans have set up the prophylaxis center because otherwise, these poor women would rot to death, and I ask, what's the prophylaxis center, and my mom, who sometimes tells me to shush when I ask questions during adult conversations, this time she explained, it's like a medical center where a doctor examines and gives injections to the prostitutes so that they don't get sick and the Americans pay for everything because they don't want the American sailors to get sick and all the prostitutes have to register at the prophylaxis center, and my mom keeps talking, and tell me, Sister Virtudes, do you know Angeles? she's a woman of about sixty and she must have been a beautiful woman, because she's still good-looking and elegant, and Sister Virtudes says, no, I don't know her, and my mom says, well she was a prostitute for many years, but she arranged things so that she was fairly independent and she saved her money and now she has her own business, I think it's a little shop, well, Angeles sometimes stops by and she tells me about her life, that she's got a daughter that she educated in Havana in the best schools and who went to college and everything and is married to a doctor and is doing fantastically, she's always lived in Havana and never found out that her mother was a prostitute and Angeles is happy knowing that her daughter is unaware and far removed from everything that she's been through but sometimes it frightens her to think that someone might tell her and when she tells me that, I always tell her, don't worry Angeles, if she hasn't found out so far, why should she find out now? and Angeles goes off feeling reassured; Santiaga continues to visit nearly every afternoon and she tells us that Cristina is living in one of her little yellow houses with one of the Guitián brothers, who is the one who pays the rent, you know the Guitiáns, right? the loan sharks that have come from who knows where although some say that they are from Havana, the thing is that they lend money at very high interest and on Fridays they go to collect from the workers from the base the money they were lent, and you should see them waiting on the wharf like vultures for the launches, they even use revolvers and everything and with them it's really true that nobody ever manages to get free because they charge such exorbitant interest; Santiaga explains all this because she also lends money because when Mamá needs any she asks Santiaga for it and afterwards she has to pay her interest each week when she pays her two or three pesos or whatever she can manage, but Santiaga says that the Guitiáns are real abusers and that the one who's with Cristina is the fattest and ugliest brother, the one who has the face of a murderer because the other one, who is the boss, is tall, thin, good-looking and speaks very softly, as if he didn't carry a gun; and my mom, but oh, Santiaga, how has that girl got involved with a man like that, and Santiaga, well, at least she's taken care of and she's crazy about him, and he says that he doesn't intend to get married, but he seems very much in love to me and he doesn't go out with anyone else but her and, despite what he says, you'll see that as soon as Cristina starts to give birth he'll marry her, and that's how it was; Santiaga has two daughters but when she speaks about one of them she always says my daughter María who was brought up in good schools outside Caimanera and who married a rich man and lives in Spain, and when she speaks of the other one, who is the eldest, she only says Norberta, not my daughter or anything; they left Norberta ignorant without going to school and the people say that when she was thirteen they married her off to a lout of a man who even used to hit her, Norberta lives in Boquerón with her fisherman husband; sometimes Santiaga comes all happy to speak to my mom, and look, a letter from my daughter María, would you read it for me? and Santiaga is really happy while my mom reads the letter to her and afterwards they go to the living room where there is a round table and Santiaga dictates a letter to my mom to be sent to María because Santiaga can't read or write, and in the living room in Santiaga's house are the photos of María who is a very beautiful woman, and of Santiaga's grandson with a very lovely, but truly lovely face, and once months went by with no letter from María and my mom wrote the letters that Santiaga dictated, and nothing, until finally her grandson answered saying that his mother was a little tired and had put him in charge of writing, and my mom found out in Guantánamo through some relations of María's husband that María died and Santiaga doesn't know, and now, when she has a letter she isn't quite so happy because it's from her grandson and she wishes it were from María, and sometimes she's really worried when she comes and she talks as if she were talking to herself, I think there's something wrong with María and they don't want to tell me, and my mom doesn't tell her anything either because María is the only person that Santiaga loves in the world, because she doesn't love either Andrés or Norberta like that, and it makes me sad to hear Santiaga dictating letters for María but I'm also glad that she isn't suffering; now I hardly ever see Emma, but one day she arrives at the swing all worried and speaks to my mom, and listen, I have a problem and the doctor prescribes medicines for me and nothing, and it seems that she's afraid to speak of this until, finally, you know, I have a tapeworm, and my mom, oh, Emma, that's not a problem, look, drink a glass full of grated coconut and grated green papaya and you'll see how you get rid of it, and Emma says, yes, do you think so? and my mom says, drink what I tell you and you'll have reason to think of me, and the next day Emma's there again, and look, what you told me is true, I discharged a tapeworm so long that I thought it was never going to end, I don't know how that animal fitted inside me, but you know something? I looked carefully and I saw that I didn't expel the head and if the head stays inside the tapeworm starts growing again, and my mom, well, Emma, then drink another glass of the same thing, the grated coconut and the grated green papaya, and Emma pulls a doubtful face and goes off with her long linen dress and her slow step so different from everyone else's, and the next day she comes by all happy, well yes, I've expelled everything, but everything, the head too, and my mom, happy to be right, you see, Emma, I told you that the coconut and papaya are extraordinary, but really extraordinary; and already the end of Summer and already it's September and the nuns and the fifth grade with Sister Lupe and now I buy more holy cards than ever that are sold by Sister Angela in a tiny little room full of medals and holy cards which are a protection for the person that buys them and soon we are going to write prayers and petitions on a tiny piece of paper and the nuns are going to put them on a very big iron plate and they are going to burn them and then God will receive all this and will grant it and what we're going to ask for is for the war to end soon and for this, in addition to writing the prayers on the tiny pieces of paper, we have to pray many more prayers; towards the end of fifth grade, my mom comes one day to Guantánamo and brings me news, your dad is out of work and next year you won't be able to continue in the Teresiano School; in August, in Caimanera, the conga makes its way along the wooden street: pin, pin, falls Berlin, pan, pan, falls Japan, and later, in *Bohemia*, the shadow that remained on a bridge like a decal, stuck there by the atomic bomb and the photos of Mussolini hanging in the main square like the beef carcasses one sees in butcheries; and the news still splashed around the town that Santiaga had been guilty of the death of Emma the Arab which occurred a few months back when Santiaga recommended some medicines to her which, when mixed with others that Emma was taking, poisoned her blood and everyone comments that bruises started appearing all over her body and within a few days she died and people still console Santiaga because the poisoning of Emma was unintentional; already in Guantánamo, I start sixth grade in Eloísa's little school to prepare me for the high school entrance exam; the table, the long benches, Eloísa with her nickname of Little Colonel, her mother, old Tulita invariably in a bad mood, walking to the rhythm of her stick and one enormous platform shoe that she lets fall to the ground with heavy beats, Eloísa's sister, so gently wrinkled, Pepe, the nephew, whom they call the son of no-one, and the spoiled, silent cat, are becoming a custom with me; now, at eleven years old, sometimes I feel like I'm in a round, circular, cylindrical, transparent prison, from which I can see everything without being able to touch it and I begin to imagine myself in the skin of everyone else; of the man who passes by me and seems so happy and I follow him and my gaze fixes on the back of his neck and I make myself smoke and I enter through there and I make myself comfortable in his body and I think about the children I have, because July 20th is Luisín's birthday and how pretty the linen dress looks on my wife, and next month, when they pay me what I'm owed, we'll take a little trip to Havana; but I can't stay too long, so much time, all the time, because always, suddenly, I'm walking behind the man and his family and the trip to Havana and the coins that he carries in his pocket are no longer mine and I return with my fear to this skin that never abandons me, and sometimes I enter a woman with long hair who walks along the wooden street, but I never put myself in her clothes nor the skin of her hand that clutches her purse; one morning like any other, blood in my pajamas, I go to Carmita's bed so that she can see the stains, oh, you're already having your period, come, you have to put on a menstruation belt, and she prepares a cotton pad wrapped in gauze, and an elastic band that you wear at hip height and, for the front and back, a small padded piece of cloth hanging from the elastic, and in the padded cloths, the safety pins pinned to the gauze and Carmita gives it all to me and I put on the sanitary napkin myself; this Summer I'm staying in Guantánamo studying with Tutú, who works in the Institute's offices and is a teacher at the American School, and every day I go with Inesita who is also going to take the entrance exam in September and during our daily eight-block walk, I discover happiness at her side; from the first day, Tutú told us to call him Mr. Pérez because if you call him Tutú, he wasn't going to answer, and that's how it was; the long table like the one at the Last Supper with benches along the sides and I always try to sit next to Inesita and if she sits down first, then, come, here's space, here, next to me; every afternoon, Tutú at the head asking things that sometimes I know and I'm not brave enough to answer, until one day, tell me, which is the only immobile and voluntary muscle? Tutú asks everyone and no one knows and me with palpitations because that one I do know, and when he asks me, I say, almost breathless, that it's the bladder, and he says, what? and I say, the bladder, and Tutú resigns himself to not answering himself and says reluctantly, yes, that's what it is, and I'm glad to have answered because not even Inesita who knows so much, well, not even she could answer; the days pass between my dream of having a career and the guilt that I feel because my mom has to work so hard embroidering pajamas and scarves with pictures of huts and palm trees so that old Pack, the black American, can sell them on the base, and the rooms in the house that she has had to rent out in order to pay the rent, and my father, collapsed on a bed reading *Carteles* and *Bohemia*, and my mom explains to me, your dad's immediate boss, Croughton, wanted to give your dad's job to someone else and they tricked him, an American asked your dad to take a pound of butter off the base and your dad wanted to do him the favor, because how many people are there who take a carton of cigarettes or some ice-cream or butter, and the soldiers that do the checks at the exit from the base turn a blind eye and at the most, they confiscate the things, but they accused your dad of smuggling and immediately black-balled him and laid him off and that's why he can't make up his mind to go to Miami, because who's going to recommend him and if he reached the position of inspector general of hydroelectric plants it's because he was an exemplary employee, in the twenty years that he worked there he never missed a day, even if he was ill he went to work; and I remember how you used to go, Papá, how you often used to walk smoking your pipe, heading for the wharf to take the launch and arrive at the base for the six p.m. shift, the midnight shift, and I was left with a little admiration and a little melancholy because I wasn't going to see you until next morning, or until the afternoon, and I imagined you crossing the salt water of the sea while the jukebox across the street played Oh, Johnny, Oh, Johnny, and the rest I didn't understand and not understanding frustrated me and I contented myself playing on the wooden floor with the Coca Cola tops, making plans for the next whirr-whirr noise-makers that were going to spin crazily between my hands, buzzing, pierced by strings; a few days after the lay-off some girls from the Teresiano School surrounded me in Martí Park and one said, my dad is a doctor, and yours, what does your dad do? and the other said, my dad is a coffee grower, and yours, what does your dad do? and they looked at one another and they laughed and weeks later I'm sitting on the doorstep of the door in Carmita's house, in Crombet Street, and the group goes by and I want to call each one by her name, but none of them stops, they start to laugh without looking at me and they take off at a run; then I began to feel the transparent cylindrical prison from which I see the open space and an exuberant vegetation like that of paradise, to see but not to touch, to see but not to be part of because the glass prison is always there, with thick glass from which I cannot escape and, at other times, when I am seated on the rocking chair in Caimanera, horrible satin ribbons begin to surround me, some of an intense violet color and others of a mustard yellow color, the ribbons multiply and form a thick wall that undulates around me, slithering like snakes; today is Saturday and I'm at Inesita's house, in a room that looks out onto the backyard, she's lying on a wide bed, made of iron, painted green, I'm sitting beside her and we're speaking in low voices and she closes her eyes and stays like that, with her eyes closed, and I move closer to her until I kiss her on the mouth and I feel a profound shudder, a melancholic happiness, and in a little while Inesita looks at me with an oh-so coquettish smile, and, listen, that kiss left me!... and one night on the hall of Carmita's patio, Inesita's sitting on a chair and I'm standing and she looks at me and I lean down and I kiss her on the mouth and when we drew apart Carmita was already coming along the hall and I think she saw us through the window with the grille, and almost at once, and what are you two doing here all alone? come on, let's go to the living room; and Inesita and I are left with a strange uneasiness; September 7th of 1946 I passed the entrance exam and I intend to enroll in the Institute because the enrollment there is free, but my mom, oh no, none of that, you're going to the American School, and a feeling of gratitude and guilt are born in me for the monthly fee of 27 pesos that will come out of my mom's embroidery; and already the enrolment in the American School and every weekend I go to Caimanera and bring back scarves to embroider in Guantánamo, but I still can't alleviate the guilt that separates me from that little girl: no, not Rafaelito, and my dress that will dry on the merry-go-round, do you love me, Mamá? do you love me more than anyone? and there are the milk stores, yes, Mamá, a pluviometer and today I didn't find any treasure but perhaps in the salt works, running around the wooden street and later, the bicycle, all the bears are the same bear, Mamá, and in the crib I couldn't call you because I still wasn't able to speak and in the afternoon I'm captaining, you love me more than anyone, don't you, Mamá? only me? and my mom smiles silently and says well, I love you but I love other people too, but that's true, you more than anyone, and my terror is lifted from me because my mom does love me and when I ride my bike I hear it very clearly, you more than anyone and when I spin the whir-whir noise-maker, you more than anyone and that's a pluviometer, Mamá; and already the Caimanera house with its posts stuck in the water, has ceased being mine and my mom's and my dad's because in one room there are two engineers who work for Snare and in another room are Clarín and Teyo and Clarín thinks I'm a genius because when she mentioned the paralyzed son of the Martínez family I told her that he was a vegetable and even more, an inanimate being and Clarín was amazed with the bit about inanimate and I'm thinking no big deal, I learned the word from a movie and that's not being a genius, and Teyo is fat, fat but really fat and he spends his day ordering Clarín around: Clarín, bring me some water, Clarín, take the glass, Clarín, I want ice, Clarín, find me that photo that we took in Bayamo three years ago, and Clarín walks meekly on the boards in the house and, yes, my love, yes, my love, and sometimes Clarín tells me how much Teyo needs her, because just imagine, Teyo doesn't like to pee or do number two in the toilet, he does everything in the chamber pot and every minute I need to be cleaning the chamber pot because Teyo doesn't like for there to be not even one drop of urine left and when he has to go I lower his trousers and his underpants and I seat him on the chamber pot and when he's finished, I wipe his bum; and Clarín always repeats, moved, that Teyo likes her to clean him; Inesita has become cautious and she almost doesn't come near me even though when we are going out with Marianita, she tells me in secret that if I don't go, she won't go, and that is sufficient, and if we're in a group I hardly talk even though Inesita is there, but when we're alone, Inesita and I, then we talk and she calls me my love and no-one's ever called me my love and now I belong to someone and one night Carmita goes with me to Inesita's house and is talking in the living room with Inesita's mom and Inesita gets an idea, come, let's go talk in the backyard, and we sit there without switching on the lights and we hug and we carry on hugging one another until we hear the steps and Carmita's voice, come on, let's go, it's really dark here, and to hide what she was thinking, she starts with Inesita's mom, almost laughing, look, Matilde, what things occur to these girls, to play like that in the dark? and I reach the living room walking in silence, and Carmita, oh, child, what's the matter with you, don't you feel well? but look at this, Matilde, her face is all fallen, and she inspects me all over, and walks around me, and soon, but look at this, you have a damp patch on the back of your skirt, you must have sat in something wet, not so? and I nod in agreement without looking at her and I walk to the door, and when we arrive at the house Carmita already has a serious expression and I go straight to my room, because now Marianita has her room and I have mine, and now with my pajamas on and now the intimacy of the mosquito netting and still feeling so close to Inesita, until I gave myself to her in the empty vastness of the bed; sometimes the nuns appear to me like transparent visions, the shadows of the headdresses forming their figures on the wall, moving in a quadrangular procession, me, in the center and the regression begins and I'm in fifth grade and the fleeting image of the math teacher appears with his mystery and his odd habits, but teaching well, always teaching well and then comes Sister Elvira with her false teeth, with her ground up English and her near goodness and the two of them disappear in a whirlwind and Sister Lupe remains, seated serenely before me while I make notes on a piece of paper, and no, the note is wrong and I throw the piece of paper and Sister Lupe fills with a dry wisdom and she points to me, things that are useful should not be thrown away like that, you should have thrown away only the part of the piece of paper that is no longer useful and remember what I'm going to tell you, the day will come when you will wish for a piece of paper and won't have any, and I keep quiet, in the rain of fear that comes from her mouth; I'm in fourth grade, in line, waiting for the sound of the castanet to enter the classroom and Josephine Fenton, who is skinny and Jamaican and taller than me, starts playing with me and starts tickling me and I laugh in the line, which is an unforgivable crime and Sister Virginia asks me with her customary fury why I'm laughing and I don't say anything and she takes me into the classroom on my own and I continue to say nothing and she starts pulling the elastic of my brown hat and tugs and tugs and now I'm choking and Sister Virginia gives one more pull and the hat elastic snaps and she's left with it in her hands and she throws it on my desk and the castanet clacks quickly and in one minute the classroom was full of girls; I'm in second grade, in the classroom on the upper floor and Sister Venancia says something to me and I didn't understand because I never understand her with her soft voice and her sunken lips but I hear her, go on, go on, don't stand there, go to first grade and deliver my message and I go down to the first grade classroom and after asking permission, Sister Lupe lets me come in and look, Sister, Sister Venancia says that you should send her all the first grade girls, that she wants to see them, and Sister Lupe, through her surprise, well, well, if that's what she wants, that's what I'll do, and I go up to the second grade classroom again, and Sister Venancia, where is what I was sent to get, and me, they'll bring them soon, and almost at once, the voices in chorus, Sacred Heart of Jesus in You I trust, and already the first grade girls are piled up in the door and Sister Venancia goes up to them in a bad mood and, what do you want? what are you doing here? and the big girl who had brought them, well, Sister, I've brought you all of them, as you requested, and Sister Venancia looks at me as though she's about to throw me out the window, and, what kind of message did you relay? what I sent you to ask for was the basket of embroidery, I'll go myself to look for it, and she leaves like a clap of thunder and the first grade girls go downstairs once more, Sacred Heart of Jesus in You I trust, and I start to feel embarrassed because only idiots don't understand but later my embarrassment leaves me because who told Sister Venancia to speak so softly and so quickly with her sunken lips, and when I saw her appear I thought that she was going to scold me but she began teaching embroidery and she didn't argue any more; learning embroidery isn't bad, but I don't like to embroider the whole tablecloth that you always have to embroider for the end of year and Agustina who's a border and is already very big with a bust in her bodice and everything and has a pointy face like a mango and is a friend of mine, always embroiders the tablecloth for me and I do her math homework; I'm in first grade and Sister Lupe sets us to doing exercises using the Palmer Method, vertical lines and circles to form a tunnel and most important of all is that you make the lines continuous without lifting your arm and now I've got it all well, but well done and Sister Lupe stops by each desk to give a grade and I get ahead of her and give myself a big zero so that Sister Lupe will tell me: no, you don't deserve a zero because you did very well, and when she's standing in front of my desk I get palpitations because she's going to say, you did very well, but Sister Lupe keeps looking at the zero all annoyed and, well, if you've graded your work, I don't have to grade it, and she moved on, and I never again gave myself a zero in anything, and now I'm at the First

Communion breakfast and I can't even try the hot chocolate that I like so much because that's what my mom told me and Carmita told me the same thing, chocolate, no, but I eat the sponge fingers because I like them quite a lot even though I kept wanting the chocolate, and now I'm at El Cayo and I'm scared of the rays and the eels that get tangled up with the posts and of the skates that hide in the mud, and now I'm in the train that leaves Caimanera when the vacations and the weekends are over and when the train pulls out I start to cry and I carry on crying until Novaliche because I miss my mom, and later, the plantain chips and the lemon cookie drops which are really tiny, well-toasted cookies with a lemon flavor, and at Carmita's house I can't look for treasure but I listen to the episodes of *Tarzan*, and of *Los tres Villalobos*, and of *Tamacún, The Wandering Avenger* and of *Spirit* or I sit in front of the portrait of my grandfather that Carmita has in her room and I didn't get to meet him because he died before my mom married my dad, because he had tuberculosis, and he was from Andalucia with a face that was really golden brown and really good-looking and he liked to get drunk in the Café La Bombilla with anis that my grandmother called *caramanchel* instead of *carabanchel* and one day my grandfather rode his horse into a store and they were going to put him in prison but they didn't take him away and I always imagine myself in that store with the pink dress that looks really good on me with my white shoes and white socks and my grandfather arrives with the force of his horse and everyone else goes weak and I'm the witness that he is a hero and then he leaves his horse and he takes me for a ride in Rufo's carriage that has a really thin and thoughtful horse because he's thinking that he's really hungry and my grandfather collects his dogs and invites them to go for a ride with us in the carriage and we go, he and I with the dogs to ride around the town and when we pass by La Bombilla we don't stop because my grandfather doesn't want any more anis and when Carmita hears my grandmother talk about that drunk, your grandfather, she always scolds her and says that the girls don't need to know the family secrets and that's why I hide in the room with my grandmother and she tells me that she was born in Arbuñó which Carmita calls Albuñol and that my grandfather was born in Gualchos and that my grandfather had a twin and she doesn't know if, when they were engaged, if it was my grandfather who came to court her or if he sometimes sent his twin and that later they went on their honeymoon and that there they didn't make toilet paper and they always used to clean themselves with clods of earth and later Carmita was born in Málaga and when she was little they brought her by boat to this very Cuba and my mother was born when they were already in Cuba; when my dad left the base I used to sit and imagine that he was going to go to Miami and there he was going to work and he would send for us and that, in Miami, the sun was like gold stuck in the air and this light so yellow obsessed me, and Mamá, let's go to Miami, we have to go to Miami, and my mom, well, yes, your dad is thinking about it, we'll see, we'll see, and one day my mom tells me the news, your dad has decided to go to Havana, he's leaving next week and there he's going to get his passport and if everything works out well, he will travel to Miami because Isabel and her husband are there and her husband promised to help him if he decided to go, so we'll wait and see, and the days pass and my mom buys him a suit for traveling and packs his suitcases and he takes a boat to Santiago to catch the train to Havana and I say almost nothing so that no-one interrupts my dream of the yellow light, and my mom, on the swing, with all those who stop to chat, well, my husband is in Havana, yes, handling some business, and it seems likely that from there he'll go on to Miami because we're thinking about moving there, well, no, we haven't heard anything yet, so he's probably already in Miami, well, he left two weeks ago but all those tasks, his passport, the paperwork, his visa, everything, everything takes time, so we'll see, we'll see; and I hardly breathe because I don't want anyone to take away my yellow light, but one morning, Mamá, it's been three weeks and not even a letter, do you think he's already working in Miami and he's going to send for us? and my mom, well, we'll see, we'll see, and that afternoon we're in the living room and the door to the street is open and my dad appears as happy as can be, with an enormous sack on his back, like those for coal, and I quickly think that he went to Miami, found work, he bought us so many things that they don't even fit in his case and that we'll soon go to Miami with good clothes and good shoes because mine have had a hole in the sole for quite some time, although they've ordered me some through the Sears catalogue and I'm waiting for them because with these shoes, if it rains, with the hole in the sole my foot gets wet, and I'm going to love the shoes I'll be getting from Sears because they're casual the way I like them and when they arrive I won't use the ones with the hole anymore, but if there are other shoes in the sack, I'll take them to Miami; and my mom is so pleased to see him, well, tell me, did you get your passport? did they give you a visa? have you already been to Miami? have you already spoken to Isabel's husband? and he says, well, no, no, I still don't have my passport, they were taking so long I decided to come back and I arranged to have them send it to me; and I feel the smallness of Caimanera fall on me and I return to the round prison that immobilizes me, as if I have to stand, locked into the enormous transparent cylinder; I approach the sack and my dad understands my movement and oh, these are some sweet potatoes that I bought in Santiago because they were cheap, and I'm thinking that what are we going to do with a sack of sweet potatoes, and I return again to my silence and I know now that Miami won't happen; my dad gets jobs selling insurance policies, working as Ship's Chandler, as the manager of a supply store and everything always ends in failure; one night, in the Guantánamo living room, I think, like so many times before, of Inesita, I'm falling into a kind of nostalgia, into that melancholy that her absence causes in me and suddenly I see her appear through the door way, and now so close to me, and she looks at me with a gentleness that's almost happy and she speaks to me with a voice of invitation, let's go and talk on the veranda that looks onto the patio? we sit down alone, without putting on the light, and Inesita's hand guides my hand to her thighs, I feel the contact of her skin on my fingers that slowly caress it, the emotion begins to carry us, forgetting everything that surrounds us, and suddenly, Carmita, so pale, before us, but what are you doing, what are you up to here? let's go, let's go, Inesita, you'd better leave, it's already late and I'm sure your mom is waiting for you, and when Inesita leaves without looking at me, Carmita turns to me, I have to tell your mom what's been going on; I remain seated on the veranda with this weakness, with all this coldness; a few days later my mom arrives and after some time with Carmita, she calls me and, look, tell Inesita that she should never again, and I mean never again, come to collect you to walk to school together, and I don't answer, and the next day when Inesita comes to collect me, look, Inesita, don't come by anymore to walk to school together, we walk for the last time in silence and that day at school, we hardly spoke; during my years in high school, each night I go into Carmita's room and from there I can see Inesita's house, some piece of furniture, a bit of wall, the ceiling lamp, but her, Inesita, I hardly ever see; the months pass and they allow me sporadic excursions to the theater with Inesita when the town considers itself visited by Culture with the child conductor who is presented as Ferruccio Burco, and Fata Morgana with her quick changes of clothes and Evita Muñoz and Tito Guízar and Andrés Segovia so indignant over the noise of the cars in the street which, combined with the comments of the audience, excited by his presence, drowned the notes of his guitar and from time to time he stops playing and, if there is not absolute silence I won't play, and the audience obeyed with great difficulty and would keep quiet, and Berta Singerman and the Vienna Boys' Choir and when the Chilean Choral Society came, Inesita and I sat in the balcony and when the lights go out Roberto comes with his red hair and almost transparent skin, he comes with his rosy complexion and he sits next to Inesita and he puts his arm around her and he stays like that while I concentrate on not feeling anguish, and now they put on the lights and Roberto leaves and while he walks away I try to imagine the marks that the operations they did on his bones have left on his legs, while I intuit what his daily chores must be like with his four retarded brothers which the town attributes to the concentrated defects of his parents who are first cousins, of the six brothers only two have been saved from defects; the return home becomes awful among conversations that try to be trivial until, Inesita, are you Roberto's girlfriend? and she says, yes, I already said yes to him; and one more question because getting to know reality is the same as controlling reality, tell me, do you kiss? and she says, no, not that, and I hardly ever see him but he gave me this little change purse which his aunt brought him from Europe, and I see the change purse opening and closing like a star to reveal and hide coins; in the days that follow I feel isolated from everything, as if deeply asleep within myself; the lethargy gives way to sadness and Carmita starts commenting to her friends that I hardly ever laugh, and sometimes she expands her comments, she's a sad girl, I don't know how she can be so serious at thirteen, and every day more closed up; at other times she speaks to me, you have to do your bit and be sociable; I remain in my silence with my eyes searching the night, looking for any trace of Inesita or locked in my room writing poems to her: I never sensed that it would be the weeping/ the last indication of your look/ with which you turned my soul into a graveyard/ where only tears will remain // I know it's unfair to love you/ with the mad passion that until today has been/ only a dream, a love in Spring/ and a support for the days I have existed// you turned my spirit into a tomb/ where lies the love you buried/ placing indifference in place of a rose/ and by way of an epitaph you left my pleas; and I always write these concentrations of sadness that I save in my notebooks, and one day I go to Inesita's house and when we're alone I give her the folded paper and, look, I wrote this for you, and she puts it away carefully so that no-one sees it and we separate and I never found out if she read it; in my wide bed I feel her scent and her breath and her mouth and her breasts so tiny and my mouth exploring her body and I'm hers in that lonely expanse; now I keep having a recurring dream, out of my brain and through one of my temples comes an umbilical cord and I see Inesita who comes floating through the air, almost made of air, and she takes her place at my side, parallel to me, with me lying on the bed, towards the edge, and she lies on air, off the bed, floating at my side, and the umbilical cord that comes out of my temple, goes into the empty hole that Inesita has in one of her temples until the cord fills the hole and we stay like that, sealed together for always, the dream follows me when I'm awake and one day, in Inesita's house, you know, Inesita, that I have a dream that won't go away, an umbilical cord comes out of my temple, and she interrupts me, yes, I know, it comes out of your brain and enters mine, here, here, and she describes everything exactly and at my surprise, she smiled enigmatically and said nothing more; in the December vacation, again the train, Novaliche, Caimanera, the wooden street, and in the living room in my house, piles of crocodile purses, piles of perfume, and my mom explains, Violeta and Dionisio sent all this merchandise for your dad to sell, you remember them, right? they're the ones who had the little stall with necklaces and other trinkets and they set it up every day on the wharf at the time the launches would arrive, and then they used to come every afternoon to eat here because they were very badly, I mean very badly off; and I say, of course I remember them, Violeta was an attractive woman, full of mystery, and Dionisio was a being lost in silence; I always wanted to know more about them, but I only found out that they were European Jews that came here fleeing from the Nazis during the war and they spent some time on that wharf, with their mobile trinket stall; every afternoon they ate in my house and my mom happy to be able to help them because no-one should want for a plate of food; now they live in Havana and they have a store which sells leather articles and perfumes; they're doing well there, that's what my mom is telling me, that they're doing very well there, and now they want your dad to sell merchandise for them here; and suddenly it hurts me to hear all this because Violeta and Dionisio were beings that lived in my imagination, how many times I tried to decipher them when I saw them behind their traveling trinkets, and now this merchandise so carefully arranged on the floor, awaiting another failure from my father and the fantasy that I lived with Violeta and Dionisio will become something else when they are converted into two more creditors like those others that knock on the door, but I don't say anything so as not to destroy my mom's hope when I hear her say, everything will go well, your dad is hard-working, in all the years he worked on the base he was a responsible man who, even with a fever of forty, went to work, and as far as Dionisio and Violeta are concerned, well, we helped them quite a bit, because your dad may be whatever he is, but he's generous, like no-one else, because I know how many people used to come here when he was working and if, at that moment, we didn't have a plate of food, he would take whomever it was to the restaurant across the road, Miguel González's, and while he could, he didn't allow any needy person who came to him go hungry and sometimes he didn't even have any money and in spite of that he used to take them to the restaurant or to the café and because he had credit with them, he would pay the bill the Friday he got paid on the base; when I hear all this I recognize my dad from when I was little, but I continue thinking that this new intent will lead him to another failure, and that's how it was; my mom keeps talking with that compassion that sometimes she shows him, he's a man with a good heart because he sacrificed himself taking care of Andrés until just recently, you know that Andrés died of cancer, don't you? and I say no, that I didn't know that, and she, well yes, Andrés died all rotten, I don't know if he had cancer of the intestines but he voided himself in the bed and with a stench that nobody could stand and every day your dad went to clean him and to help Santiaga with Andrés because when push came to shove, nobody appeared in Santiaga's house to confront this terrible thing, and until the end it was dreadful, because he spent days in agony and there was no way for the spirit to finally detach itself, until I made up my mind and I spoke to Santiaga, listen, Santiaga, I know that you're very catholic, but I've heard it said of cases like this one, when the spirit can't let go of matter, and Tinita, the spiritualist, has prayed for them and with Tinita's prayers their agony has ended, because Andrés has been in agony for days and days and he can't manage to die in peace; and can you believe that Santiaga agreed, and as it turns out, I spoke to Tinita and she went there to pray for him, well listen, I don't know if it could have been coincidence or what, but that same afternoon Andrés died and the one who dressed him and took charge of the whole rigmarole of the funeral was your dad; and I ask, and now, Mamá, Santiaga lives alone? and my mom says, no, Santiaga lives with Norberta, because you know that Norberta was widowed a few years ago and lived alone in Boquerón, but now Santiaga asked her to come and live with her and Norberta's there; my mom is quiet as if remembering, and suddenly, look, I don't know whether to tell you something that Santiaga told me, because she had never told anyone before, but I know that you wouldn't tell anyone; I feel close to my mom in that tone of intimacy, and I say, no, I wouldn't tell anyone, and she says, well it has to do with Norberta and Andrés, it's such an incredible story that it's like one of those novels from last century, it turns out that when Andrés died, Santiaga told me, look, I want to tell you something that I haven't told anyone, it has to do with Norberta, and I told her, well, Santiaga, in town it has always been said that Norberta isn't your and Andrés's legitimate daughter, but it must be unpleasant for you to talk about that, so it would be best to leave it alone, and Santiaga says, no, no, it's not that, it's that Norberta is Andrés's daughter, but she's not my daughter, let me explain, I was a servant to a family of aristocrats in Spain, and Andrés was the family's coachman, and as life would have it, the daughter of the owners of the house became pregnant by Andrés and when the little girl, who is Norberta, was born, the family gave us money, a lot of money so that Andrés and I could get married and adopt the baby girl, but with the condition that we leave Spain, and that was how we came to Cuba, and that was how I was able to buy those little houses that I have, and if it hadn't been for all this, I never would have married Andrés; February 8, 1948, Ernesto Milá, who is with me in high school, comes and says, look, he's in love, do I want to be his girlfriend, and I don't really want to be his girlfriend and anyway, Ernesto, even though he doesn't have any money yet, spends his life playing the part of the future heir to the Yateras' farms, and talks about his grandfather's cattle and says that his father is going to be the mayor some day and then, just imagine, you'll be the girlfriend of the mayor's son; and if only I could fall in love with Ernesto and shake off all this loneliness, and I decide to be his girlfriend and he's as pleased as anything, and for Ernesto, being my boyfriend means kissing me until my mouth goes numb and I acquiesce to try and accustom myself but I don't get used to it; if Ernesto and I could only talk, but no conversation is possible, because everything's about how one day I'll be the mayor's son and you'll be the girlfriend of the mayor's son, and one day I'll inherit all the Yateras' livestock; I should like Ernesto, with his blue eyes and his wavy brown hair and his pretty face, above all, his mouth and his teeth; one day we went to the Actualidades cinema without Carmita's permission, and Ernesto, at once, his arm behind me, and kissing me, and I submit although actually what I really want to do is see the movie, but the night passes without me being able to see anything of *National Velvet*; I keep waiting to see if I will fall in love and still nothing, and during the Summer I'm in Caimanera and Ernesto is coming this weekend because my mom allows me to have Ernesto come and visit, and she says that she knows that we're boyfriend and girlfriend and that it is best for us to see each other here at home and not out there somewhere, but I haven't said anything to Carmita because Carmita is obsessed with the family honor and says that if she even sees me speaking to a boy one day, that she will immediately send me to Caimanera in case I end up with a round tummy and she doesn't want any responsibilities and anyway, honor is everything, and during the week I can't go out and when I do go out I have to be at home by nine p.m. and on Sunday I have to be there by 10 p.m. while the Martí Park band plays the national anthem and when the musicians with their faded uniforms play the first notes of join the combat *bayameses* as the Motherland looks on with pride, everyone stops and puts their hand over their heart and Marianita and I start running to get to Carmita's house, if possible, before to die for our country is to live and definitely before to arms, brave soldiers, run, and as Carmita lives half a block from the park, we always arrive on time, although sometimes, when one of the patriots with his hand on his heart sees us running, and starts shouting, the anthem, more respect for the anthem, and we keep running so as not to have to listen to Carmita go on about honor because once I arrived at ten past ten and Carmita began to cry because arriving at ten past ten is to stain the family honor and that night she kept touching my stomach as she does when she thinks I've lost this virginity that I still carry around with me, and Carmita, from one sigh to the next, tries to guard the family honor because if something happens to you, you know, if you stain the family honor, right away I'll send you to your mother, and above all, don't do anything that has them talking about you because if people say that you're loose, you might as well be; and I always have to be very careful because if Carmita sends me to my mom in Caimanera I can't study anymore; on Friday Ernesto arrives in Caimanera with a briefcase and a very serious face, look, I was going to visit every day during the weekend, tomorrow, Saturday, and also Sunday, but they're having a stock breeders' meeting and as my grandfather can't go, I'm going in his place, the meeting is in Santiago, and can you see this briefcase here? well, there are thousands of pesos in it because we're going to make deals that run into thousands, but thousands of pesos and all this I have to do on behalf of my grandfather; and I know that even if Ernesto were thirty instead of sixteen, his grandfather wouldn't entrust the simplest transaction to him; what I do know is that it is Carnival in Santiago and Ernesto is off to party through the streets, and it makes me enormously happy to be free this weekend, and when it is time for the boat to leave, I say goodbye with thankfulness, and well, I hope everything goes well for you in the stock breeders' meeting, and I'm relieved because the Carnival lasts a week and if Ernesto returns exhausted from so much partying, most probably he'll need to rest and won't need to bother me for a few days after his return; the months pass and I'm still not in love and now it's September and I can't take this any more, until look, Ernesto, this can't go on, and Ernesto insists on those explanations that the girlfriend traditionally has to give when she breaks off the engagement, and if it's the boyfriend who breaks it off he doesn't have to give any explanation because, by disappearing, the romance is considered over; Ernesto continues insisting on knowing why I want to break up, and I have nothing to say, until he says, well, that's fine, and he leaves with his hands in his pockets, assuming the role of wounded man, maybe even proud of the drama that he's playing out; a few days later he started going out with a girl who looks like a little hornet and who luckily isn't in the same school with us because the imaginary love triangles and unnecessary jealousy would have been awkward; I ask myself what Inesita must have thought of this relationship, because we never spoke of it and I ask myself if Inesita will have intuited that with boyfriend and everything, I never stop being hers in the lonely narrowness; I carry on wandering through this third year and the months accentuate my silence; I start thinking that I'd like to study astronomy or medicine, and Carmita says, no, what would really suit you is to be an architect, and I think that I won't know how to do the house plans and when they're finished they will collapse in on themselves from the center of the roof and I always see them falling until they become dust, and each time that Carmita says anything about being an architect I think about the collapse and look, Carmita, better not, let it not be architecture, and at other times I think that worrying about the career I'm going to study for in Havana is a type of dreaming, because how are they going to send me to study? now they've offered my dad a business, they've given him a general store to administer and little by little he'll buy shares until he's bought all of them and he becomes the owner of the store because there are various shareholders who own the store and who want to sell it and my mom is excited because outside the store is a gas pump and my dad also overseas the pump and also, with that huge fire that there was in Caimanera, that burnt even the market square and the main general stores, imagine, your dad's store has to be a good venture until they rebuild the square and all the other stores and, when they've built all that, your dad will already have customers who will keep buying their groceries from him, and I'll tell you the truth, what I'd like to do is to work in the store with your dad because if I'm in the business and take charge of the cash register, I know we'll improve our lot but he's against me working in the store and he won't even allow me to set foot inside, he's forbidden me to go there and I even have to buy groceries in one of the few little stores that are still standing after the fire; I'm happy that, at least for a while, my mom is excited, until one day I go to Caimanera and my mother's miserable, the minute I get off the train her complaint starts, your father lost the store, he wasn't taking care of it and he was spending the money on women; a little later in Guantánamo, I'm seated on the rocking chair in the hall, my dad arrives and I don't even move from the rocking chair nor do I look at him and he, for the first time, draws up a chair and sits down in front of me to talk to me, as if to give me an explanation, you know what's happened? and I shake my head to say no, and he says, well, I lost the store, and I was really lucky because I could have gone to jail and I sit in silence thinking that this man that I have before me has no right to eat the plate of beans, nor the rice, nor the meat, nor the soup, nor the potatoes of so many lunches and so many dinners that arrive at the table through my mom's sacrifice, and the pain caused by this chasm between us, begins to invade me; third year marches on with my preoccupation of not being able to study in Havana, because I sometimes feel that my life carries with it a destiny and I must be in Havana to meet it, but there's also all that's imposed, that which is still hanging, still to be resolved, the knowledge that I don't want to spend my life in this solitude, and during my nights in an empty bed, sometimes Inesita appears suddenly; at one of those dances that happen without a warning at the Union Club of Guantánamo, Carlos Barceló with his sharp nose and his Fred Astaire feet comes up to me and I allow myself to be carried off by his rhythm until he imposes a claustrophobic proximity that has me spending the rest of the night trying not to feel his hardness between my thighs until I'm saved by Carmita with it's getting late already and we have to go; we go down the stairs, cross the park in the night air and we're already in Crombet Street, between Pedro A. Pérez Street and Martí Street and the furniture store on the corner and the door to the Hotel Venus, known in town as the door of sin, because they say that the hotel, which is above the furniture store, is a house of rendezvous although I've never seen any woman entering through the narrow and half-open door which allows a view of the stairs, and now already, in Carmita's house, and the respite of not feeling Carlos imposing his hardness; in the weeks that follow, Carlos multiplies on street corners, I have to see you, I have to speak to you, and his repetitive insistence, I'm in love, I want you to be my girlfriend and the demand that I explain to him why I don't want to be his girlfriend; days of insistence and harassment follow until I tell myself that perhaps with Carlos I will get used to it and I became the girlfriend of this son of a shoe store owner; on Sunday nights, the park and the open-air concert and the pairs circling and circling, and the men standing, ringing the ambulatory circle of women that stroll in bunches, arm in arm, and as they circle and circle, the men's flirtatious remarks reach them, what killer eyes, have mercy, you're slaying me; bye, pretty; hey, don't give yourself such airs; oh, mama, you're so hot; or, if not, they begin whistling and panting and they fall into a sexual trance; when I see Carlos I have nothing to say to him and he comments on my silence, sometimes without knowing what to do with it, and at others, reciting Neruda, I like you when you're quiet because it's as if you're absent; I'm no longer interested in going to dances with him because he ignores the music and concentrates on trying to pierce me with his hardness and when I went to the América movie house with such anticipation to see *For Whom the Bell Tolls*, Carlos appeared to try and impose his sexual entertainment and I was only able to see, from time to time, the faces of Gary Cooper and Ingrid Bergman; at each meeting, Carlos becomes a limpet without a voice or feet, only his way of latching onto me and my boredom that ends with look, Carlos, this can't go on, nothing, it's not because of anything, it's that I can't carry on, and in my fifteen years of life the transparent cylinder, that I wish to break with my death, continues, but suicide is difficult in this town and I've known that since I was thirteen and I wrote a letter to Carmita, I don't want anyone to cry for me or to suffer, because if I've committed suicide it's because that's what I chose to do, and the letter folded in the pocket of my uniform shirt, and in the pharmacy on the corner I tell the person who dispenses to give me a vial of potassium permanganate and if it comes in capsules, even better, and he says, well, wait a moment, I can't sell you that, and he disappears into the back and returns with the owner of the pharmacy who is fat and tall with a pink face and who asks me why I want it, and I say, I don't know, that Carmita sent me, and he says, unless Carmita comes to collect it herself, that he can't sell it, and I insist that Carmita said that, even if only a small dose, and he says, unless it's to Carmita herself, that no; I go to other pharmacy and the same thing happens, unless it's to Carmita herself, then no, and I head home clutching in my hand the money that I had collected to buy the permanganate and in my pocket, the letter that I will never give to Carmita; in the chest of drawers in her room there's a revolver that

Carmita told me belonged to my grandfather and I tell myself that I have to get bullets but two years have passed already and still no bullets and when I want to die, I lock myself in Carmita's room and take out the revolver and I stand in front of the mirror and place the mouth of the revolver on my right temple and I squeeze the trigger several times, click, click, click, and always I tell myself, if this had contained bullets, everything would have ended by now and I am calmed by the possibility that everything could be over; in the Agriculture course, in the fourth year of high school, the professor, a country man with the title of Doctor of Pedagogy, whom we called *el sijú*, the little owl, insisting that we learn to distinguish the different classes of earth, squeezing them, looking at them closely, even takes us into the countryside, to a farm and shows us the implements of agriculture and from time to time he bends to gather up a fist-full of earth and gives a lecture on each handful; I feel especially close to Inesita and the country and nature and this waiting that so silently I feel in me; we've come in several cars and upon our return, Inesita gets into the backseat of the professor's jeep with me at her side, cornered near the window, and, as if it were of no importance, I rest my left arm on the back of Inesita's seat and I start to caress her and she moves her arm a little, making space for my hand, while *el sijú* speaks between each bounce and bounce of the jeep; the next day, at school, we treat each other with a distance that wiped out in a moment our closeness of the day before; months later, a trip with the school to Uvero beach, we leave at daybreak in an open truck and we travel all seated on the bed of the truck, Inesita, absent today; for me this is a magic journey that takes me away from this house and this town, I'm still a little sleepy and I allow myself to feel part of the morning, to be, a little, the freshness through which I travel, to dissolve myself in space, to be space itself, and now on the beach I choose my patch of sand from where the images unravel: the vision of the sea, the principle of the school in culottes, like an English huntress directing, with dignity, a safari in the heart of Africa, with her red hair, her blue eyes, her soft and definitively authoritarian English, the sea between headlands of rock, I follow with my gaze the space that becomes distance as if I wished to enter it, to confuse myself with the sea, to leave forever this shore, time flows gently, I stay seated hugging my legs around the knees and suddenly, Marcia running quickly in front of me, and her happiness and her laughter and behind her, Saúl, the Polish Jew; they're throwing sand at each other and they laugh and Marcia's happiness makes me anxious, perhaps because, if the sand Saúl throws touches my skin, I could also laugh, I have stopped confusing myself with the sea because life could be here, on the shore, and it could be mine if I were to touch it; I enter the skin of the laughter and I catch Saúl's happiness with his teddy bear walk, his black, curly hair, his brown eyes, his small mouth, his teeth so even and that kind of pride that he knows how to wear; in the open truck, on the way back, Marcia sings a song repeating over and over, he's my man, he's my man, and in the tune of the wild Parisian tango I intuit her passion; now back home, I write a love letter to Saúl that I save carefully in my wallet having no intention of sending it to him, and on Sunday in the park, circling and circling in the inner oval, and with each turn, the vision of Saúl, standing there, until he comes up to me and speaks to me and I become almost drowsy when he accuses me of indifference, and why do I hardly even answer him, and, when the national anthem begins, before I start running, I give him the letter and I declare, if I were indifferent, I wouldn't have written to you like this; the next day, Saúl, as if delirious, because no-one's ever written him a love letter, and from now on we're together whenever possible and we study together at Carmita's house and she keeps a close eye on us and each day we write each other letters and when I turned sixteen he wrote me a poem and brought me a bottle of perfume; sometimes I ask myself if I entered Marciass's skin and I felt myself run in the sand with her feet and I laughed with her laughter and I fell in love with Saúl through her eyes, and when I worry because we're from different religions, Saúl assures me that it isn't a problem, because by my converting to Judaism everything will be resolved and he tells me that, during the wedding, we'll throw two wine glasses onto the floor to be stepped on and they shatter into shards that symbolize that our marriage cannot be dissolved until all the little pieces once again unite; sometimes I dream about the ceremony with the broken wine glasses and about a little boy that we have who always wears little, black velvet shorts and a white silk shirt and who is already two years old and who walks all over the place and wants to grab things and with me behind him; now every weekend I go to Caimanera so that Saúl can visit me; one day, while seated on the floor in Carmita's house, escaping the heat through the coolth of the mosaics, I'm suddenly invaded by an anguish for Inesita and Saúl disappears along with the ceremony of the broken glasses; that afternoon I go to the Church of Santa Catalina in Martí Park to the *salve*, the prayer with which one petitions the Virgin Mary, and I pray at length and with such anguish and I try to make the little boy with the little velvet shorts appear, but he doesn't come; now, at the end of my fourth year, I'm in Caimanera for the Summer Vacation, Saúl visits daily and suddenly he's gone and my worry and uncertainty until Marianita brings me a message, that Saúl broke an arm playing ball and that Jenny, who lives near Saúl, told her that at night Saúl would wake up shouting my name and that Saúl's parents were alarmed by this and that they would never permit him to marry me because if it isn't to a Jewish girl, they aren't going to allow him to marry; I go to Guantánamo to see Saúl and his sister is on the veranda, polite, come in, come in, and as if to mollify me, my parents are in the remnant store and they never close before six; I enter this house that is so spacious, into this vastness, and on the left, a bedroom, Saúl in his pajamas, with his arm in a cast and complaining about the pain, I stay with him a little while, a little nervous because I'm afraid that his oh-so serious parents will arrive, especially his father who never laughs, we arrange to see each other as soon as possible; once again in Caimanera, the weeks pass, Saúl doesn't come and I send him a letter with Marianita and a few days later he appears with the news that he is coming to say goodbye because he's going to study in Chicago; that night my mother tries to comfort me but she doesn't know that my sobs aren't for Saúl, but for this shattered hope; now in fifth year, my mother's promises, even if I have to make sacrifices, I'm sending you to study, bring me the almost certainty of being able to go to Havana where I might be reborn; one day a classmate says, yesterday I got a letter from Saúl, he's as happy as can be in the United States, and then he looks at me, he asked about you in the letter; it's time to resolve this situation between Saúl and I through some form of communication, so that this doesn't end up as a deep cut, like something hanging, inconclusive, and I ask him, seeing as Saúl asked about me, can you give me his address? and he says, yes, with pleasure; now in my room I try to write a letter that doesn't sound like me begging or demanding and all I can produce is a weak pretext for writing to him, since they'd told me he was asking about me, and that I thought he'd forgotten about me and that maybe it was better like that, and I waited hoping that he would write me anything at all that would establish a dialog, a means to understand one another, but his letter never arrived; in the December vacation, here's Saúl, marching around Guantánamo park where you can still see the statue of Periquito Pérez, Santa Catalina Church, the benches, and the people walking in circles in the park on Sunday; Saúl has arrived with the air of a traveler, with a cigarette in one hand and waving about a box of matches with his name printed on it; after a few days of waving to one another from a distance, he approaches me one night in the Union, his happy face, cigarette in one hand; I need to know if he received my letter and he says yes, and that when he read it he thought I was mad, and I smiled to myself because I realized that he had nothing to do with my life and that I had invented this entire relationship, I know that Saúl did not understand my smile when I moved away soon afterwards and left him, showing his name printed on his box of matches and waving about the cigarette with which he appeared to proclaim: now I am indeed a man; fifth year continues with 11 subjects and close to the high school diploma in Science and Humanities, my letter to the president of the University of Havana, sent to San Lázaro Street, asking that he send me a list of courses and, on the back of the envelope, my name and this address which I wish to leave behind, Crombet Street, between Pedro A. Pérez Street and Martí Street, I examine it for some time so that this becomes a ritual of goodbye; now I always walk with my eyes on the horizon, involuntarily drawn there; and now the list of University courses and I spend much time on each syllabus and I keep coming back to Diplomatic and Consular Law because this will lead me to infinite journeys, I spend hours studying the list, reading it and rereading it and when my mom comes to Guantánamo, look, Mamá, what I want to study is Diplomatic and Consular Law, and Carmita hears this and comes running, but child, do you know what you're saying? around here diplomatic posts are only obtained through political influence and who do we know who can recommend you? listen carefully to what I'm telling you, a diplomatic career would be nothing more than an ornament for you, a bauble, something very pretty but nothing more, that's fine for rich girls who want a university degree for that purpose, as an ornament, or to have something with which to keep themselves busy, or because they know the politicians that one has to know to get them posts and give them recommendations, but you, where do you intend to get with a degree like that? if you like law, study Civil Law so that at least you can earn something with wills and divorces; I understand that Carmita is right and when she moves away and Mamá tells me with affection, listen, child, study whatever you want, whatever inspires you, I feel a profound gratitude, but I know that I can't permit myself the luxury of choosing a career that will be nothing but ornamental; I begin the procedure, I've already chosen my subjects in the fields of Civil Law and Diplomatic and Consular Law and now I go to Rosalía's house because she's been studying in Havana for a year and she's going to advise me about which guest house I can stay in and now I've lost that sense of embarrassment that I felt around Rosalía because, when we were in fifth grade at the nuns' school, I used to use supports and when I walked my feet came out of my shoes a little and when Rosalía was in line behind me, she was always laughing and I think it was because of that, that my feet came out of my shoes, but, although it made me very embarrassed to have her laugh at me, I never laughed at her because she didn't know how to pronounce "ch" and instead of saying *Pancho*, she said *Panso*, and instead of saying *muchacha*, she said *musasa*, and now she's speaking to me and telling me that a classmate from Philosophy and Humanities has written her a letter and do I want to read it and I say, yes, and when she gives me the letter I'm careful not to sit in the armchair near the door to the street which is where people say the leprous uncle sits during his afternoon visits; I open the letter, words like a spider's footprints, open, spilling out onto the white paper; there's something attractive and liberating about this letter and perhaps it's because it comes from Havana, I would have preferred that this letter be for me; while I read, I hear Rosalía, in the guest house where I stay there's no space, but, as you can see, Marisol has written to me asking that I find students for a guest house that a woman she knows is going to set up and I'm telling you, Marisol is delightful, I know you'll love her, if you want, you can stay at the house where Marisol will be staying and when there's a vacancy in mine then you can move, I reread the letter and am a little taken aback when it says: we're looking for decent, moral young girls for a new guest house, there are only going to be six of us girls in total, if you know of anyone, let me know, I continue looking down the page to the signature with its expansive letters, Marisol, and I want to think that she wrote the letter to me and that she sends a hug to me and not Rosalía; about this time Marianita marries Albert, her American boyfriend; the wedding, in Carmita's house because Albert is a protestant and refuses to marry in a church, and the cake and cider and the guests and the witnesses and everyone hugs Marianita when they've finished signing the register and when I go to hug her, a deep sob escapes me because she's eighteen years old and she is going to an unknown world to escape this fixation with honor; soon I'm going to Havana; Mamá buys me some Samsonite suitcases that someone brought her from the base and already it's October 6, 1951, and the farewell and the taxi at the door and the plane to Santiago and from there the bus to Havana and I'm happy to make the journey with Rosalía and her sister because this way I don't feel quite so lost, all night we travel past towns in the bus, in this almost darkness I intuit Camagüey, Santa Clara, Matanzas, until, the freshness of the morning and the bus terminal and I can hardly believe I'm in Havana; Rosalía and her sister drop me off first, at the guest house on the corner of Escobar and Aramburu streets, there's something sad in these streets but the apartment building seems nice, I knock on the door and it's answered by a black woman who, I imagine, is the maid, now I'm in the sitting room and I wait for a space of time that seems long to me, really long, finally a fat, almost repulsive woman appears, with a matronly figure, with a mouth like the gizzard of a bird and that moves a little to one side when she talks, after greeting her I give her a brief introduction, I'm the new girl, recommended by Marisol, and the woman, somewhere between shy and authoritarian says, please sit down, and I sit on the Samsonite suitcase with all my 17 years of age and all the fear that accompanies me; the wait, once again, stretches on until a brown-haired girl appears with eyes almost closed as if she still hasn't quite woken up yet; when I see her I get up and ask her if she knows Marisol, and she says, well, Marisol is arriving in a few days, she let me know she'll be arriving in a few days, I'm also a Law student and Tomasa is my boyfriend's aunt, Pedrito Alvarez, do you know Pedrito? and I say that I do, yes, I know him, but of course, I don't tell her that a few days ago they gave a bash in the Union, one of those dances that happen without advance warning, and there, Pedrito inviting me to dance and me allowing myself to be carried by his

rhythm until he starts to come on to me, to try and kiss me, there's
something attractive about his mouth, his sensual lips, but I maintain
my distance, and in the following days, Pedrito asks, do I want to be
his girlfriend and I say, look, Pedrito, in a few days I'm going to Havana,
so don't keep insisting, and he says, and what's that got to do with
anything, look, sometime soon I'm going to Havana on a business trip,
give me your address and I'll come and pick you up and we can go out
in Havana while I'm there, and I, kindly, that no, that thank you, but
I can't; now I have Marta before me on this corner of Escobar and
Aramburu, so you know Pedrito? well, it just so happens that he's
arriving today, he's going to spend a few days here in Havana because
I don't know how long it's been that we haven't seen each other, of course
Papi and Mami and my brother have come from Ciego de Avila and
they're going to stay here in Havana until Pedrito goes, and well, I'm
going to get ready because he let me know that he was thinking of
getting here early, but come, let me show you your room; we go to the
room and my bed is up against the wall, on the left; near the window,
the other bed and Marta explains, this bed is going to be for Zenaida,
also from Ciego de Avila, and in the other room it's Marisol and I, this
semester we've only managed to find four students, but in a few months
time another two are moving in; I investigate the large, pleasant
apartment, at the entrance, on the right, is the room where Tomasa and
the black woman sleep, after that comes Marisol and Marta's room, next
is the bathroom and after the bathroom, my room; Tomasa's room
opens into the living room and the other two bedrooms and the
bathroom are off the dining room; I start to unpack my cases and to
put away my things, and now the cases are empty and I'm ironing a
striped linen shirt and a white linen skirt and I'm thinking about the
fright Pedrito will get when he sees me here and while I'm thinking this,
someone knocks on the door, I see Pedrito enter and hug Marta in his
role as loving boyfriend, with his eyes closed, forcing a gentlemanly
tenderness, and me standing there, with the iron in my hand,
contemplating the hug until Pedrito comes back to himself, sees me
smiling at the scene and he jumps away from Marta as if he has seen a
ghost, and I say, hi, Pedrito, what a surprise to see you around here and
he stammers, that yes, yes, yes, what, what, what a surprise, and as if
with an urgency to up and disappear, well, Marta, shall we go? and she

says, well, Papi and Mami and my brother should be about to arrive, they're coming to pick us up because my brother brought the car, and Pedrito, ah, so your parents are here? and Marta, yes, of course, they're going to stay until you leave, and Pedrito grimaces, as if they had trapped him and had stuffed him in a sack, and shortly thereafter Marta's family arrived, the fat father, the insipid mother, the thin brother, focused on the importance of belonging to a wealthy family, and Pedrito among them like a fish out of water; as they start filing out, he looks at me as if wishing to say something to me but he ends up going out with the group that carries him along as if they had found in him a precious bauble; now the house is empty and Tomasa and Julia spend hours in their room, whispering secrets and laughing, the day goes by and I'm alone in my room and I don't dare go out because if I leave I'll get lost, I think it's awful not having someone who loves me; the loneliness grows until at two in the afternoon when I can stand it no longer and I begin to cry and I decide definitively that I'm going back to Guantánamo, I have to tell Tomasa, but how do I interrupt her fun with Julia, then I decide and, look, Tomasa, I have to go back to Guantánamo, and Tomasa, with her mouth twisted to one side, no, you can't do that, wait a few days, Marisol will be here soon, and this afternoon what you need to do is call that friend of yours who brought you and tell her to come and collect you to go out with her for a while; I'm not enthusiastic about the idea because I have nothing in common with Rosalía, but I can't bear this loneliness any more and I call her, look, I want to leave, I'm all on my own and I don't know anyone, and she says, more condescendingly than enthusiastically, well, look, my sister and I will come by and we'll go for a walk, we'll collect you at around six; knowing that they're coming calms me a little, I'm fine until they're here and we leave to walk through streets that are unknown to me and the beauty of the city doesn't alleviate this sad loneliness, we go to Rosalía's guest house, the building is almost new and the neighborhood much better than the one where I live; we sit down to chat and I say, I want to go back to Guantánamo, and Rosalía starts laughing and she tells me, you'll see how in a few days you'll get used to everything, and then, when you're comfortable here, you're never, and I mean never, going to want to leave, believe me; and deep down I know it's true, that it's a question of surviving these days until Marisol arrives; the next day Pedrito greets me and I know that at that moment he feels more friendly to me because he's realized that I haven't said anything to Marta about his declarations; today, all day, the loneliness of my room; at night, when Marta and her group of relatives are in the living room, Pedrito arrives and I see him endure the boredom; when they're getting ready to go out, he turns to me and invites me, come, come with us, you're not going to stay here alone, as it is we should have invited you along from the first day, and I do want to go so as not to be alone, but the others haven't invited me and I don't dare accept, until Marta's father, oh, so you're the only student here? well, of course, naturally you must come with us, and the mother, yes, of course, she should come; I didn't take much convincing and I was grateful to Pedrito for his gesture of friendship; we go around and around in the car, Pedrito is friendly and chatty with me, and I feel less alone; at about eleven we head home, and Marta, tonight I'm going to sleep here in your room but from tomorrow I'm going to be in the hotel with my parents until they leave for Ciego de Avila; I sleep protected by the corner where my narrow bed fits, I sleep protected by my wait for Marisol and now this dream without interruptions that lasts until the light of day, and this crystal laugh that reaches me from the living room, and this voice like the tinkle of a bell that is joined to words that I half hear, that's Marisol, I know it's Marisol because along with her came Spring; after exchanging greetings with Tomasa and with Julia, the footsteps approach, and now Marta stands up to greet her and I'm seated on my bed in my green and white, and tobacco-colored, checked pajamas of shrunk cotton, my legs together, my hands on my thighs, and this innocence that returns to me as if I were being born, Marisol has already passed my bed without seeing me and now her back is to me, hugging Marta, oh, so your family is here? well listen, I came sooner than I intended because I thought that you weren't going to have anyone to go with you when you went out with Pedrito, but anyway, I'm glad I came in any case; I'm dazzled by her happiness and it hurts me that she came to be with Marta and not because of me, and already I love her right down to her white dress with blue and tobacco-colored brush strokes and I love her black hair, and when will she notice me, but this is the time for waiting and for silence and my hands are still there, resting, without daring to gesture, until Marisol turns around and, oh, you're the new girl? and I nod my head when I feel her smile directed at me, those incredibly beautiful eyes and her hand on my right shoulder, and, as if she knew the exact words that I needed to hear, her voice reaffirming, you're going to be happy here, don't worry, you'll like it here; the sound becomes a symbol of a new beginning, of making my way into life for the first time, of rebirth; now her voice talks to Marta, words that aren't for me, but which are a presence in me; I enter a dream state that brings me to myself gazing into the mirror in the bathroom, while I finish the automatic task of brushing my teeth; a lukewarm shower, my cotton dress, a cup of coffee with milk, delicious strips of bread with butter, the baguette cut into four strips for dipping into the coffee and everything becomes luminous; and Marta, listen, Marisol, I'm so sorry that you came back because of me, but look, if you want, come with all of us; and Marisol and her oh-so beautiful smile, no, never mind, I'll stay here, I'd go if you needed me to, if you were on your own, but I prefer to stay here; and she looks at me, and if I stay, the two of us can go somewhere, what do you think? the happiness in her eyes, a light that illuminates me from the inside, demolishing all my deaths to draw me into life, and I agree from my almost silence, I know that Marisol intuits what I feel, what others don't see, and right now, here, in the living room, we're sealing our own mystery into which no-one else can enter; Marta's family arrives, Pedrito with his look of resignation, Marisol exchanging greetings, friendly, polite, welcoming and I can hardly pay attention to anyone else; finally the moment when they file out, I see them disappear through the door, and now Marisol beside me, let's get comfortable, do you like walking? and my almost silent reply, yes, I love it; now Marisol has put on her moccasins and I've put on mine; we leave behind the apartment to walk through the daylight, and that love of Marisol's for the air that she breathes and of being alive and her way of accepting this silence of mine while she points out to me, look at these stones, how ancient, I love these stones so laden with history, look, look, and she shows me, look, don't you agree that the steps at the University are beautiful? look, this is my college, the College of Philosophy and Literature, look, this is your College of Law; and now in Carlos III Street, look, the College of Medicine; I open myself up to life and I begin recognizing the beauty of things as her voice touches them and this luminosity that wraps itself around my hundred and twelve pounds; in my bones, the wisdom to make the cobblestones, the old buildings, the L and 27 coffee shop show off for the first time, come, let's go have the most tasty hot dogs they make in Havana; the wide sidewalks, the tarred roads, the promise of Radiocentro, look, this is where we'll come, here, apart from the movie, they always put on a really good show; now it's getting dark, if only we could hide away in a solitary cabin, but it's time to go back and my fantasy stays amidst the wide avenues; now dinner with Marisol telling stories with that happiness of hers that's so charming, and well, I'm going to get comfortable; she enters the bedroom and comes out wearing white, silk pajamas, the collar finished with a thin, wine colored trim, and I'm also in my pajamas, plaid, and we're all in the dining room, Tomasa seems entertained by Marisol's stories, and Marisol says, I have no clue about dancing, do you? and I say that yes, I do know, and she says, oh, well you have to teach me because I'm a disaster on the dance floor, in the past, what I did know how to dance was the Aragonese *jota*, yes, I think it was the Aragonese, right? but now I can't remember, and with that she starts dancing the *jota*, her laughter so clear, and, well, I thought I knew how to dance the *jota* but now I think I look like a Chinese greengrocer, don't you think? Tomasa laughs and Julia keeps walking around Tomasa's chair, with her tight, mean face until Tomasa notices her and, well, it's ten thirty already, I'm going to bed, every night we go to bed early, now I'm locking the front door because Marta isn't coming home tonight; we say goodnight; Marisol goes into her room, calls me and says, close the door, let's talk a bit, what do you think? she gets into her bed that is near the window, I sit on Marta's bed that is almost right next to Marisol's, and Marisol, come here, why don't you come closer so we can talk? I sit on the floor with my legs under her bed, my head, at the same level as her head, we talk in the semi-darkness until Marisol asks, looking at my eyes, how do you feel? and I don't dare tell her how I feel in Spanish and it comes out as "wonderful," in a deep voice; Marisol smiles, almost happy, and we don't say anything else about this because it isn't necessary, the night slips away from us until Marisol says, well, I'm not tired, but we have to go to bed sometime, don't you think? and I agree, but how difficult it is to leave her; now standing up, well, goodnight; in my room, I'm filled with a beautiful feeling at the same time as I long to be with Marisol, and suddenly, Marisol in the door to my room holding her pillow, listen, seeing as Marta isn't here, I'm going to stay in your room so that you aren't all by yourself; and this serenity that enters me and this gratefulness and this intensity as I perceive the silhouette of her small breasts that insist on standing out against the white silk of her pajamas; and Marisol, sleep well, don't worry because I'm here; she falls asleep in the other bed and I in mine; I surrender to sleep with this meekness until what remains of the night leaves me and now, the light of day, and this freshness that comes to me; I sit up in bed; the joy of seeing her sleeping so close to me, I stay close by her to keep her company while she sleeps until she opens her eyes and her smile, and hi, did you sleep well? in a tone so warm, and we both anticipate this day of ours meant for walking through streets that become beloved; coffee with milk, bread with butter, Tomasa, seated at the table, makes an obscene joke and Marisol and I stay serious while we wait for her grotesque laughter to end; with breakfast finished, we get ready to go out; someone knocks on the door, Marta and her family arrive with Pedrito, Marta calls Marisol and they speak in their room and Marisol calls me and, listen, Marta wants me to go with her and Pedrito to a ball game that Pedrito wants to go to because her parents can't go with her, nor her brother; I hear this and something clouds over inside me; Marisol rescues me from my sadness, don't worry, I've already told Marta that you have to go too because you're not going to stay here alone, so we'll be together, it's an arrangement I can't get out of, you understand, don't you? I look at her, grateful for this confidence that she gives me; we go out, Marta, Pedrito, Marisol and I; now in the stadium, an enormous line to get in; after the long wait, we're in our seats, the game that I don't understand begins and Marisol takes great pleasure in explaining to me what home and first base and a strike are and is amused by my comments that are so wide of the mark and she is excited because the Almendares team is playing and she's a big fan; the hours and days fly by and classes have already started; I've decided to take my classes as an external student so I can take ten instead of five classes each year, it's vital that I get my degree soon because I don't know until when my mother can keep me in Havana; when our money from home arrives, we pay Tomasa, what we have left over, Marisol and I pool and that's what we use to go out for an afternoon snack, or to the movies, to find private moments outside the apartment; we're always by ourselves, she and I, and it becomes increasingly difficult to sleep in separate rooms, she with Marta and me with Zenaida, with whom I have nothing in common, although sometimes she tries to be nice to me, hey, you're like a bear when you sleep, and that's how she starts calling me *el oso,* the bear, and Marisol tells me that she likes this *oso* thing and repeats, *oso, osito,* little bear, my little bear, *mi osito, osi, mochi, Mochi*; on the afternoons when Marisol has classes and I don't, I'm overwhelmed by sadness until she gets back; at night we sit apart to study and Marisol says, come, put your chair facing mine, here, closer, and I move my chair and we're facing each other, we speak to each other, and look at one another, she with her feet on my chair, brushing up against the side of my thigh; sometimes, in the bathroom, I hug to me the clothes Marisol has worn so that fluids, now dry, from her body impregnate me with her scent; this morning we got up to go to the University, leaving each other is becoming difficult, we continue talking and Marisol suggests, hey, why don't we walk for a bit along the jetty, *el malecón?* and so we allow the sea to accompany us; in the bus on the way to Galiano and San Rafael, a thin boy, with black hair, and very pale skin says, hi Marisol, it's been so long, how nice to see you again, say, where are you staying? in Marisol's happy cordiality, I hear our address of Aramburu and Escobar; we get off, the boy stays on the bus; among all the people in the street and the elegance of the stores, something inside me hurts, I know that Marisol intuits this because she looks into my eyes, blurts out an explanation; this boy, Ricardo, was in love with me but he wasn't my boyfriend or anything, he's a nice guy, he used to write me love letters in which he called me little doll, but I've always thought of him as a friend, that's all, anyway, I've never had a boyfriend, in all my twenty one years, no-one's ever kissed me; I stand there looking at her mouth, that oh-so quiet need becomes almost pain on my lips, a controlled sensuality keeps me company during our snack in the Ten-Cent; Marisol's purity, her almost naivety, her adolescent air, make her seem younger than me; in the bathroom the smell of her clothes that I hug in secret becomes routine, all of this that I never mention becomes routine; Zenaida goes out almost every night with her boyfriend and tonight Marta has gone out and privacy will be ours; we're in Marisol's room, with the door closed and already in pajamas, there's a knock on the door; Julia's twisted face appears, hey, Marisol, there's a young man looking for you; Marisol chooses a dress quickly, changes in the bathroom and heads for the living room; in the bedroom, this coldness that invades me, the waiting that stretches to become anguish, now it seems to me that Marisol has left forever and I'm defenseless to hide my anguish; the door opens and her smile and her worried gaze and hey, Mochi, are you feeling OK? I was worried about you in the living room, Ricardo came by to visit me as a friend, to chat for a bit, but nothing more, he knows I don't like him in any other way; I feel lighter and this moment becomes beautiful; when we continue to be plagued with the presence of others, I ask myself if Marisol has become aware of this thing we feel, if she intuits this need I feel for her mouth; one morning, hey, do you want to go to Old Havana? that way we'll have a walk and you can see that part and on the way we can go to the Post Office, because I want to send a registered letter home; now the bus and the streets so ancient that I walk among dreams and the post office and the line and two boys who come over to strike up a conversation; one, very good looking, what did you say your name was? Marisol? well I'm Eduardo, yes, I study Medicine, so Escobar and Aramburu? OK, so we'll call for both of you around eight thirty, is that OK? and Marisol, fine; I glance at the one who will be my date, a blond guy with blue eyes and the face of a friendly little monkey, one of those you could find behind the bars of any zoo, we say goodbye, and the bus, and the apartment, and Marisol washes her hair and talks to Marta, hey, Eduardo's got a really good build, a gorgeous face, but even more, he's got a chest that looks like a Simmons mattress; and I think that it's time I forgot about all this stuff that I thought I perceived in Marisol, all this stuff I invented for myself; I make an effort to maintain a serenity that's really resignation and disappointment, I make an effort not to think about what I will feel when I see Marisol with that man; with the precision of clocks that mark the hour with bells, I'm reminded of hey, Eduardo's got a chest that looks like a Simmons mattress; now at night we're waiting in the living room, between my cold hands and the persistent phrase, a Simmons mattress, for the arrival of Eduardo and Ruby; the waiting continues until nine, until ten, until ten thirty and just when I thought Marisol was going to be disappointed, I hear her laugh, well, I knew a while ago they weren't coming, and I ask, are you disappointed? and she, laughing, says no, why should I be disappointed? relief returns to me along with the intention of accepting that I invented something for myself that doesn't exist; a few days later, Tomasa, with her mouth twisted to one side and the rhythm of her enormous body says, listen, girls, we have to move out of here; she gives a few vague explanations, something along the lines of the owners want to live in the apartment, but everything explained in a strange and complicated way; the move to this other, almost new apartment in K Street between 19 and 21 takes place quickly; now they've put me in a room with Elvira, a new girl from Cienfuegos and with a friend of hers whom they call *la Rubia*, the blond girl; Marisol is in another room with Marta and Zenaida; at night Marisol and I stay in the living room studying, we start at about eleven, when everyone has already gone to bed and we close the door to the corridor that separates the bedrooms from the rest of the house; one night, Marisol says, listen, I don't feel like studying for my classes, do you want me to read you a little Roman Law? I hand her my book, to read aloud we have to sit close together so as not to wake the others, we sit on the floor of the passageway, she reads to me, the laws pass through my head, sometimes like a serious liturgy, at other times, like a song; in the murmur of her voice I'm affected by the same light-headedness that we get when we're hungry, because Tomasa keeps us hungry with little food, enough for two or three people served to eight; when we receive our money each month we eat out at different cafés or restaurants or we buy something to eat in the apartment, the last few weeks of each month we only have Tomasa's meager rations; night after night, seated on the floor, so close, when Marisol isn't reading aloud, we sit there gazing intently at one another, her hand in mine, now her hand is always in mine, I draw it to my mouth, I kiss it and I feel my open mouth, almost absorbing it into me; I spend the day waiting for our moments alone, tonight, after reading, Marisol says, come, let's go out on the balcony, I want to show you a star, I follow her as if in a daydream, how lovely the night is, and she says, look, isn't it a beautiful star? that's our star, we breathe in the night before going back in, as if to preserve it, and now in the half-light of the dining room, we hug in this slow way, tightly, the heat of my hands exploring her back, the moistness of my open lips on her neck, on her ear, our deep and restrained breathing, an intensity that almost hurts, a letting go towards surrender, and suddenly, Marisol's voice, we'd better go to bed, don't you think? without speaking, we go to the passageway and walk along it, her hand in mine, and now the door and now the farewell and I ask myself if Marisol realizes what's happening between us, if she's aware of everything that we never mention; now, Marisol seated before me in this dining room where we have hugged so many nights, her legs on the seat of my chair, so close to my thighs; the grey afternoon that beats with its rain on the windows intensifies, my warm, grey daydream intensifies, beautifully melancholic, unexpectedly shaken by Marisol's voice: yes, he was my first love, whenever I saw him I thought I would faint, we always coincided on the same summer beach, but I don't think he even noticed me, just imagine, he was about seven years older than me, and I was just a kid can you believe it?; her voice fades away as she writes a strange, beautiful poem, about rain that beats the windows, about rain that brings back nostalgia for that love; and once again her voice: Mochi, when I get married and when you get married, our two couples could live in the same house and that way we wouldn't have to ever leave each other; I hear her from within an astonishment that grows in me as I tell myself that I must definitely have invented those things that don't exist; now it's night, we return to Constantine I, who moved the capital to Byzantium that ended up being called Constantinople, my hands empty without the touch of her hand; the night is well along and I decide, I think we should go to bed, and she says, yes, it's late; I go to the door, she stops me, and, well, aren't you going to give me a hug? I hug her trying to insure that my touch be one of affection and friendship, that it be the hug of a friend or a parent, and she, hugging tighter, not like that, hug me like you always do; the intensity hits me suddenly, my moist mouth on her neck, drinking her in, until I hear her voice, well, we should go to bed, and now the passageway, her hand in mine, the passage door, and, goodnight, yes, goodnight; it's December, the vacations are nearly here, what will my mother say when she sees my ninety eight pounds and leaving you, Marisol, and now the errands, and the ticket and Rosalía and her sister and the bus and the plane and the train and Caimanera and my mother on the wooden bridge, crying, oh, child, what has happened to you, you're almost transparent, your hands are transparent, and I say, well, they don't give us much food, and my mother, well here you have to eat well, and when you're in Havana I'll send you boxes of food, you know, canned things so that you can eat properly, oh, dear; and she starts crying again and during this time my mother's care, and the food and the tonic, Vitaferol, listen, child, you're taking a bottle of Vitaferol with you to Havana and I love Vitaferol because ever since I was a little girl they gave it to me and I always wanted more because it's like molasses; December 31 draws near, I don't want to go to the dance so that nothing will separate me from Marisol, not even the insignificant act of dancing with someone who doesn't interest me, but perhaps this need to be faithful to Marisol is something that I've invented for myself because she still talks about the day when she'll get married and also that we should go out with boys, that we never go out with boys; one day when we saw Ruby, Marisol invited him home and Ruby arrived with a friend, we went for a ride and Ruby explained to Marisol that, on the night he and Eduardo were going to go out with us, they didn't come by to pick us up because something came up and it was impossible, and that any day they'll come by to take us out, but they never came; now in Guantánamo, Luisín invites me to go out on the 31st, I accept without wanting to, without knowing why I've accepted, perhaps because Luisín is the best looking boy in Guantánamo and all the girls are crazy about him, and Carmita and everyone will ask why I don't go with him to the dance on the 31st seeing as I have a date and a chaperone, I also don't know why Luisín has invited me, perhaps out of curiosity, to find out if what they say about me in the town is true, and now it's the 31st and now at the dance and it's true that Luisín is a handsome man with his eyes and hair the color of honey and his complexion like a rose and his perfect mouth, he's not mannish, not even masculine, he doesn't dance badly although with short steps, holding tight, and I'm waiting for some moment when this gorgeous man says something interesting but he says nothing, not about himself, nor about the Medicine he's studying, he just stands there, tamely vain; now alone, the darkness keeps me company, this waiting, the moment when I'll see Marisol again, the certainty that this year of 1952 doesn't begin for me until I'm with her; the wait continues until the day of the trip, and now in Havana and our meeting that's almost silent with so much to say; we go for a walk to be alone, and I say, hey, Marisol, on the 31st I went to a dance with Luisín, and Marisol asks, is that the boy Rosalía talks about so much, that everyone's crazy about him? and I say, yes, it's the same one, Marisol goes pale and in her eyes that I love so much, I recognize the pain, and look, Marisol, I, we didn't even kiss, nor did I let him come near me, I told you I went to the dance because I wanted you to know, but not because it was at all significant to me; relief overcomes her as she listens to me and once again, the need to be together, we decide to eat out and later, go to the movies and return to the apartment at night; in our need to be together sometimes we forget to go to classes, and on the days that I do go, while I eat a guava pie in the Law cafeteria, I think about the moment I will return, of hurrying down the streets to speed up our reunion, but Marisol always insists, we have to go out with boys because everyone else does; one afternoon I arrive back from the University and Marisol, so happy, says come, let me show you, she takes me to her room, shows me a box of pastries, and look, Uncle Pedro brought them for me, I didn't want to open them until you got here; upon opening them, this whole array of tasty Cuban confections, the delicious cappuccinos, the San Jacobo sticks, square and round rum cakes, the almond candies; and Marisol, and that smile, and isn't all this a dream? and I still haven't told you the best part, Uncle Pedro left me some money and tonight we're going to the Radiocentro café and we're going to have an unforgettable feast, what do you think? and I say, finally, well, Marisol, it can't be tonight, because I met up with Luisín and he invited me to go out and because you're always saying that we have to go out with boys, well I, Marisol, she interrupts me, oh, yes, well OK, of course, go out with him; I see the sadness in her eyes and in her frown; I try to study in the living room during what remains of the afternoon and suddenly, Marisol says, hey, I'm going to go out with you and Luisín, I am sure he knows that no girl goes out alone, and I accept because the best thing that could happen to me tonight is to be with Marisol; now it's eight thirty, Luisín smoking and walking with his George Raft steps, are you ready? and I say, yes, but we have to wait for a friend who's coming with us; Marisol enters the living room before Luisín can say anything and Luisín says, we're going to the fair ground, we catch the bus and the three of us travel standing up, and from time to time I look at Marisol, her face so solemn; at the fair ground Luisín wants to ride on everything, the crazy cars, the roller coaster, the merry-go-round, and Marisol always stays on the ground, waiting, with sadness in her eyes, until I say, look, Luisín, I don't feel well, I need to go home now, and he says, but it's still so early, the night is just beginning, we can go somewhere else, and I say, but I feel sick, and he says, if that's the case, that's OK, we'll go; in the apartment, Marisol's voice, it's true what Rosalía says, he's a very good looking boy; and I reply, for all his looks, he bores me enormously; she looks at me with an almost resignation as if she had just lost, irredeemably, something very important to her; that night we didn't study and when I went to hug her, her voice, goodnight, and she didn't return my hug; in the following days, an emptiness has come between us that little by little dissipates; tonight Elvira's not here and *la Rubia*, as so many times before, has gone to spend a few days with her family at Los Pinos; it's time for bed and Marisol comes to my room; the light's off and Marisol is in Elvira's bed, in the semi-darkness we listen to the music of André Kostelanetz, I'm seated on the floor like that first night, in an intense, shared silence in which we gaze at each other for ages; we begin closing the distance and my mouth, open on her neck, on her ear, I feel my lips slipping across her skin to the rhythm of deep breathing; something almost like pain as I unbutton her blouse and I start to caress her breasts through the satin, a moaning sound that escapes her, a mixture of soft violence and tenderness, and suddenly, her voice, this shouldn't be happening between us; I feel a coldness that debilitates me because I think that definitely, I invented something for myself that doesn't exist in Marisol, and the anguish of my error, and the sob that bursts out of me, uncontainable, forgive me, Marisol, it's my fault, for not having seen that; Marisol, with her poignant tenderness says, no, it's not your fault, I don't want you to feel bad, it's just that we have to speak about this, we've never talked, but we have to say it, we can love each other in some other way, because to me you're like a little sister, don't you feel the same? and I, yes, because it's true that I love her in many ways, and Marisol says, I'm glad we talked about this because this way we can try, isn't that true? with the serenity that begins to surround us, we're also faced with how to dissipate a feeling that, so absolutely, envelops us; one night, after trying to study, we go to say goodnight to our star, and Marisol asks, aren't you going to give me hug? don't you want to hug me? once again the dining room, the semi-darkness, the mixture of soft violence and tenderness and, as always, Marisol's voice right on time, we should go to bed, don't you think? another day, at around two in the afternoon I'm in my bed and Elvira's in her bed; Marisol comes and gets into bed with me in this narrow bed, our bodies so close, and protecting our intimacy a blanket that covers us in the intense heat of our climate, Elvira laughs her little laugh of naïve child and between yawns says, oh, I'm so tired, why don't we just have a little siesta and she closes her eyes and Marisol and I are left in silence, looking at each other for I don't know how long while, from some nearby apartment, we hear the music that accompanies us, Liszt's *Dream of Love*; now no-one can take away from us what must happen, I move closer so that she can try out on my mouth her first kiss, this force that is so soft and that unites us, this serenity that is so full that it stays with us when Elvira opens her eyes and says, hey, guys, didn't you sleep? I died; Marisol doesn't answer and I say, in the half silence, no, no we couldn't sleep; without saying anything to one another, Marisol and I know that we have to go out because today everyone else would become intolerable; the most isolated table in the café, the slow stroll down avenues, night has fallen without us realizing; we return, and now I'm in my bed with Marisol in her room, and that voice of hers that has stayed with me, we needed to get out because we just had to talk, right, *mi vida*? what a beautiful thing, my first kiss, I had imagined it so many times, what my first kiss would be like, but I never dreamed it would be like that, so beautiful, when you kissed me I felt as though I was becoming detached from the world, as though I stayed floating in space with the music of *Dream of love* accompanying me, I know at which exact moment it was that we kissed and from now on and for always, each time I hear it, I'm going to remember that moment, and I have to tell you something, my love, that the other night when you were caressing my breasts, I wanted it too, didn't you realize what I was feeling? but you won't believe this, I was ashamed to think that you were going to see me naked in front of you, because I never... but there's also the other thing, the thing I've fought so hard not to see, but since the beginning, from when we started to study together and you used to hug me and you would kiss me on the neck, I was filled with such intensity that when we parted it made me ask myself, but dear God, what is all this, sometimes I tried to not think about what I felt for you and at other times I would ask Saint Joseph to help me, I used to ask him to make this not what I thought it was, because I was so afraid, but today I don't want to spoil this happiness, this beautiful thing that was my first kiss, that mouth of yours, what a mouth, I adore your mouth; now in my bed, Elvira insists on talking and I say, look, Elvira, I'm really sorry, but I'm dog-tired, and finally Elvira is switched off and I remain in my daydream, repeating to myself Marisol's words, taking them in through my skin, because I don't know what the future will throw at us but the fact that her first kiss was mine, now no-one can take that away from me; it becomes difficult to occupy this love among so many people, and Marisol's constant preoccupation, we must go out with boys, now more than ever, we have to date; whenever I gaze at her, she always warns, be careful, don't look at me like that, they're going to find out, I look away and ask myself in silence if one day I will stop being bothered by the invasive presence of others, so many pairs of eyes watching; the need to kiss, we have to wait for that late hour of the night when everyone else is asleep and my Roman Law book is left, open in the passageway; one night when saying goodnight becomes too difficult, still holding hands we head for Marisol's bed and the tender violence of our kiss is prolonged while I caress her and save her moisture in my hand, my mouth slides on her neck, on her breasts, our breathing deep and contained, a shiver that runs through me and the low voice of Marisol trying to calm me, slowly, slowly, they might wake up; in the semi-darkness I look over at Zenaida's bed perpendicular to me, about a meter and a half away, to my left, so close, Marta's bed, I don't want to stop and think about whether they're asleep or not, if they've felt my shiver and the low voice, slowly, slowly, I try to relax, on my back, my arms at my sides, I stay stretched out, stretched out on the bed, I start to calm down, I begin to separate myself from everything that surrounds me, just me and thought, nothing more, I leave through my eyes, I wander off through the ceiling's quadrilateral, this quietness that penetrates me, this otherness that envelopes me like an involuntary act of letting go of the piece of lime and of cement and of bricks where Zenaida and Marta also breathe, I return to myself through my eyes, I feel the shell of the cranium and all this that is skin and blood and lime too, and the idea of being free outside of myself, something other than myself, air and space; the silence stretches out until, well, Marisol, goodnight; in my bed, the insistent need for freedom, and the question, why do I have to pay for my bread with the blood of my brow, with the blood of time, with time, how many pieces of time do we have to spend for one piece of bread, how many pieces of this time-life do we have to give for a hole where our privacy is protected; if only one day I could live in time without having to hand it over for a piece of bread, if I could only paint or write or freely love a woman; the obsession with living inside time surprises me here, in my plaid pajamas, it's time to lead myself into sleep, I hug my pillow, I'm lying on my right side, my right hand beneath the pillow where my head rests to be able to sink myself into this not being; night passes and I don't feel it until the light of day, I begin recognizing myself, everything the same, the plaid pajamas, Elvira, the watchful eyes, I go to the bathroom, my pajamas lowered and my pants and the act of urinating privately; seated on the bowl lighting my first cigarette of the morning, to smoke in private on an empty stomach to feel the dizziness that nicotine gives me, I'm interrupted by the first knock, and I say, it's occupied, and another knock, and another, it's occupied, and now this isn't urinating in private and now this isn't smoking in private; the piece of paper brusquely torn from the roll, I dry myself, my pants in place, my pajamas buttoned up, I come out, the apartment's traffic is always the same and these desires for kisses that are half given behind closet doors, Marisol, to alleviate the denseness that envelopes us says, hey, Mochi, I think I should buy myself a maternity bra, what do you think? her laughter, ringing like crystal, makes me forget for a moment all these limitations, the watchful eyes that peer at walls to attack our intimacy; one morning we're all in the dining room and Tomasa says, I have to tell you all something, I can't continue with the guest house, I don't feel well, so you'll have to move soon, she doesn't tell us exactly when; Marisol takes the news with her usual attitude, in which she doesn't consider things that have a solution of any importance and when we're alone, don't worry, I'm sure we'll find a house that's much better than this one, the days pass, March 10th the sound of gunfire in the streets, people talking about the coup d'état, that Fulgencio Batista was really quick off the mark and where will Mary Tarrero and Prío Socarrás end up; Marisol and I have been in the streets since early, we pass by little groups of people; everyone's nervous and the University is turned upside down; Marisol and I have decided to return to the apartment, now we're walking along the sidewalk, we hear gunfire and don't know where it came from and Marisol says, lie down, lie down on the ground; we lie on the ground, face down, until the ringing of bullets is over and now there's silence and we still don't know where it came from; we're in the apartment waiting for news about the student strike until we receive confirmation, the University is closed indefinitely, on this 11th of March we decide to go back to our towns, and Marisol asks, why don't you spend a few days with me in Las Villas? that way you'll get to know my town and then you can go on to Guantánamo; the invitation arrives like an unexpected stroke of good luck in which it's difficult for me to realize that the cylinder made of thick glass has opened, liberating me to experience a plenitude that has never been mine; our suitcases packed, the station, the train moving and I'm worried because all I can see are seats and I thought we were traveling in a sleeper car, and Marisol, yes, don't worry, they'll make the beds now, and in a short while, the beds are ready, and now in our bed, the curtains tightly closed, the vibration of the train, to sense the countryside in the swift and dark race of the window; this intimacy all our own here, where no-one bothers us, and if living meant sensing the countryside, to travel the night dizzily in an infinite journey, in this rectangle that contains us, to stop time in this act of making love; how beautiful is Marisol's paleness in the semi-darkness where our bodies begin learning to recognize each other in the intensity that leads to a clearly identifiable peace, and, goodnight, my life; goodnight, my love, and we stay like that, embracing, skin to skin, in that desire that prevents sleep, and once again we begin and we're surprised by this violence so full of tenderness, and afterwards this peace, this definitive serenity, and we begin again and again and the seventh time the light of day begins intruding and the deep voice of the conductor announcing the name of the town; we dress quickly, I feel my tiredness plastered on my face when the station's already there, Marisol's family, the house; and her mother says, oh, you poor children, how gaunt you are, it's that those train trips are terrible, I'm sure you couldn't sleep, right? and we say no, we couldn't sleep; I find myself observing her figure fifty eight years old, so absolutely diminutive, behind thick glasses, her feet joined at the heels and separate at the points; the breakfast, Marisol has asked the cook to make me a hot chocolate that tastes delicious, with bread and butter, towards the end of the breakfast, Marisol's mother insists on talking but when faced with our absolute exhaustion she relents, well, I can see that you want to rest, well, yes, go to bed then, we'll put our guest in the other room, everything's ready, and Marisol, no, Mami, it's better that she sleep with me because she's afraid of sleeping alone; her mother doesn't really agree but she also doesn't want to challenge Marisol's emphatic decision; now in this wide bed I lay my hand on hers to fall asleep like that, and Marisol, shocked, be careful, we have to be very careful, at any moment when the notion takes her, Mami may come in, until tonight, wait until it's night; I accept this promise, I fall asleep; these past days we've wanted to stretch out time; in the moments in which we're not surrounded by cousins and relatives of Marisol, we go out to walk through the town, after we pass the country houses we find ourselves in the open countryside, we share the silence or speak in low voices; the countryside, uncontaminated by people, we can look at each other, and Marisol says, what a sweet gaze you have, and that smile, I adore your smile, do you realize that at your side this path between the grass seems beautiful to me? no-one's ever spoken to me like that before and then we didn't need to say anything more and now amongst the crowd of cousins and little nieces and the sister-in-law and the brother and the father and the mother, what we shared on the beautiful path opening through the grass stays with me; at the rectangular table, lunch, Marisol's father tells me stories, he speaks with an accent as though he's just arrived from Spain but with a diction impaired by asthma, when I don't really understand what he says, Marisol interprets my gesture and repeats the story; Marisol's brother, seven years older than her, about five foot four, the belt of his pants at the height of his small breasts, a huge moustache, huge sideburns, there's something alert and noble in his gaze; Marisol makes an effort to make me feel welcome, have you noticed how my whole family accepts you? Mami waits on you all the time, Papi, who never speaks to anybody, stays behind at the end of the meal to talk to you, my brother has already told me that, when you leave, he's going to take you to the airport which is quite far from here, my brother who never leaves the store for any reason, not for anything, just imagine that when he was fourteen years old he said to Papi that he didn't want to study anymore so that he could dedicate his time to the store, and can you believe that he doesn't even go home to eat lunch because, seeing as our house is right next to the store, he saves time by having lunch here; Marisol and her family protected within the safety that money provides, the store that's so big and through which file the peasantry and the town folk, houses that they own here, apartment buildings in Havana; Marisol, unsoiled by ostentation within her wealth, free of the weight of sacrifice, how comfortable it must be to be born like that, without this guilt that poverty brings us; if only one day I could have money so that she could live by my side as peacefully as she lives right now, without even realizing that survival is a prolonged, painful act, an impossibility, a limitation; my anguish finds words, Marisol, if we could live together one day, how do I dispel this poverty that is always with me, because right now I can't even dream the house that I build for you, the one I always surprise you with, and your happiness and profound emotion when you see this space that will be ours, today I can't dream it because I feel poverty stuck to my bones; and Marisol, but treasure, don't you realize that the only person I can be happy with is you? if it were only about poverty, I would go with you to the ends of the earth; resignation fills me as I listen to her, a bitter taste because now I can't say it, that when I grow up I'm going to be a man and marry you; Marisol continues thinking about marriage as if it were, for her, an act of inescapable compliance with society, because, as Mami says, even if I get divorced later, a woman should get married; I know that we'll never live together, I'm overcome by an urgency to emigrate so that the watchful eyes are blinded to my whereabouts, and I dare to mention this, if this could happen, Marisol, if I could go somewhere far from here, would you come with me? and Marisol, I don't want to speak about our separation, but however far apart we are, nothing will ever separate us, even when my skin gets all wrinkled I will still love you because our blood unites us, do you want to see how our blood unites us? she picks up the knife that was resting on the bedside table, she cuts her hand and bleeding, she passes me the knife, now you, and I, as if possessed by this strange ritual press the knife into my hand until it begins to bleed and we join hands tightly, like a seal; we speak about blood transfusions, so that my blood runs through your veins and your blood travels through my body; these pacts that we make in time won't occur in space, because Marisol will never take flight and it will always be the same, the rectangular table, Marisol, her father, her mother, her brother; the day of our separation will come too soon, it will arrive violently, to remove my mouth from her body; this beautiful afternoon, the sun of our earth, and Marisol, come, I have to share something with you, before you leave me, come; I follow her up stairs to the roof garden, Marisol breathes deeply and opens her arms to receive all the purity of the air, look, come, these are my doves, for a long time now I've had my dovecote, isn't it true that my doves are beautiful? she begins showing me her favorites; I share the moment in near silence, and I think that how good it would be if Marisol never lost this healthy naivety, how good it would be if I never had to say to her, Marisol, it's better that I leave, it would be better that I leave tomorrow, and the two of us are touched by this sadness, and Marisol says, well, yes, I understand, your mami will be impatient for you to arrive; I don't say to her that in truth I can stay longer, but I've noticed that every time Marisol and I say we're going for a walk by ourselves, her mother's mouth forms a little trumpet of protest; every morning at daybreak, her mother comes into her room and let's go, let's go, Mari, get up now and have your orange juice, Marisol sits up in bed half asleep without it occurring to her to ask not to be woken up so early; every night we have to allow enough time for the others to fall asleep and if we feel her mother's footsteps we have to separate at once, because she can come into the room suddenly to say any old thing to Marisol; now we breathe the air that reaches us in the roof garden, and Marisol says, tonight my brother was going to take all of us to visit my aunts who live about fifteen kilometers from here, I think that between the trip and the visit they will be away for about two or three hours, I'm going to tell Mami that you want to see *The Hunchback of Notre Dame* that's showing here, in the cinema on the corner, we'll insist that you haven't seen the movie and that you want to see it, we'll go into the cinema before they leave, wait a bit there and then we'll come back here, that way we'll have the house to ourselves, what do you think? her voice reaches me like a promise and I'm amazed at Marisol's habit of finding a way to compensate pain; now her voice, so happy, let's go down and have a guava jam for our afternoon snack that's divine, just divine, you'll see how much you'll like it, and we drink coffee, and there are crackers that you call Cristina crackers, that you like so much; now at the rectangular table, the food's delicious, Marisol's father drinking his coffee, her mother walking without stopping in her high-heeled shoes with the toes pointing outwards, and Marisol, hey, Mami, tonight Mochi and I are going to stay here so we can go to the cinema because she hasn't seen *The*

Hunchback of Notre Dame and they're showing it in the cinema on the corner, and now the little trumpet, and well, if you two aren't going, we'll leave the trip for another day, and Marisol says, no, Mami, why should the rest of you not go, anyway the aunts are already waiting for you and it's not at all necessary, it's silly for you not to go; and her father, exactly, that's how I see it, we'll go to your sisters' house and they'll see the movie; the little trumpet in place, tight in the silence, and Marisol says, Mami, I think you'll be back before we are, but just in case, leave me a key; now it's night, her mother, her father and her brother are getting ready to go, and Marisol says, well, Mami, give me a kiss, have a good time, and don't worry about us, OK? in the cinema, all that about the hunchback of Notre Dame that I had already seen in Guantánamo, for all that it moved me so, now I'm impatient with the hunchback, and now Marisol who knows that I can't stand being there and without me having to say anything to her says, calm down, we have to allow enough time, until finally, now, let's go; we cross the street, we enter through the doorway and Marisol says, let's check the house to be sure that there's no-one here, we search it, it's comfortably empty, when we reach the bathroom with the floor tiles we start kissing each other, there, in front of the sink, so close to the shower, in front of the toilet bowl and the bidet; a long hug and a prolonged kiss, and I say, let's take off all our clothes and get into bed, and Marisol says, no, no, we have to be dressed so that if they arrive we can tell them we've just got back from the cinema, again a hug, and a noise at the door, the key turning, the brusque separation and Marisol, that must be them, thank goodness I switched the lights on when we came in, her hurried steps towards the living room and me there in the bathroom, inside a rebellious silence, and Marisol's voice, but Mamaíta, you're back already? let's see, you old dear, did you have a good time? and the voice of her father, yes, your mother wanted to come back at once, as soon as we arrived she wanted to return; I come out of the bathroom with a forced smile, and hi! did you have a good time? how are your sisters? and the mother, as if disgusted, well, they're well; and I say, we've just arrived this instant because we didn't like the movie; and now to sit in the living room until it's time to go to bed which keeps getting later until Marisol says, Mamaíta, we should go to bed now because tomorrow she has to get up early, and Doña Florida says, well, OK, and Jacinto has to take her to the airport? because he has a lot of work at the store, and I rush to answer, no, because Marisol says that the bus that will take me to the airport stops right here on the corner, and Florida, yes, that's right, you can catch it right here; and I say, well, goodnight, and Doña Florida and Don Alvaro say, well, goodnight; in bed, time to wait for Don Alvaro's snores, the silences of the high-heels, and I say, hey, Marisol, how did your mother end up with the name Florida? And Marisol says, well, she doesn't like her other names and she got rid of them herself and decided to call herself Florida because she says that she always liked that name, and I say, what's she really called? and Marisol says that her mother doesn't like other people to know her names, and I insist, tell me, until finally, Marisol says, well, they called her Tiburcia Agripina, can you imagine giving those names to a little angel who's just been born? we found the way Marisol said this funny and we laughed quietly, suddenly, Doña Florida was there, planted in front of the bed, well, if you're going to get up early tomorrow you won't spend the night talking, will you? and Marisol says, no, Mami, I'm going to sleep now, because I'm sooooo tired! and she starts yawning, and you, Mami, aren't you tired? and Doña Florida says that no, she's not at all tired; she leaves, I'm left thinking that if it occurs to her to spend her insomnia walking about the house, what a night we can expect, I don't know how many hours pass, the worn-out music of the slot machine from the café on the corner reaches us, and finally, silence, our naked skin, and how soon the morning arrives, the high-heels echoing throughout the house, the door open, the glass in her hand and that diminutive figure, let's go, let's go Mari, the orange juice, and Marisol drinks it without protest, enjoying her mother's care and afterwards that childlike and spoiled tone, Mami, it's still very early, I'm going to sleep just a little more, only a little more; the clicking of heels moves off, the glass, the diminutive stature; I open my eyes to look at us a little while longer, and Marisol says, in a low voice, do you know what? every now and then they change the position of my mattress but I'm going to tell Mami that they mustn't touch it because if they don't move it, I'll always now exactly which is your spot and it will be as if you're here, as if you hadn't left; time to get up and now at breakfast and my suitcases in the living room and the moment to cross the street to catch the bus and now in both of us the sadness of absence and the hurdle of a cordial goodbye in order to confuse with formulas our deep love; the shaking of hands with Don Alvaro, the hug to Doña Florida, thank you very much, Doña Florida, for all your generosity; and Marisol and I holding ourselves back in this discipline imposed on us by renunciation; we avoid looking at one another, Marisol comes up to me, have a good trip, and, under her breathe, a telegram, send me a telegram, I need to know that you arrived safely, and, out loud, well, so long, best wishes to your Mami and others in your family, now in the bus and Marisol there, on the sidewalk, until is becomes useless watching her because the movement steals our images, makes towns disappear for us; on the road, absence fills with memories, Marisol, I've never been given a birthday gift like this, what a morning, that 12th of March; Marisol, and if one day I were to move far away, would you come with me? this poverty that always accompanies me: Marisol, what hurts most is what I've never told you, I'm going to grow up and be a man and marry you; this acquiescence of hers and, at the same time, the way she loves me, if there's anyone I can be poor and happy with, it's you, don't you realize that with you this path between the grass becomes beautiful? and the loud voice of the driver shakes me from my daydream, the airport, checking in the suitcases, boarding the plane, the noise that shatters the serenity of space, the acidity, the sleep that Dramamine brings, Santiago, another plane to Guantánamo and my mom and Carmita who are waiting for me, what can I talk about now, no, the riots didn't affect me, no, I didn't hear even one shot, no, I didn't set foot outside the apartment nor show my face at the University, everything well, there are no problems; I try to listen to stories about people I hardly know, and oh, child, how happy I am to see you, and you, aren't you glad to see us? you're so sad; and I say, no, it's just the trip, the trip has made me really tired, how could I not be happy, before I forget, I have to go to the post office to send a telegram because my friend's mother said that she would be very worried if I didn't send a telegram to let them know that I arrived safely and this woman was very kind to me, so, as you can imagine, I must do this, and my mom says, child, of course, of course, but why don't you send it tomorrow, if you yourself say that you're so tired, you know what's involved in going to the post office now? and I say, well, for me it's a commitment and it's a pain to have to go out now, but she insisted and it's better that I send it today; and my mom says, but lie down first and rest for a little, and I say, no, I don't want to have this hanging over me; I leave before the explanations can become any more complicated, while I walk the blocks to the post office I think about the telegram, my love, I arrived safely, you've no idea how much I miss you; my life, I've just arrived and already I want to be with you, yours always; the steps of the post office, the window, and yes, may I help you? send a telegram? look, here it is; I fill out the paper, name, address, date and the text, I arrived safely, Mochi; the man at the window counts the words, and that's how you want to sign it? it says here Mochi? and I say, a little ashamed because everyone else can hear his voice which is naturally loud, yes sir, just that, I pay, the steps, my return along the same sidewalks, and of course it should be just Mochi, it's the only thing I can say; in Caimanera, everything's the same, so many mosquitoes on you, hovering around you, the mosquito invasion that intensifies towards six in the afternoon and doesn't leave us until morning, it's those stagnant waters, that's what people say, it's those stagnant waters that breed the mosquitoes and we'll never be rid of this stench, it's always there because the toilets flush into the sea, right there, underneath the houses and when the tide is low, everything ends up on the shore, just think, how could it not smell; in my house we now have a toilet bowl, but in many other houses what's there is a crate, when I used to sit on it I would feel the sea breeze right there and I would do everything in the blink of an eye because often the boys from the town go beneath the houses and one never sees them because they hide behind the posts; my mom and I continue making pajamas, the dragon and the hut, the embroidery of the letters, Cuba, and are you already finishing that one? well, give it to me so that I can iron it, Pack waiting on the swing and hurry up because the American launch is leaving and Pack travels in the one that leaves for the base at three in the afternoon; my dad's in the little bed on the veranda of the lattice patio, lying face up with the *Bohemia* in his hand and I ask myself if enough pajamas and scarves will be sold to cover my trip to Havana and to cover the cost of the guest house, always this anxiety, always will I be able to go or not, the days pass and a letter from Marisol that my mother gives me opened because she wanted to participate in the excitement of receiving a letter from Havana, from somewhere that is not mosquitoes nor Pack nor ironing nor embroidery, I'm going to complain, but I leave it like that, in surprise and silence; a few days later another letter from Marisol, saying that Tomasa has already left the guest house, but look, Mochi, I've already found another one in a building on N that you'll love, a gorgeous building, quite new, that's near the café Cibeles, it belongs to a country woman who lives with her daughter, they seem like nice people; Mami and I have already gone to have a look at everything; we'll be Marta, you and I in one room and Elvira and *la Rubia* in another, Zenaida is going to another guest house, hope to see you soon, love, and her signature which is like a definition of herself; time seems to stop until the moment finally arrives to send a telegram, in two days I'll be in Havana, I re-read the date, the address, the text with my time of arrival and my signature, Osito, the man behind the window counting the words and excuse me, the signature is Osito? that's what it says here, Little Bear? his naturally loud voice and me in my half silence, yes sir, that's what it says, I pay, I imagine to myself Marisol waiting for me at the bus station and now the taxi and now the plane to Santiago and the bus to the station in Havana and Marisol isn't there; I travel in the taxi thinking that it must be that it's over; now the house, and in the entrance, Marisol with her smile, and my face so serious, and I don't have to say anything to her because at once, the explanation, I've just arrived too, I was desperate to get here before you to be able to wait for you but I couldn't, I couldn't get here any sooner, but what bliss to be together, am I right that you're going to lose that serious expression? look, when I got your telegram with the bit about Osito, I felt like you were giving me kisses like this, like this, like this, oh-so many kisses, her happy laughter begins erasing my seriousness that's like stone and I come out of my confinement; it's true, this building is gorgeous with beautiful plants all over the wide entrance way, the floors so polished and at the end, the entrance; we climb to the third floor, and look, Mochi, this lady is Nievita and this is Claudia, her daughter; Nievita is a stocky woman, a country woman, who seems like a nice person, Claudia is thin and pinkish, like the color of new-born mice, with long, stiff arms, half squint, not quite normal, profoundly shy, and I say, to Nievita, a pleasure to meet you, and to Claudia, a pleasure to meet you; we go to our room with an extra bed left over, waiting for Marta, Marisol intuits my protest and looks at Marta's bed with resignation, what could I do, just think, what could I do, how do I tell Marta that I want to be alone with you; when our resignation starts becoming unpleasant, Marisol comments, Marta is going to arrive a few days late and till then, the world is ours; the walks through the Prado, the oh-so delicious flying saucers that they make in a kiosk near there, we always like the ones with strawberry jam and cream cheese and we love watching how they place the two slices of bread with the jam and cream cheese in the round iron, and later, we savor the flying saucer with a shake made of anona or mango or sapodilla plum which Marisol calls a *mamey* shake, or if not, a vanilla or chocolate shake, we explore so many places ending up suddenly on the jetty or in the Cathedral, Marisol always wants to go by the Cathedral, it's true, isn't it, Mochi, that the Cathedral is exquisite? it moves me to see it, I swear it moves me; sometimes, the tumult of the downtown area, Galiano and San Rafael, and to dream in front of the store windows, to stare at the wedding rings until I find one that I like for Marisol; this afternoon we're heading for the Café América, we drink a chocolate frozen and Marisol repeats, you see how thick and tasty they are? we even have to eat them with a spoon; I really like these long spoons that they give you; I'm entertaining myself with this when suddenly, Marisol says, look over there, now how's this for luck, look who's just come in; I look and it's a black woman wearing a green satin suit, with an elegant air, and Marisol explains before I can ask, it's the Marquise, have you never heard them talk about the Marquise? and I reply, that yes, I've heard of her and also the Gentleman from Paris, *el Caballero de París*; the Marquise goes up to the counter and sits on a stool near Marisol, Marisol starts talking to her, Marquise this and Marquise that, and the Marquise is quite comfortable hearing her title repeated with such enthusiasm; the bus and N Street, we're walking towards the apartment and Marisol says, hey, Mochi, do you realize that our conversation with the Marquise was an historic moment? do you realize that we've lived history? her question starts us on a series of stories about our towns, she tells me about her characters, about one who's called Callejas, like the old publishing house, for all the stories he tells, and that at home they also call her Callejas because she likes to tell stories and to talk a lot; and sometimes when she doesn't stop, hey, isn't it true that I'm worse than Callejas? and I say, no way, that I love listening to her; and in Guantánamo, also, we have Cloud Burst, *Aguacero*, because when he speaks he spits on everyone, and there's Big Head, who has an enormous head and the boys shout Big Head at him and he shouts back obscenities that rhyme with Big Head and he keeps repeating, ed, ed, ed, and there's Virula, who, when they say Virula to him, he answers, you must call me Felix, and for some strange reason, in my town they've taken this phrase to mean that one doesn't have anything to do with what's being said to one, and instead of saying, I wash my hands of that, they say, you must call me Felix; and there's the mulatto woman who's always hitting herself on the cheek, quite high up, almost in her right eye, she hits herself with her fingers held tightly together and she's already given herself an enormous bruise, like a black circle around her eye, and whenever someone says, excuse me, what happened to your eye? she always answers, it was Ampallo's mule, it kicked me in the eye, and that's how to get her started because then she keeps repeating, Ampallo's mule kicked me, Ampallo's mule kicked me in the eye, and we hear her repeating this litany until she's out of sight; and then there's the old woman who sells tickets and who gets furious when you call her Bichí Bichí, and one day I called her Bichí Bichí and carried on walking as if nothing had happened and after a little while, I had already forgotten about Bichí Bichí and as I'm passing the columns of the pharmacy building, I feel someone lay into my head with a stick and it was Bichí Bichí who had been laying in wait for me and who got her own back with a blow to my head and I never said anything to her because she had every right to do that, I tried to be composed, as if the beating hadn't affected me at all, but, to tell the truth, I was even dizzy and the fact is that I never again called her Bichí Bichí; Marisol and I start laughing, imagining Bichí Bichí hitting me on the head with a stick and laying in wait for me among the columns; in Guantánamo there's a crazy woman called Severita, whose face is full of wrinkles and furrows and who's always made up to the nines, her mouth painted with a red, bright red pencil, as if she were a clown, and rouge all over her face, she always wears a sun hat and five or six dirty skirts, ragged and smelling, they let her ride the train from Guantánamo to Caimanera for free, and she's taken to telling people that she's the lover of a doctor in Guantánamo, when Severita arrives in Caimanera, the people shout out to her, hey, Severita, how did it go with the doctor last night? Severita laughs like crazy and says, and the doctor, everyday he's more in love with me, and last night he did such and such a thing to me, and she lets rip with a stream of foul language, and people fall about laughing, and one day, there are some boys in the veranda of my house listening to Severita, because Severita comes every Sunday to say hello to my mom, and one of the boys says, how about if we give Severita a bath? they ask my mom for permission, and my mom says, well, if she wants one, in the patio there's a hose; they take her to the patio, and, let's go, Severita, it's to get rid of some of your fleas, Severita accepts with that innocence that's so defenseless, I saw them ready the hose and I left, because the bath seemed too painful to me; and there's old woman Panchita, the one with the bundles, who wears long dresses, and who always carries a bundle of clothing like the tramps in the movies, she's mute and people say that she's mute because they pulled out her tongue, but no-one knows why, she goes from house to house asking for bread with her wrinkled face and her toothless mouth, and even though you can't hear her voice, you understand that she's asking for bread and when she receives any she puts it in the bundle with the clothes and when she has her mouth open like an enormous oval to ask for bread, she wears an expression of surprise, almost happy, she's not like Severita, who sometimes laughs insanely and at other times sits down in the chair and cries indefinitely with a sadness that becomes profound; in Caimanera we have Cosita, Mr. President, a mulatto about fifty years old, with a white beard, who uses a walking stick, and who looks like a patriarch, always impeccably clean, people who walk by him, and so, Mr. President, how goes the government? and, listen to me, Cosita, what we need is for you, as President of the Republic, to make a good speech, Cosita gets up from the chair where they're cleaning his shoes, happiness in his eyes, his fine-looking figure, and begins to speak, immune to the taunting and the laughter of the people who surround him; and suddenly, I'm amazed at the thoughtlessness with which we mock these beings touched by madness; I'm assailed by a need to meet the Gentleman from Paris and to live in his world; and now Marta's here and luckily she's one of those who always goes to class and in the mornings we have the room to ourselves, I've convinced Marisol that we have to lock the door because Nievita walks into rooms without knocking, and Marisol asks, but if the door's locked and Nievita tries to come in, what will she think? and I say, well, just think, what if the door's not locked and Nievita comes in when she shouldn't; one night when, happily, Marta's out, we're in

Marisol's bed, her body under mine in a prolonged kiss that has made us lose all sense of time, suddenly, the doorknob, noise, someone trying to come in, Marisol stiffens in an attempt to stop so as to obey the order given by Nievita who's determined to open the door and I embrace her more tightly and refuse to remove my mouth from hers; Nievita is now beating on the door, Marisol trying to get away, I keep kissing her so violently between cries of oh, Lord, Claudia, Claudia, call someone to help us open this door; her shouts detach me, I head for my bed, pretend to be sleeping, Marisol opens the door with a sleepy expression in her face, and oh, Nievita, I'm so sorry, it's just that last night we studied until late and we were exhausted, and Nievita says, oh, my Lord, what a fright, and the other girls aren't here because if they were I would have asked them to help me open this door, and Marisol says, we're really sorry, tell me, Nievita, what did you want? and Nievita says, well, I, let me see, well, child, I don't even remember, with the shock, I can't remember, it was nothing important, but now I don't know, child, with the shock, now I don't know; we don't mention this and I'm left wondering whether Marisol would have been angry with me for the anxiety I put her through, but one day, while we're having our afternoon snack, that smile of hers, the joy in her eyes, and her voice, what a kiss that was, my love, what a kiss; and I say, which one, and she says, that kiss, the one with Nievita shouting, and with our laughter, this happiness that attends us; Marta, with that sour expression she always has, has changed with us and each day it becomes hard for us to live with her; I don't think she knows that Pedrito has a girlfriend in Guantánamo and that now people say that Pedrito and Lidia are getting married; Elvira sometimes looks at me with her smile of naïve idiot, she half says something to me, as if pitying me, as if saying, well, despite everything, I forgive you, but she quickly realizes that I'm not interested in her forgiveness because she has nothing to forgive me for; at other times she takes on the role of savior and she goes with Marisol to present her to her brother Rolandito, as if Rolandito could save Marisol, look, Marisol, you'd make a marvelous couple with Rolandito, why don't you talk to him? as I listen to her, I think about Rolando, about his doltish smile just like Elvira's and I wonder whether Elvira realizes that she's wasting her time; Rolando and some other boys come here every day to eat lunch even though they don't live here, and Elvira insists, look, when Rolando comes to lunch speak to him, because if you don't, well, he is too shy to ask you out; and she sticks on her face that smile where she lifts her upper lip and you can see the inner part of her lip as if it's trying to get to reach her nose; Marisol is still not interested in Rolandito and Elvira is left with no-one to save; now Marta spends days away from the guest house and when she returns, she brings with her a bitterness and a resentment that becomes aggressiveness; one day we enter the room, Marta's crying, she tells us that she received a letter from Pedrito and that Pedrito's broken up with her; Marisol, moved, tries to console her but Marta keeps her distance; Marisol tries to approach and Marta, withdrawn, says, I'm leaving here, I'm moving the next few days, but from today I'm gone from here, I'll be back soon to get my things, and she leaves with her bitterness that's so acidic, without looking at us; the relief of not having to live with Marta's resentment, and on the other hand my concern for Marisol, who's been affected by Marta's attitude, and, Mochi, I think Marta knows about us and that's why she became so bitter, aside from what happened with Pedrito, I think she left because of what's between us; I try to calm her because it's pointless to allow ourselves to be eaten up by her resentment; Elvira is still on about, girls, you never go out with boys, with all the boys who come here for lunch, and you already know, Marisol, that if you want, I'll speak to Rolandito; I don't want to hurt Elvira reminding her that she doesn't go out with boys either because they don't invite her; Nievita has changed with us, she looks at us with a suspicious air; the circle is closing and now we go out more then ever because we need the pleasantness of a matinee or the mystery of Chinatown, lunch at the Pacífico or an afternoon snack in some café; in the apartment we feel under scrutiny, something unpleasant that filters through to us; one night, Marisol says, listen, Mochi, if Marta and Nievita and Elvira and I think everyone reacts this way to the two of us together, it must be something that we should give up, let's promise Saint Joseph that nothing will happen between us from now on, we have to go to confession, but above everything, to promise Saint Joseph that we'll never ever be close in that way again; Marisol has chosen the Church of the Sacred Heart on Reina Street, tonight I can't sleep thinking about the possibility of getting one of those priests that is always talking about hell, if that were the case, I would have to tell him that how can I go to hell for a love that is so beautiful, I'm still a little intimidated by cassocks and it would be horrible if the priest came out with the devil and hell; now in the bus, at the back, a coldness in my chest, this fear that I recognize in the silence and in my sweating hands, in Reina, the beautiful church, now on my knees, the terror, and look, Father, I can't remember how to do confession nor can I remember the Act of Contrition; a soft voice which filters through the lattice responds to me, well, child, not to worry, not to worry, repeat after me, and I repeat what he says to me; faced with the benevolence of this priest who's so old I confess all these things without being sure that they're so terrible; and the old man says, well, child, that happens a lot in the convents, between the nuns, don't torment yourself, my child, go in peace, I keep waiting, until finally I ask, Father, what is my penance? and the priest says, well, if you want, you can do some Hail Mary's, as many as you think necessary; Marisol there, in the confessionary, minutes later comes up to me full of relief, now together, on our knees, we're praying; and now standing up and now in the isle and the street and, Marisol says, God bless that dear old man, what a pure soul, what a feeling, tomorrow I can take communion; that night Marisol in her bed and me in mine; and I'm thinking that this love can't be a sin and about the irony of finally having a room to ourselves and that it should be accompanied by this abstinence; the voice of Marisol that wants to occupy the night, you see how we can love each other like this too? and I think that yes, we can love each other in this way too, although I don't ask for how long, in this silence, Marisol's excitement, tomorrow we take communion, sleep well; and you too, goodnight; and now the light of day and we don't have breakfast so we can take communion, and now our cotton dresses, the high collars, turtleneck, sleeves down to our elbows, skirts to our knees, Marisol in total concentration, and now Reina, and now the Church, the solemn and unfamiliar mass, it's time to take communion, the fat, unpleasant priest, comes from my right bursting with flab, he takes a host and raises it and another and another and starts placing them in the mouths open like mailboxes, I listen without understanding the hasty words that he pronounces automatically, I look at his fingers moving towards mouths, like pork sausages, and what if this priest urinated before offering the host and didn't wash his hands? I lower my eyes and now, before me, the wide skirt, I imagine the host raised and the words said in the blink of an eye, I open my mouth, I remain with my mouth open and the host which never arrives, the volume of the skirts before me, and the loud voice, get out, get out of here, you shameless creatures, it doesn't occur to me to close my mouth because I don't realize that the priest's shouts are for me and for Marisol who's at my side, I remain motionless, and Marisol's hand touching my arm and her voice, let's go, let's go, we have to leave; now in the street I ask her what happened, if it could be that the old priest who listened to our confession could have told this priest, and Marisol says, no, no, dear God, because that old man is a noble soul, the priest insulted us because we aren't wearing long sleeves, didn't you hear him say something about the naked flesh of arms? and I say, the truth is I didn't hear anything, perhaps because it didn't occur to me to think about our nude arms when the sleeves reach almost to the elbow; but it's better that I didn't understand while there, so that I didn't lose my temper there, in the temple; our brief immobility on the sidewalk, our first steps and now the bus and the trip back and Marisol, pensive, and her voice, priests like that are the ones who drive people away from the Church; and me thinking that from now on my search for God will be alone, and my moments of meditation, in empty churches, bare of priests and automatic litanies; restlessness filters through the promise-sacrifice because not giving in to this love that we carry is a way to die a little, the austere dryness in our room, the wasteful emptiness; Marisol has taken out the metal box that she keeps in her closet, she opens it and says, we have to throw out this cotton; with the wave of hand, now the cotton is there, in the wastepaper basket, and that oh-so beautiful night comes to me, when it was time to rest, and Marisol said, I want to save this surrender that comes out of me for you; the moist cotton on the bedside table, and the next day, we didn't speak about this when she placed it in a corner of her metal box, and I was made happy by this idea of solidifying memories; our self-sacrifice becomes bitter, our laughter goes away, we're overcome with loneliness, the need for relief, and well, after all, we can sleep holding hands; this afternoon, in our room, Marisol studies, seated on the rocking chair, I enter, I stand behind the chair and her head inclines backwards as if to look at me, I lean forwards towards her and in this moment, our gaze becomes a prolonged kiss, the door locked, our naked bodies, skin to skin, the movement of her surrender in my mouth, the pressure of our hands drowning out our screams; we're not completely suffused with serenity because we've broken a promise but we experience the relief of knowing everything is still the same, that absence has yet to surprise us; now dressed, the door unlocked, Marisol's in the rocking chair and I'm standing, something makes me look through the window, there's no-one down there, in the empty backyard, I keep looking around and I focus on the apartment building that's across the yard, I scrutinize all the windows and suddenly, look, Marisol, look at that window, what do you see there? and this coldness that invades us because we recognize it, a telescope pointed at our window, iciness turns to words, Marisol, could they have seen us? and Marisol says, I don't think so because the bed is way below the window and that apartment is at the same height as this one; but I know that, like vultures, they've wanted to devour the vision of so many kisses that we thought protected by our walls; and now, this new concern, this surveillance of the window; now the exams are here and I'm short on time, a dose of Benzedrine to keep me awake, to try and complete ten subjects instead of the five or six usually taken; the course finished, the farewell and this absence that is Summer; in Caimanera, everything's the same, the satin pajamas, the scarves, the embroidery; in the afternoons, I choose the images that I'll keep with me in this part of the afternoon, I don't know how long I've been here, standing, my mind, lost in water, setting itself free, freeing itself, and my body's so still so that no-one interrupts this means of escape; a presence approaches timidly, the soft voice of my father, what, child, are you thinking? I don't respond at all and when I feel his arm on my back with almost tenderness, as if to keep me company, this hardness emerges from me as I move away from him; his eyes down and this silence of his that I feel so deeply; I watch him move off with a sad step and I want to shout at him, forgive me, Papá, forgive my hardness, why have you fallen, tell me, why have you fallen, tell me so that I can understand you; I keep watching him and I leave him to his sadness, I remain standing, without moving, my mind escaping out to sea, until I can't any more, and here, with me, this loneliness that's so solitary; Marisol's letters, sporadic, and mine to her are also few for everything that I have to remain quiet about; in one of her letters Marisol tells me that Nievita has closed the guest house, that she went to Havana with her mom to fetch her things and that she's already found another guest house that's in H Street, an old house, but nice, that she and I will have a room to ourselves; this urgency to leave this place, the need for my freedom, not to be a burden to anyone, what roads will I have to travel in this life, how does one free oneself; the comments in Caimanera, the gypsy's here, the gypsy has arrived, and only twenty five cents; I want to visit the gypsy and my mom says, look, let's do this, I'll go first and a few days later you go because if we go together she'll say the same thing to both of us; and I say, Mamá, who is the gypsy? and she replies, well, no-one knows where she's from, she's already been here once when she stayed for a few days, but I've never been to see her; my mom goes to see her and when she returns, I ask, so anxiously, what did she say to you, Mamá, tell me, what did she say to you? and she says, well, child, she told me such great nonsense that I wouldn't even let her continue, just imagine, according to her your father is about to die and I told her, look, madam, stop right there, because my husband has never suffered from even one headache; now, child, if you want to go, go; I want to go and I cross the town until I get to the house where the gypsy is staying, a type of hut but without a roof of palm leaves, instead it has a roof of zinc; the gypsy lays out the cards for me and look, you want to leave here and you're studying and you're going to go overseas but later on, before you leave you're going to get married and one day you're going to finish your degree, although I don't know when; and now the gypsy becomes very serious, and look, there's something here but I don't know whether to tell you; and suddenly I'm frightened, but of course, yes you must tell me; and the gypsy says, well, look, your father's about to die, we're at the beginning of October, I don't think he'll make it to next month, no, he won't make it to November, this is now a question of a few weeks, something that's going to happen suddenly, as if at the wrong time, because he's still a young man, not so? and I say, he's forty nine, and she says, well look, on your father, for years now, they've cast the evil eye and now they've decided to do it, to kill him, because it's not yet his time to die, but what they've done to him is too strong; I leave there, carrying with me this bewilderment through the streets and now my house and my mother in the living room and I see my father in shorts, on the veranda that looks onto the patio, at the moment when he's about to pick up something that's on the table, and at that moment I knew, Mamá try to see that they give him a spiritual cleansing, try to do something so that he doesn't take darkness with him to his death, can you take care of that Mamá? will you do it? and my mom, indecisive, says, well, let's see if he wants that, I'll try; now it's time for me to go and this hardness that prevents me from saying to him, Papá, take care at the hour of your death, Papá, take this light, take my light, to accompany you; the house on H has its charm, an old house, with a garden and an wrought-iron gate, but so many people, and the room Marisol and I share has a door that opens like in the movies about the Wild West, like those saloons in the ghost towns, with a little latch to keep the two halves together, the lack of privacy and the surveillance await us, and Marisol says, do you know that Nievita told Mami about us? Mami told me and I was able to convince her, although I don't know if deep down she'll believe me, and now you know how careful we have to be, we have to go out with boys, we have to make friends with the other girls, we can't isolate ourselves because they're going to end up saying the same thing, it would be best to try again, to try and give this up, I know we can do it; Marisol will only be in Havana for a few more days because she's come by a position as a music teacher in a small town of Las Villas, Marisol's father had to buy her the position, I don't know how much he had to pay for her appointment and she has to spend a certain number of days giving lessons in the town, and the rest of the year she's free; you know what, Marisol? before I left Caimanera I should have spoken to my father and I didn't do it, I said goodbye so coldly, and now I have to tell you about him, Marisol, because I've never done so, because that time you asked me where he worked, I gave you a dirty look and we never mentioned it again, I didn't want to recognize his existence, because he embarrassed me so, like a social being that didn't fulfill his function as bread-winner, but he's there, Marisol, he's always been there, and I never tried to understand him, to walk in his failure since he was sacked from the Base, to understand him better, and when he dies so suddenly, he will be even more present, because of all the things I never told him, I won't have time, Marisol, I won't have time to see him again; Marisol's tenderness reaches me like relief, don't obsess like that, you'll see that you will, you'll see that you'll be able to speak to him and the two of you will be able to talk, everything is going to be alright, you'll see; and when all this obsesses me, I tell Marisol about it and she repeats for me that everything is going to be alright

and I begin calming down; a few days and Marisol isn't here, I begin
getting to know the girls who live here, Quica has become my friend,
she's good, uncomplicated, generous; her friend Matilde, with whom
she shares a room, is egotistical, with the face of a mango and with a
boyfriend who also has the face of a mango; in the same room with
Quica and Matilde, is Hilda the Arab, so quiet, so intelligent, such a
country girl, such a good person, who speaks to almost nobody, only
with her boyfriend, who's also an Arab; Zaida is from Matanzas, bad
tempered, rude, with a room to herself; and Leyda and Bibi and Nenita
in another room; Bibi told me that Nenita is a homosexual and that the
owners are going to get rid of her under the pretext that they're going
to close the guest house and she's so worried because she's a friend of
Nenita's and she cares about her, but the owners have told Bibi that she
has to tell Nenita that it's true, that they are going to close the house
and if Bibi doesn't cooperate with them, she can go too, and Bibi tells
me, it's just that I really care about Nenita and I don't care if she's a
homosexual or not, they don't have the right to do that to her because
she never hassles anyone, why have they put me in the position of having
to trick her, but at the same time, I would prefer that she leave here,
without knowing why, I know she has to leave; the owners are the
daughters of Doña Filomena, who is now really old and never gets
involved in anything, the ones who are in charge of everything are Niní,
who's about forty years old, the fiancée of a thin, bitter, dry doctor with
little frameless glasses and an old-fashioned moustache, Niní calls him
Cuchi, but Marisol has already christened him Tamarind between
Bitterness and Loneliness; the eldest daughter is Cuquita, who's about
forty three, and is a lawyer but doesn't have a practice and works in the
Fiscal Section, her boyfriend, from a millionaire family, red-haired, as
fat as a barrel, who speaks like a retard, has his medical degree and is
installed in a small clinic on the outskirts of Havana; a few weeks ago
Marisol and I had to chaperone Cuquita when he took her to see the
clinic; the two fiancés are almost in their fifties and can't make up their
minds to marry the two sisters; they come courting every night, Niní
and Cuchi sit on the chairs in the living room and Cuquita and Orlandito
sit on the chairs in the dining room, we always ask ourselves what
Tamarind and Niní talk about, so bitter are they; but what Orlandito
and Cuquita talk about, everyone knows because Orlandito speaks at

the top of his voice and even though we can't hear Cuquita, we know what they're talking about, now Orlandito has got it into his head to study Pedagogy and he studies at the top of his voice in the dining room and when we ask him to lower his voice because no-one can study, he says, oh, shaw, thash OK, but continues shouting, and Cuquita, who's so intelligent, is aware of the spectacle that Orlandito makes of himself but tries to hide it because for her and Niní what's most important is to get married, the two are so dedicated to their boyfriends, that they cater to their comfort, and ensure that nothing bothers them; Cuquita is prepared to do her duty, to get married and to listen for ever to Orlandito's solemn speeches: wook, wook, I have a pashient thash verwy shick, wove, and I shink, wove, that he needsh penishillin, wook, wook, wove, I shink that wif penishillin she'll be cwured, what do you shink, Cuqui? and Cuquita agrees, Cuquita always agrees, yes, Orlandito, try penicillin, we'll see; and Orlandito says, good, Cuqui, now we're gowing to shtudy Pedagogy; and there he goes with the pedagogy until eleven at night when he leaves us after making us spend hours looking for a corner where we don't have to listen to him; Bibi, also has a boyfriend because she's decided that she has to get married, but Bibi knows, if she marries, that will be her death ritual, to fall into Ricardo's asphyxia which will control her socially, officially and physically, which will also control her mind that's so clear; her Miss Dior perfume, her elegance, to get all dressed up to go courting with Ricardo and to return weighed down with tedium, withered by Ricardo's mediocrity, because, for Ricardo, coming into this world means studying Commercial Science and some day to run his father's hotel, there, in Santiago, with Bibi locked up at home, obeying his every command, obeying his mother, his father, his sisters, and the whole close clan of a family; Bibi sometimes talks to me about these things, like a half complaint; I ask her, are you in love with Ricardo? and Bibi replies, no, not me, but Mamá and I have spoken about it, Ricardo is the man I'm going to marry; Ricardo and all his money, and that haughty air that he wears in his impeccable clothes, in the quality of the clothing that covers him, but also, that insecurity that he tries to hide between the brusqueness and the silence; one day Bibi says, do you know something? Ricardo has forbidden me to mention you to him, he's forbidden me even to mention your name, because sometimes language comes out of me that he finds strange, and his surprise, and I say, that that language is yours, that's how you speak, and sometimes I get it into my head to repeat your litanies, and his surprise, and I say, that these litanies are yours, that that's how you speak, and at other times I come out with your sayings, and his surprise, and I say, that these sayings are yours, that that's how you speak, and today he's forbidden this, that I should never again mention your name, that I should never speak of you, that I should never speak like you; the sparkle in Bibi's eyes, and her smile because no comment is needed, and my satisfaction, that of knowing that Ricardo feels threatened, that he should feel the need to forbid Bibi to mention my name, but that, despite everything, I'm there; the room's empty without Marisol, Quica comes to keep me company as if she knew that someone needs to try and take away some of this anguish caused by absence; now, at dawn, when I wake up, I go and sit in the living room, and Bibi's always there, we look at one another, we find ourselves in that language that's now become ours, there's something in these mornings that relieves me of so many sorrows; now I'm going to class and I always meet up with Eddy in the Law cafeteria, while I eat my guava pie and drink my Coke or coffee, I'm touched by his protective attitude and when I go with him to the Radiocentro café, between the pork and ham sandwich and the ice-cream, I'm glad to be doing what Marisol wanted; we're in the last week of October, I'm haunted by worry, I'm haunted by fear; the morning of the 30th, the extended ring of long distance and I almost wake, I know I should get up but don't leave my bed; the ring is transformed into voices that I hear in the distance, a murmur of voices draws closer and now standing before me, Doña Filomena, Cuquita, Bibi, Hilda the Arab, Matilde and Quica; and Cuquita says, look, get up now, they've called, and your dad's not doing so well and you need to go there, and I say that I want to know, is it serious, and Cuquita says, no, not at all, they just want you to be there, but he's out of danger, and I insist that I want to know what's wrong with him, and they don't tell me, and Cuquita says that she doesn't know; I get up quickly, I need to get everything ready for the journey, the ticket, everything else, and Cuquita says, no, Bibi has already arranged everything, get dressed and pack your suitcases, Hilda and Bibi will go with you to the airport so you're not alone, just so that you're not alone; on the way, the almost palpable compassion of Hilda, that hurt inscrutability of Bibi; the plane, to Santiago, the plane to Guantánamo, white clouds under me, an oh-so diaphanous space, it's my meeting with a truth that's so serene, my father's dead, I know my father's dead; the airport made out on a bird's flight, we land, and as I leave the plane, that man there, standing, I know that he's waiting for me, perhaps it's my father who has come here so that I don't get a fright, so that I can see that, in truth, nothing has happened; I hurry, I approach, and it's Inesita's father who has come to meet me and he hugs me, and look, I came to wait for you, we have to go to Caimanera, I'll go with you; and I ask, and my dad? and he says, well, your dad couldn't come, but you'll see that he's well, you'll soon see, right now we're going to Caimanera by taxi; in the taxi, a friend of Carmita's and Inesita's father, a closed silence the whole way, now we're near Caimanera, in front of the hillock that's the cemetery, a group of men are standing in the road gesturing to stop the taxi and Inesita's father gets out quickly and takes them aside and argues, no, no, and returns to the taxi and his voice, to the driver, look, carry on, carry on to Caimanera; I know that they're burying my father, I don't allow myself to think about that; the taxi's moving and the town, the veranda of the house, all the people, and my mother comes out crying to meet me, and I ask, where's my dad? where's my dad? she gets control of herself for a moment, and, they've already buried him, child, they've already buried him; the crowd draws closer, watching out for my tears that they want to collect for their catharsis; I don't cry and those faces contracting into a sob that has nothing to do with my father nor with me; Mamá, tell them to go, I need to be alone, I go to the sofa couch, I lie down, close my eyes, and my mother asks, are you feeling ill, child? and I say, yes, Mamá, the people, all the people, tell them to go, and my mom says, no, I can't tell them that, they've come to be with us, but almost immediately, apologizing, she speaks to them, please, she's not well, almost faint, someone's already gone for the doctor, please, I appreciate you having come but she needs to rest; the contracted, damp, unknown faces begin leaving, I remain in the silence without crying, the doctor examines me, she's fine, perfectly fine, and he leaves with his black bag; I ask my mom to leave me there alone; I lie on my back, so straight in the bed, and stay like that, for who knows how long; now well into the night, I get up, I explore the house where he no longer lives, remains of death rituals, a crucifix, the candles, that smell of burnt wax, my mother's explanation, child, we couldn't wait for you, we kept vigil over him here, but with this heat, we had to decide; a few sleeping pills to help me sleep in this house of mourning; the light of day, and on the bedside table, his ruby ring and his pipe; I wander through the house as though looking for something in the corners, and when my mother isn't looking, I go to his room, open the closet to see his clothes, I touch them, I remember how this shirt looked on him; and now this clothing of his so empty, and me before the armoire, as if each day I came to look for him in his clothes and I don't find him, and this sob that burst out of me, so mine, I let myself cry because there are truths that enter us in fragments and today his death has matured in me; I begin breaking my silence, tell me, Mamá, how did it happen, and my mom asks me, didn't you receive my letter? and I say no, and she says, well, I wrote to you a few days before he died, I told you that he bought a little boat and that he would go fishing everyday with a man who lives in Nunque and that they took the fish to the market and made a little money, and your papá gave some to me, and the rest, to pay for the boat; in my letter I told you that he had changed so much, that it was as if he had begun to transform himself, oh, child, what strange things happen in life, the 29th of October your father was going fishing and I begged him, please, not to go, because of this strange dream that I had, that he died suddenly and that hundreds of workers from the Base asked for permission to leave work to go to the funeral and that there wasn't time to bring the hearse from Guantánamo and that they took him in a type of huge truck and when I woke up, I told your father that he shouldn't go fishing that day and I told him the dream and he laughed but I insisted that he shouldn't go and when the fisherman from Nunque came to look for him he made his apologies, said that he wasn't feeling well, that he couldn't go; we stayed here he and I, talking about his death, and he asked me, if he were to die, what was I going to do, and I told him, I would leave here at once, I'd go to another town or another country and he stayed like that, very sad, and he said to me, no, stay here, don't struggle all alone in a place where no-one knows you; here you may have more or less to deal with, but you won't have that loneliness of the unknown; just think, child, we even talked about that on that day and then in the afternoon he began to feel ill, I was in the living room and I saw him on the veranda that looks onto the patio walking, jerking, and I thought he was playing, you know how he liked to play like that, but he kept staggering, I go up to him and I see he's in a bad way, a really bad way; he went to lie down and I lay down at his side, I fell asleep and at midnight, something woke me, I don't know how to tell you what woke me, something awful that was happening to him, and he couldn't move from the bed, and I was so frightened and he almost couldn't talk, but he said to me, with such effort, stay calm, you have to be strong, you only die once; I went to find the doctor and left Luneida here, she's the one who washes the dishes for me and helps me to embroider, Luneida sleeps here because we don't rent out rooms now because ever since he started with his boat we decided not to rent them out anymore because we needed this peace; when I went out and fetched the doctor, on the way I told Santiaga so that she would come with me, when we got back here he wasn't able to talk and the doctor said to me, this is an embolism, but very bad, so bad, that if he lives, he's going to be a vegetable; almost at once he died, and afterwards it was like I saw in my dream, so many workers began to ask for permission on the Base to go to the funeral that at two in the afternoon they had stopped giving leave and didn't want to give any more; I've never ever seen a funeral with so many people; and just as I saw it in my dream, there wasn't time to bring the hearse from Guantánamo and they had to take him to the cemetery in an enormous truck; my mother keeps talking and I'm offended by this grotesque aspect of death, the inevitable process of conducting a funeral in whatever form of transport turns up, and my mother, grateful, says, you know how everyone here loved your father, you can't imagine how good they've been; I continue to listen to her and I'm still hurt by this enormous truck; and now it's time to embroider, to embroider incessantly because that way, if I embroider piles of pajamas, perhaps I can return to Havana, November is almost over and we've decided that if I return, it will be after the December vacations to avoid the cost of so many trips; I'm worried about my mom being on her own, but a divorced woman who works on the Base is going to rent a room from her, what she'll pay is a joke, but what a relief, my mother isn't going to be alone, and now this sad day in December when a new year is going to dawn; soon I'll be in Havana and before I go I want to see my father's tomb; I accompany my mother to the hillock on the outskirts of Caimanera; before me, this piece of marble, the name of my father and the date, 1903-1952, I'm not moved by the stone and I'm not moved by the date and that name of my father's that seems strange to me, as if it weren't my father who was there, in that pile of earth; it's time to go back and with me goes this incredulity; and now it's time to leave, the ticket, the plane, Havana, and it's January and Marisol hasn't arrived; Bibi is waiting for me at the house with her almost tenderness that's so flirtatious, with her happiness that's so gentle, her welcoming hug, every morning we get a head start on the others, Bibi and I in the living room looking at one another, defining ourselves, look, Bibi, I can see you in the circle of light from a projector, in that smaller world, with the light that goes with you in all your solitudes, in that solitude that you inhabit with Ricardo, sometimes we speak volumes without talking, because we have this way of understanding each other; days pass, Marisol arrives, and look, I've been keeping this letter for you; it's my mother's letter, your dad bought a little boat and now goes fishing every day; he goes with a fisherman who lives in Nunque; your dad's changed so much, from what they make from fishing, he always gives me something, and the rest goes towards paying off the boat; the letter now folded back in the envelope, my hand covering the envelope as if wishing to retain something, and I don't know what it is; Marisol is on again about abstinence, that we have to go out with boys, but above all, that we have to abstain and make friends with others and not isolate ourselves; I'm saturated with the guilt of my mother's struggle to survive, to keep me in Havana, and now the guilt of feeling all this that I have to give up, the weight that comes to me with guilt, this anguish that never leaves me, this unpleasant wait; at night we spend ages gazing at one another, with controlled urgency, Marisol in her bed and me in mine, tonight the look stretches on, and it's tenderness and it's intensity just below the surface and in my mouth, an almost painful insistence; Marisol, slowly opening her blouse, and her breast waiting for me, now the two of us in my bed, I want to forget that this happiness can be so momentary, tension leaves us, and now Marisol in her bed, we talk about our promise and abstinence and our lack of willpower; and I say, Marisol, I can't believe that this love could offend God, nobody brings to the surface this nobleness, the best of me, like you do, this can't be a sin, I know this, and Marisol replies, I feel the same way, I know that no-one knows how to love the way you do, I'm sure that nobody would know how to love me like you, but other people, and suddenly, a light that descends upon us like goodness, like the most pure, infinite love; do you feel it, Marisol? yes, a presence, and I say, yes, the presence of infinite love, and we fall asleep in this blessing; now we still go out as before but when we haven't any money left to go to a movie or to go out for a snack, we no longer have anyone to sell our clothes to, because before we sold the dresses we didn't like to Claudia and with that money we could go out; here on the corner is the Viennese restaurant with its European atmosphere and the owner who speaks to us with her German accent, tonight, in the Viennese, the piano with its music so lonely, almost classical, always sad, the pianist with his old-fashioned clothes, that have come out of some old trunk, and now the menu and this light so intimate that half illuminates us, giving us a yellowy-orange reflection, Marisol, looking at me says, I so like the reflection of this light on your face, in your honey-colored eyes, do you know, Mochi, that ours is one of those great loves of history? and I begin asking myself if, in other reincarnations we would have loved one another, but in this one, it was destined to happen, because, just think, Marisol, to coincide in time and space to find ourselves here, now; the waiter with his little notebook, our order, for Marisol, broiled steak and for me, roast chicken, wine to keep us company, the waiter recommends dessert, the specialty of the house, that sounds something like cheese strudel, a delicious cheese pastry with cream, we enjoy ourselves in all this so slowly, and now coffee to cap off the dinner in these moments that are so ours; a few weeks later, Marisol is no longer here and Quica often comes to keep me company; in the early morning, I meet once again with Bibi in the living room, and always in the afternoon Bibi and I in her room; Bibi places a small towel with ice in it on her breasts to keep them firm, and me there, while she moves the ice in concentric circles from the nipple to the base, what beautiful breasts Bibi has, she knows it and each afternoon after the ice she looks at them in the mirror, and I'm always astonished by this strange ceremony; one morning, at around eleven, Bibi comes up to me in the lonely corridor where I'm searching among the piled up letters on the long table, to see if there's one for me, and Bibi, with a naughty look in her eyes: do you know what I was going to do? I was going to kiss you on the mouth, what would you do if I kissed you on the mouth? I know that Bibi's only playing, a momentary flirtation that appears just to suddenly disappear and become distance and I speak without looking at her, if you'd tried to kiss me, I'd have pushed you away; now it's exam time, once again my ten subjects, and after the exams, a letter from my mom, saying that I should go and see Marianita, that she will pay for my ticket because we have to know how Marianita's making out in a strange country, as young as she is; I'm filled with fear as I continue reading, you decide what you want to do, but if you go to Texas, most likely you will have to stop studying because it's impossible for me to meet both costs; and here I can't carry on without telling the true story, I can't continue without saying that I'm not an only child, I can't continue without saying that Marianita isn't Carmita's daughter, because Marianita is my mother's daughter, like me, and that's why, although my letter clearly states that I want to carry on studying, my mom insists, I need to know how Marianita's doing, so go to Texas directly from Havana to save the fare, and we'll see how we sort out your studies; last year I had already gone through the process of getting my passport in case I had to go and see Marianita, because my mom wanted it like that, in case of anything that might occur, and Marisol was with me for all this with the photos and the trips to the lawyer's office in Old Havana, until finally, Republic of Cuba, passport number 15691; place of birth, Guantánamo, Oriente, Cuba; date of birth, March 12, 1934; civil status, single; profession, student; height, 5'1"; color of skin, white; color of eyes, hazel; color of hair, brown; document number 20353-52; receipt number 4278; and this certifies that the bearer of this passport is a Cuban citizen and in light of this we beg the civil and military authorities of the countries through which the bearer travels to recognize the citizenship of the bearer; issued in Havana on July 18, 1952; the ticket, the clothes I'm going to take, my cases packed, Marisol at my side in Rancho Boyeros, look after yourself, Mochi, take care, and that deep sadness in her eyes when it's time to say goodbye; the lonely flight, Miami airport, a stamp that they stick in my passport, U.S. Department of Justice, admitted July 24, 1953, Immigration and Naturalization Service; I'm in line, waiting my turn to go through customs, I hope they don't search much because in my suitcases I have green plantains for Marianita, and here it says that they don't allow plants or anything like that, and suddenly the voice, will everyone place their suitcases on the platform, I see them there, open, while time passes until I say, look, please, in twenty minutes I have to catch another plane to Corpus Christi, I have to go to another airport to catch it and I'm not going to have time, please, check my suitcases quickly; I show him the plane ticket, the customs official shuts my suitcases and, OK, you can go; I run for the exit, a little afraid when I take the taxi because where is it going to take me, I say in my English to the blonde, chubby taxi driver, that I know the other airport is nearby but if he gets me there quickly, I'll give him five dollars more, five dollars, five dollars, and I show him the note and chubby says OK, drives like crazy, we arrive and finally the plane, what joy those plantains are going to give Marianita; no smoking, safety belt, landing, Corpus Christi airport and a small fear, will they be waiting for me or not, and if not, what should I do, how do I get to Kingsville, how do I find their trailer; I go down the stairs, walk towards the building and there, Marianita and Albert; hugs, the happiness of seeing one another, the happiness of saying, Marianita, you won't believe it, I've brought you some plantains; Marianita imagines and enjoys these fried plantains that are so tasty and she tells me that she can cook now, that in the beginning all she did was open cans and, as she didn't know any English, each time she opened a can it was a surprise and, in the beginning, sometimes Albert got back from work and found her with her cases packed and saying that she was going back to Cuba, especially the day they had just moved into an apartment and she had to clean it because it was all greasy and when Albert arrived he found her seated on the stairs, with her suitcase packed and crying because she wanted to go back to Cuba; and I ask if this has happened often, and she says yes, but that after Albert was there she would get over it and would unpack her suitcase and that now everything was different, but just imagine, without speaking English and almost without understanding what Albert was saying, and Albert opposed to learning Spanish and he never sat down to teach me English, what I've learned, I've learned from the television and guessing what people were saying to me; Marianita and I speak Spanish the whole trip with Albert there, at the wheel, stiff as a mummy; Kingsville, the trailer, a tedium sprinkled throughout this trailer park; in the streets of Kingsville that we pass through, everyone seems like country people with boots, spurs, cowboy hat; Marianita's trailer has one bedroom, a bathroom, a kitchen and the living room where there's

a small dining room table and a sofa bed where I sleep; we speak for
hours without once mentioning what she had said to me so many times
in Cuba, I, in this house full of old people, am not staying, who's going
to look after them when they're old, my two aunts, my mom, my dad,
my uncle, at the time, my grandmother will already be dead, but what
about everyone else? to live with these two aunts for whom everything
is bad, for whom everything is a sin and who are always on about how
we're the walking stick of old age? and if not, to go to Caimanera to do
what? me, I'm going to marry the first one to appear, and I know,
Marianita, the first one to appear was Albert, and I know, Marianita,
that you would have married him anyway, even if my mom wouldn't
have lashed out at you when you were walking with her through the
streets of Guantánamo and she asked you if you were getting married
and you told her with that way of yours of not giving explanations, that
you didn't know, that you had no idea if you were getting married and
the day of your wedding I hugged you and cried deeply for the innocence
of your eighteen years, I cried deeply for my mother's smack, she had to
choose, you know, the scarves and the pajamas with the dragons and
the huts, made in Cuba, weren't enough for all the bills, and my
university career, Marianita, what's it costing you? but you know that
my mom loves us, that she loves you and that's why I'm here, on a trip
paid for by the infinite hours shed on dragons and huts, all made in
Cuba, for us, for the two of us, Marianita, you can see; now, surrounded
by the absence of imagination in Albert to whom it doesn't occur to go
anywhere, I miss Marisol with an almost sob that accompanies me
because we're separated by time, so many weeks before it's time to go
back; if we go out in the car, Marianita and Albert ride in the front and
I ride in the back, dressing Marisol in white, transparent night dresses,
and her breasts right there, waiting for me, always a white, transparent
top, and her waiting for me; from time to time, Marianita notes that
I'm so quiet and I tell her yes, quietly as I can, so that nothing distracts
me from this thing I feel so frequently; the days pass and our trips are
to the market and to buy some screw or fishing rod, and I say that I
want to see King's Ranch, that when they called this town Kingsville
it's because King's Ranch must be important, and I want to see San
Antonio and I want to go to Dallas and to Austin which is the capital
of Texas but Albert stays quiet; finally he decides to take a trip, he takes

us to his parents house in Mercedes, a small town in the country, we visit the little cotton farm with the wooden house where there's no bathroom or toilet and Marianita and I have to go out every morning to see behind which trunk we can take shelter because we don't dare to go to the outhouse that they have in the yard because Marianita says that there are snakes and rats and at night we urinate in a can and in the morning we throw the urine in the yard; Marianita and I decided to call Albert's mom Severita, because she has a face full of furrows and looks like Severita, she makes dresses out of flour sacks that now they print with little flowers so that the country people get all excited and buy them; we're amazed by this ingenuous old woman who's set in her tradition of ignoring the rhythm of civilization; the refrigerator and gas stove are there because Albert paid for them; the old woman makes delicious little cookies with chocolate kisses and also, okra coated in breadcrumbs; Marianita and I call the old man Maca-Maca and he seems like a character from a country novel with his pipe and his dungarees, seated on his tractor all day; I spend the night hours without being able to sleep because the old people have made the mattresses with raw cotton and they're hard and full of lumps, and they say that there are some rats that are so big that they kill them with a shotgun or they set enormous traps for them, that they're the size of rabbits and that they walk along the crossbar of the roof which is above the bed where I sleep, I spend hours watching the crossbar so that, in case I see any movement, I can run out; in the mornings Marianita and I go out for a walk around the farm and we go to the hut of some Mexicans who, when they see us, always say, here come the little mistresses, and when we arrive to greet them they always thank us with great gesticulations as if our presence there constituted a great honor; Marianita always takes them something, especially clothing, and sometimes she gives them a dollar that has managed to escape Albert's strict control over money; when we're in the trailer, I keep insisting on when we're going to go somewhere worthwhile, and one day, Albert says, well, that he's going to take us to a very famous beach, Padre Island, I see myself enjoying the sea, sitting on the sand, pretending to be asleep so that they don't interrupt my meeting with Marisol, but Albert announces our trip at night, explaining by the way, what I want is to go there to fish; the oh-so long journey, Albert talking about the coyotes in Texas and didn't I hear the howls of coyotes on his parent's farm and that maybe on the road we'll see one, and I say, I never heard them nor saw any on the road, although I have seen rabbits, dozens of rabbits and with that the conversation ends; at the totally deserted beach, it's as black as the mouth of a wolf, I lie down to sleep on the back seat of the car and Marianita lies down on the front seat and we fall asleep until morning comes to wake us, Albert, who's now back with all his fishing gear, so happy with how much fun all this has been for him, and as soon as he gets in the car, starts the motor and we're on our way back to Kingsville, to pass the days playing cards with Marianita and to wait for the nights and to feel the insects hitting the glass of the window looking for light; another day, perhaps to get away from my insistence, Albert decides, OK, we're going to San Antonio, and I'm so happy on this Sunday because I'm really looking forward to seeing the Alamo, but when we get out, the sign, *closed*; and Albert immediately, well, let's go back because there's nothing else to see in San Antonio; the car started, the unpleasant return journey, the midday heat; now I see Marianita laughing before a shelf in a kitchen cupboard that she's just opened and calls me, come here, you have to see this; I look and see cans and cans, all empty, piled up, filling the shelf, and I ask, hey, Marianita, what are you guys doing with all these cans? and Marianita says, that's one of Albert's ideas, because according to him, if a war comes, we already have cans where we can store water and other things, just imagine, I have to throw out cans on the quiet because if I left it to him, we'd have this trailer full of cans, from the floor to the ceiling; and she laughs again somewhere between rebelliousness and condescension as she shows me a collection of fishing rods and rifles of every kind; September 3, my trip, the stamp in my passport, Republic of Cuba, port of entry, Rancho Boyeros; in my suitcase, the present I've brought for Bibi, a little nylon petticoat, pleated, with some very fine pleats in different shades of yellow as if they were different shades of the sun, and Marisol's present, several records, the *Warsaw Concerto* by Richard Addinsell, *La Valse* by Maurice Ravel, and small records of forty five revolutions with *High Noon* and *Ruby*; letters to my mom, that Marianita's well, not to worry, that she can cook now and has the trailer well organized and very clean, but I don't say anything about the collection of cans, fishing rods and rifles, because this is a report, Mamá, so that you can be at peace, because this is a report, Mamá, so that you can say, between pride and resignation, I have a daughter there, in the North, married to an American; since I got back I've been out with several boys to the movies and I've managed the best I can the pressure it puts on me to strike up a conversation; one night Marisol and I go out with two boys to dance at the Tropicana and at Sans Souci with two other couples; the crowds, strange to me, jumping or holding each other tight to kill time between the Cuba Libre and the smoke of lighted cigarettes; sometimes Marisol and I set out to listen to the records I brought her but now, if she goes sometimes to class or stays at home, I go out on my own from time to time so that people see that we're not always together; one day I went out on my own, wherever the first bus that passed took me and I get off on the corner where the synagogue is that I've always wanted to see, I walk towards it, I stop at the foot of the flight of steps, I stand looking at the undecorated façade and suddenly, this presence behind me, I half turn and there, so close, the Gentleman of Paris with his cape, his filth, his fly open, his tangled hair, his gestures of baroque elegance; we greet each other as if he were a great gentleman and I a great lady from another century; I speak to him, because to whom better, look, Gentleman, I know that soon they're going to take me away from Havana, something that is not me takes me because I don't want to leave, but before I go, before my absence, I want to see a synagogue; the bows of the gentleman agreeing and our parallel steps ascending, I knock on the half-open door, no-one answers, I enter, a man walks through the empty hall, and my questions, is it alright for me to enter and see the synagogue, and he says, as if he weren't answering anyone, no, there's nothing to see here, if you would like, call by telephone and ask the rabbi, no-one's here now; he turns his back on me and disappears; the Gentleman is still there, I call him over and, you see, Gentleman, I haven't been allowed to see the synagogue, but what a privilege, to meet you; again his bows, his smile of satisfaction at hearing my words, and our goodbye; I walk the streets to lose myself in time and I think, if it rains tonight, I'm not going to cry because I have to get rid of the terror of imagining the water filtering into my father's tomb to fill his bones with cold; now it's night, the heavy shaking of the rain and a sob that escapes me to remain between Marisol and I; at night we continue with our abstinence and the same need as always and each one in her bed when we start to talk about what we would do if it weren't for abstinence and we end up talking to each other as if we were making love, and suddenly, Marisol's breasts, waiting for me, until we interrupt the abstinence; we enter the heart of the night always late because Quica comes into our room after going courting with her boyfriend and she doesn't leave us until one, until two, until she feels like it; and Marisol insists to me, we can't say anything to her so that they don't think we're trying to be on our own; in the morning, at six, here's Matilde, to use the wash basin that's in our room, to wash out her mouth, to wash her mango face, to enjoy interminable gargling and gargling, and this invasion of our privacy and my indignation, but Marisol has already said, we can't tell anyone not to come into our room, we can't isolate ourselves; the semester advances and one of these mornings during our abstinence and guilt, we hug for ages in the bathroom, we stay standing, next to the wash basin for this new meeting and now we don't say that we didn't have enough will power, because a peace comes before guilt, once again the Presence, like a light, like an infinite love that touches us; Marisol, do you feel anything? and Marisol says, yes, the Presence, what incredible peace, God is here, with us, He's here so that we know that our love isn't a sin; the vacations draw closer and there's a new worry, my mother writes to me that Teófilo, Emma the Arab's nephew, is competing with her in the sales of pajamas, a man so immensely rich comes to snatch from us our only livelihood; now Pack buys his pajamas from Teófilo because Teófilo has them embroidered on a machine and they cost him less and he sells them to Pack cheaper than my mom can, and without selling pajamas, how can I continue studying, how are we even going to survive, and each time more so, this departure of mine seems not to have a return; the afternoon I have to leave arrives, in a few hours I'll be far away, and already, in the morning, Marisol and I know that this may be our last time, and the two of us in my bed and our surrender that intensifies with the thought of separation, until we're at peace, as if we'd touched infinity; now in the airport, and Marisol says, how sad it is to see you disappear in an airplane, when you went to Texas and I saw that the plane was almost out of sight, separating you from me in this space that's so big, I felt as if something were breaking inside me; again today you're leaving me like that, for me the airplane is a symbol of separation, what takes you away from me; and I reply, so that our separation doesn't sound so definitive, yes, Marisol, planes take me, but they also bring me back, and she repeats, they also bring you back, we stay like that, looking at the horizon, between hope and resignation, waiting for my flight, that arrives so soon to separate me again; in Caimanera, my mother struggling to make ends meet, selling shoes, clothing in installments; I have with me all my books from this Law course and as the months pass I continue studying in Guantánamo, in Caimanera, perhaps I can go to Havana for the final exams, but it's almost time for the final exams and I'm still in Caimanera, and my mother says, look, I don't know if I should write to my sister Amparo, the one who's lived for so many years in New York, or perhaps it would be better if you wrote to her, because the two times she's come here, well, it seems that she liked you, ask her to lend us eighty pesos, tell her just how grateful we'll be, that I'll pay her back bit by bit, because child, it hurts me so to see you lose this year after studying so, I write the letter with this shame that poverty brings, and almost at once, the reply, I received your letter and I'm writing to tell you that I'm not up to paying for anyone's university career; I'm left with this disbelief after reading the letter, as if the situation were to be sorted out anyway, at any moment, but nothing changes and I write to Marisol, it seems definite to me, I can't go, not even for the exams, we haven't been able to find the money; a few weeks later, a letter from Marisol, I've taken so long to write to you because I've been trying to find out how you can continue studying, I've spoken to a woman with a guest house who wants to sell it; it's a well-known house and you won't have any trouble finding students, also, I could help you find them, but it's imperative that you and your mami go to Havana and speak to the owner as soon as possible, and Marisol insists with that insistence that I've never seen in anyone but Marisol; I speak to my mom, and my mom says, well, let's see who'll lend me the money with interest for the fare because ever since Santiaga died I've no-one to borrow from, because even though with Santiaga, that's for sure, I paid her interest and high at that, the other loan sharks are even worse, but if it means that you can continue studying and that we can survive, let's see, child, let's see how we can find the money for the fare, and a few days later, another loan shark lent her the money; we're in Havana and I'm horrified at the idea that Marisol, my mom and I will share an apartment; Havana has turned sad without Marisol and this moment in which I see my mother so helpless has turned sad as we walk in Vedado towards the guest house; now in the apartment and the woman, oh, yes, I'm going to sell the guest house, of course, I'm referring to the business on its own but without guaranteeing you that the students who live here now are going to stay on with you although I imagine that they will, why not, naturally you have to buy the furniture and pay the rent; my mother, a little intimidated by the outlay she feels we won't be able to afford, says, well, and how much are you asking for the business? and the woman says, well, four thousand pesos will do fine; my mother, in a very little voice, as if frightened, says, well, there must be some mistake, we could never pay that; and she looks at me and says, well, child, shall we go? I accept her suggestion in a silence full of shame; now in the street, I pass by a building and I remember that in one of its offices, a dentist took out one of my teeth; I ask my mother if she wants to see something of Havana and she says that, no, it's better not to stay so as not to spend money on hotels, that we should just go to the bus station now and that we'll take the next bus that leaves for Santiago, and I'm glad that she didn't take me up on my offer because it would be painful to show her Havana through this sadness; how could Marisol not have come with us to guide us in this, how could she have insisted that we make this useless and expensive journey; I don't say anything to my mom as the taxi takes us to the station in this awful failure that envelops us; now my mother and I are back and people are asking, well, are you finally leaving? and my mother, with the timidity of one who asks with what we're going to pay our debts, always answers with the same sentence, no, the business didn't work out, so we'll see, we'll see; my letter to Marisol saying that the woman asked four thousand pesos to allow us to rent the empty apartment and what she meant by selling us the business, was exactly that, an empty apartment that we would have to rent and furnish without any guarantee that the students she had living there would stay on with us, and even if that happened, we'd never be able to pay an amount like that; Marisol replies almost at once, saying that she must have misunderstood, that she thought that this was a reliable business and that she's taken all sorts of steps to see if she could find us something, that she's really sorry that we didn't succeed, and that she'd only tried to find a way for me to continue my studies; my mother, who hasn't said anything until now, says to me as if deep in thought, how could that girl not have been better informed before making us take that trip; I can't find an answer, I only think that Marisol doesn't know how difficult it is to survive and that for her a trip to Havana is nothing; the months pass, I take courses in typing and bookkeeping; if I could only work, to help my mother; as soon as I feel a little prepared I start applying for an exam on the Base to see if I can work in one of their offices, I go to the first exam, and the clock, and to type so many words per minute and these things that they ask always between minutes and seconds, I don't pass the first time I try, nor the second, finally I pass on the third try and a few days later they tell me to go to the Ordnance Department; I start my automatism without knowing what the Department is all about, without being interested in finding out; for my boss I get Coughton's son and so often I look at him and ask myself if he knows how much his father has made us suffer; Pete Croughton is skinny and tall, wears glasses, is always in shorts, with thin, compressed lips, always neurotic, always somewhere between condescension and bad temper; I run on automatic when he says something unpleasant, I keep quiet as if he hadn't said anything; one day he calls me and, hey, I have to speak to you, I prepare to hear him, and he says, you know that no homosexuals are allowed to work in this Department? I keep looking at him without expression, as if I hadn't heard anything, and he, a little frustrated, continues, homosexuals are not allowed to work in the Department, not even if they've only been homosexuals as children; he carries on about how the Department is very secret and very important and that's why they can't have even one homosexual here; I stay expressionless and ask, if he has anything more to tell to me, because if not, I want to finish what I'm typing; he's disoriented, and no, he doesn't have anything else to tell me; I continue typing all this that for the Department is so secret and so important and that for me is boring to the point of tedium; Marisol's letters, so sporadic, my letters to her, sometimes so pessimistic and pained and at others, so dry, because if she loves me, it's better that she forget me, what can our love offer her now, if I can't dream anymore like when Marisol used to say to me, I'm going to tell you our story, you're Pablo and you're a painter and we live in a small apartment far away from everyone, from all these people that bother us and I'm your wife and I'm very happy with that, with being your wife, and do you know what I might do? perhaps I'll dedicate myself to writing, you paint and I write, what do you think? now, an expression of sadness marks my face, this automatism, the miserable wage with which at least I can help my mother, I don't buy anything for myself that isn't absolutely necessary to begin saving little by little, because some day I have to go away from all of this; the lack of sleep to take the train from Guantánamo to Caimanera, in Caimanera the launch to the Base, because the few times that Marisol writes to me, she writes to me at Guantánamo and I almost always make the journey wondering if there'll be a letter for me, there almost always isn't, I go to the post office frequently, to beg the employees who work at night, to check and see if there isn't a letter for me, I always have to explain, it's an important matter, it's an urgent matter, but they look and look and there's never a letter for me and my explanations become useless and the pretexts that I have to find for Carmita, that I'm going to the little store on the corner, that I'm going to the pharmacy, that I'm going window shopping, and Carmita is always suspicious because, for her, if a woman goes out alone at night to wander the streets, and she always repeats the bit about to wander the streets, she's staining the family honor; to avoid her litanies of honor, I go to the movies and I keep the ticket so that I can come and go several times to go to the post office, to see, but I always go home without a letter from Marisol; if I stay in Caimanera, the mosquitoes, my impatience for a letter, pain like a bitter lump between my throat and chest, my obsession with the circular prison from which I can never escape; perhaps if I marry an American and we leave here and I divorce him in the United States, then I can send for Marisol, but these are things that one thinks and never does and I know that Marisol will never leave her family and all that security she has to share her life with me and my monotonous job and my paper bag with the sandwich that is my lunch; this sadness is my destiny, prison, pain, and my silence; for some days now, an American has been after me, he wants to marry me, I tell Marisol about this man and she doesn't ask anything of me, if she were to need me, but she doesn't say anything to me and on August 19th I decide to get married, two years after the last time I saw Marisol; a brief note in which I don't mention that so many times I fall asleep crying during these nights without her; the ritual in the Catholic chapel in the Guantánamo parish, honeymoon trip to Santiago de Cuba, a room in the Hotel Casablanca, a wide bed in which I precipitously lose my virginity in a violent act that has me gripping onto the bars of the headboard to withstand the pain and afterwards, running to the bathroom to try and stop the stream of blood that runs down my legs to my ankles and he acts as if it were nothing, let's go out, I'm hungry and a little later we're in a seafood restaurant recommended by the taxi driver where we find the lobsters moving slowly in a tank of water and that pass to our plates to be eaten in a dinner without happiness on my part, in an enthusiasm that seems grotesque in him, without the freshness that children have, without the depth of a man who has done some maturing, as if he were there, with a strange, false, irrelevant smile; now in Guantánamo, a few weeks have passed since the ritual and people ask me when they see me if I'm ill; the American and his constant jealousy and his lies and his irresponsibility and always saying that if he even suspects that I'm going to leave him, he'll kill me and everyday he presents some perfect way to kill me so that no-one suspects him and that his preferred method for killing me would be drowning because that way he could say that I fell into the sea and that he tried to save me but he couldn't and everyone would feel sorry for him when they saw him cry, inconsolably, over my death; one night his fury around my neck, the strong pressure of his hands, I stay still because it seems right to me that this should be the hour of my death; my immobility removes the incentive to keep squeezing, as if it weren't an achievement to kill someone who offers no resistance; weeks later, my decision to divorce him without saying anything to him; I take him to the lawyer under the pretext of arranging my passport and between his surprise and my calmness, we become legally separated; November happens upon me and if I could only go and see Marisol, and my letter, I don't know what you will think of this, but perhaps I can come and see you next month; the quick reply, so explosive, come, I'm waiting, it will be my Christmas present; on December 31st I'm in the plane that takes me to Santa Clara airport, and from there, the bus to Marisol's town, and now, the bus stop in front of the pharmacy, Marisol appears, so radiant, so spring; we hug each other without effusiveness because I bring with me a dryness, something so faded and so without shine, Marisol is struck on seeing me like this, with the look of someone who has just had a long convalescence; we spend the afternoon walking around town, and afterwards, the New Year's dinner at the same table as before, the father, the mother, her and I; it's time to go to bed and Marisol and I are in the same bed, like last time; we speak in low voices without mentioning what is happening between us, without saying one word that has to do with that love so big, until this closeness becomes an embrace and our bodies, as Marisol would say, recognized one another; a few days pass, I feel as if my youth has returned to me again, and Marisol says, do you know, you're a different person? I'm amazed, you arrived so faded that I was shocked to see you, and now you're once again clear, fresh, what a beautiful night that was, with which we saw in this year of 1956; and then my question, tell me, Marisol, if I could leave here, would you come with me? Marisol becomes somber, no, I can't leave, let's not talk about that again; here everything is the same, the orange juice in the morning, the little trumpet, I ask myself if Doña Florida isn't becoming saturated with my presence and I decide to leave in two days time, on January 9th; in one of the few moments that remain to us, Marisol takes me to her room and shows me two beautiful photographs, look, take these photos with you; she kisses them and after kissing them she gives them to me; that way, when you look at them, you'll remember that they carry my warmth; tomorrow is my return journey and perhaps tonight we love each other for the last time; the thought occurs to both of us, this absence that always takes place so soon; we let the hours run out without mentioning our separation and now it's morning and now my bags are ready, there's a bus strike and political unrest in the streets, Marisol's brother takes me to the airport repeating the whole way that he's only doing this, because it's for me, because during business hours he doesn't usually move from the counter, and I thank him for his sacrifice; now on the road, Jacinto in front, driving, Marisol and I in the back; Marisol takes one of my hands and holds it between hers the whole way, and now the airport and our goodbye in front of her brother, half affectionate, almost polite, thanks for everything, say goodbye again to your parents for me, and I walk towards the stairs of the plane to disappear once again in space; January 25th, a new job on the Base, in the Naval Supply Depot, the tedium of these desks and these calculators and the typewriters and the discipline that I impose on myself to be able to stand it and the escape of reading tirelessly, a biography of women that includes Gertrude Stein, twelve volumes of Freud, *Les Misérables, La Pelle* by Curzio Malaparte, books to learn Italian, to learn French, in the train, on the launch, in the forty five minutes they give us for lunch; time passes until April and your letters, Marisol, so sporadic; this weekend, in Caimanera, in the living room, I hear the voice of Quiqui asking for me, our greeting and then Quiqui says, I came to wait for my dad who's about to arrive from the Base, so right now I'm heading for the quay, but first I wanted to come by and say hello, I came to spend a few days in Caimanera; we quickly remember the days of our almost childhood when he would come by daily when Marianita and I and other friends from Guantánamo came to spend the summers and the weekends in Caimanera and Quiqui was always with us, wherever we went; and so, how's it going at the University? do you like Medicine? and he says, you know that I, from a little boy, said that I was going to be a doctor, but the truth is that the course is difficult, oh, before I forget, my girlfriend's staying in the same guest house as Marisol, so I see her almost every night, her and her boyfriend; my voice comes out like an echo, oh, I didn't know that she had a boyfriend, there must be some mistake, and he says, no, what mistake? I know him too; cold invades me and I can't escape from my silence and suddenly Quiqui hugs me and he starts kissing me and I'm paralyzed in his kiss because I've lost all possible reactions, when he lets me go to give himself time to pull himself together to go out to meet his father, I watch him leave, with his blonde hair and his green eyes, his guayabera shirt that's so clean, his breathing still a little ragged, and this friend from my childhood, suddenly, is unrecognizable; I've had to wait a few days before writing, Marisol, Quiqui told me that you have a boyfriend, I can't explain to you what I felt, I know that all of a sudden he started kissing me; Marisol, in her letter, is indignant with Quiqui, that he had no right to tell me she has a boyfriend and what a cheek, to kiss me like that, that when Quiqui gets to Havana she's going to let him have it, and about the other thing, I, yes, it's true what Quiqui told you, but I haven't wanted to tell you I have a boyfriend, because what's between him and I doesn't have anything to do with you and me, I will always love you the same; I keep forcing myself to stick to my work routine without conquering this desolation and now in May they warn me that the Department will be cutting back on personnel and that on the 18th

I won't have a job and before I leave I go with the official to get a letter of recommendation because to get work you have to arm yourself with recommendations in which they emphasize as if it were a great achievement the fact that I've used and held sway over all the keys, the ones on the typewriter, the ones on the adding machine, the ones on the calculator, and when they say that I've always responded when duty calls and I've never missed work, I feel diminished, as if they've said to me that I'm wonderfully, perfectly mediocre; that same month I find accounting work in the office of the Officers' Club, Commissioned Officers' Mess Open, with a salary of 150 dollars a month which is reduced by the cost of daily transport, but I can eat lunch at the Club for free; my boss is a nice Cuban who was a pimp for many years, almost from when he was a boy, he always had some prostitutes in the Caimanera area who worked for him, he's thirty three and the girls think he's gorgeous because he looks like Robert Taylor with his black hair and his green eyes, he's married to a teacher; the old American woman who works in the office with me, he and I get on well; the atmosphere here is nice because the office in the Club is welcoming with glass windows that look over gardens of oleander and green lawn, always well cut, there are several rooms and a bar, it's like a colonial mansion of wood painted white and everything's clean and so elegant, the office isn't separate but is like a small room in the mansion; the old woman, Bernice, has become my friend, she wants to be my Pygmalion in the way she thinks she should mould my life, that I have to get more dressed up, and above all, to wear more makeup, because who has ever seen such a young woman who isn't interested in wearing makeup, that I have to go out with men, that she can introduce me to some, and I thank her, but I always find some excuse; almost the moment she met me she told me that she was in the Armed Forces and that she started going out with the man who is her husband today and that she got pregnant and that almost at once they kicked her out of the Armed Forces with a dishonorable discharge and maybe it was because of everything she suffered, but she lost the child, and that she would say to herself, well, at least I have him, when we get married, this whole disagreeable experience will be left behind, but one day when they were chatting on a bench in the park, he told her that he never had the least intention of marrying her, and that she, in the midst of her shock told him, I can't believe you would be capable of doing this to me, I've coped with everything that's happened because I always loved you and my love for you was bigger than my fear of this shame I'm suffering, what I don't understand is why you had to play with me like that, but if you don't love me, you're free to go; he got up and he left, I stayed on the bench crying for I don't know how long; suddenly, I see him standing before me, and, Bernice, I've decided to marry you; and so you see, we married years ago and here we are; I love Bernice's stories and her sense of humor and her agreeable disposition; the steps taken to leave here once and for all and the procedures extend until July of 1957 when my student passport is renewed, Ministry of State, Office of Citizenship and Passports; this passport is valid until July 18, 1958; fees $2.20; signed by Francisco Ugarte, Chief of the Passport Division; and the exit permit, Republic of Cuba, Ministry of State, valid to leave National Territory until July 28, 1957, in agreement with the provisions of the Law-Decree number 1463 of June 10, 1954; the visa in the American Consulate in Santiago with the stamp in my passport, none quota, 0-1; Immigration visa No.33, dated July 8, 1957, American Consul at the American Consulate at Santiago de Cuba; my letter to Marisol, I'm going to the United States on July 21, I'm telling you so that, if some day you decide to write to me, your letter shouldn't fall into strange hands; the morning of the 20th, the postman, Marisol's handwriting in a love letter that's so beautiful, phone me when you get to Havana, right near the airport there are hotels, we can spend a few days behind closed doors, loving each other, until we die from love; the afternoon draws to a close, the last dusk that I will spend in my land and in the definitive goodbye, perhaps a meeting with Marisol; eight p.m. and there's a telegram from Marisol, I've decided to leave Havana, when you get here I'll be in Las Villas, it's better that way, write to me, hugs, Marisol; in the last few hours, the contained sadness of my mother, I would like to see her laugh like that time here, in Carmita's house, when Marianita and I were little, and Drina, the black girl who ran errands had just arrived with the chicken and fish my mother sent her for, because when my mom spends days in Carmita's house she always buys food to help, and when Drina comes in with the shopping, Marianita goes up to my mom and starts talking about the Betty Grable film they're showing in the Actualidades Cinema in the five o'clock showing and that Betty Grable is a really famous actress and that she wants my mom to take us and my mom says, oh, if I'd known that I wouldn't have asked Drina to buy fish because all that's left over is my fare to Caimanera; and Marianita says, well, I think it's better to go to the movies than to eat fish, and my mom looks at me, and well, you also want to see Betty Grable? and I say yes, me too, and I don't say that the truth is that I want to go to the movies to see the second film in the five o'clock showing, which is *The Invisible Man*, because they told me that this invisible thing means that no-one, but no-one, can see him, and I've often wanted to be invisible and I think that if you're invisible it isn't necessary to use doors because you can even walk through walls; I stay quiet to see what my mom will say, and my mom says, well, I think there might be a solution, I'm going to return the fish and the three of us will go to the cinema, listen, Drina, go to the market square again and return this fish, tell them that it smells bad and that it's off; and Drina says, but excuse me, you told me when you saw it what good fish it was, that it was magnificent; and my mom says, no, but now I've looked at it again and it's off; Drina goes to the market square again to make the return and my mom tells Marianita and I to take care not to tell Carmita that she returned the fish to take us to the movies, and Marianita promises that she won't say anything and I promise that I too won't say anything, and I worry and say, hey, mom, why don't you keep the money from the fish so that tomorrow you won't get back to Caimanera without a cent? and my mom says, no, no, your dad is about to be paid, I'm sure he'll get paid tomorrow, and of course I have to be there when he arrives, if not, when I get there he'll have spent all the money; and she bursts out laughing, really happy because the three of us can go to the movies and because she pulled a fast one with the fish and Carmita didn't even notice; in the afternoon we're already bathed and dressed and when we're on the sidewalk, walking on our way to the cinema, I give my hand to my mom and I stay like that for a bit because I'm pleased that she knows that it's better to go to the movies than to eat fish, and in the window on the corner of the street where the cinema is, my mom buys us a *real's* worth of orange gum drops and I hold really tightly to my bag and I think that I'm going to save these gum drops until the movie about the invisible man starts, and now we're in the Actualidades cinema, we sit a little towards the back, the seats are wooden, they're long benches with a back, because in the Fausto Cinema there are individual seats but here they're benches like the ones in church, but really ugly; now it's half dark and Betty Grable comes on the screen, and I say, look, Mamá, that's Betty Grable, she's a really famous actress, and what she always does is sing and dance and she's always smiling, tell me, Mamá, haven't you ever seen a Betty Grable movie before? my mom hesitates a little and says, yes, I think I've seen one, it's true that Betty Grable's really pretty; I see that my mom's really happy and I am too, here, waiting for the invisible man to start so I can open my little bag; now it's time to leave and I know that after her controlled hug, my mother will end up crying and Carmita, with her face of strict mourning; the taxi, the airport and now Santiago and now Rancho Boyeros, the announcement that the plane for Miami is leaving, the noise of the engine removes me for always from this land; the traffic of the air hostesses, the champagne, two little packets of chewing gum, one Dramamine, the seat right next to the window now reclined; my silhouette becomes detached from me, it slides to the empty seat on my left, it occupies it, it gets ready for a speech directed at me although it stares straight ahead, its expansive gestures, its grotesque and open demeanor: "the train from Guantánamo to Caimanera went slowly, stopping in Novaliche and in so many other sections of the twenty kilometers; ticket, they shout, and I give it to him and the conductor doesn't even look at me and he makes a few useless holes in the piece of cardboard and continues collecting the ticket from the man, from the woman and from so many others in the small worm of the train; the stop in Caimanera, I get off and now I have to run and catch the launch at the quay and there's always this stink in Caimanera and the launch crosses the bay and the soldier asks for my pass at the entrance to the Naval Base and I listen to English all day and the tedium and the boredom and the day started at four in the morning, and the typewriter and a few minutes to have coffee and forty five minutes for lunch and once again the typewriter and the accounts and sums and subtractions and one arrives in Guantánamo at seven at night and that huge house where an old woman dressed in mourning multiplies into many old women dressed in black, look, they've never stained the honor of our family and you haven't menstruated yet, you should already have had your period; and there's no way to tell them that my period is always late and that their honor is locked away near the opening from which I urinate and the old woman dressed in a black so somber looks at my tummy until she can no longer contain herself and she touches it proclaiming out loud that they've never stained our family honor, I don't bother to tell her that I've always had a hard, fat tummy, that sticks out and that sometimes I go for four months without having my period and that through the closed hole only sea water has entered when I go to the beach; with her black fabric, she's ecstatic, she raises the side of one nostril and half of her top lip as if anticipating a bad smell, she touches my belly again and with a quavering voice says, we could never allow any dishonor, if they dishonor you, we'd have to send you to your mother; the woman dressed in a slightly less rigorous mourning rolls her eyes until white shows as if she were surrendering an orgasm to some imaginary knight whose iron armor, the lance, hands and all his flesh and all his bones have become invisible; trembling with a virginal and venereal pleasure, she teaches a doctrine that is also sick: to be someone's girlfriend means only kissing on the lips, I'll die single and a virgin like everyone who has never ever stained the family honor, and she falls into a convulsion of sadistic pleasure as if she were enjoying herself in the presence of a sin, between tears and intermittent and quick moans the smiling dentures parade, savoring her oh-so bitter victory of going to her grave untouched, intact, and she lashes at me with words, girl, why don't you answer, look at her, sister, how she goes to her room without saying a word and she's put herself to bed; there stay my mother's two sisters, dressed in mourning, Carmita and the virginal one I haven't wanted to mention until now, I go to bed without saying a word because words are useless to the two women in mourning; it's late and tomorrow morning again, at four in the morning I'm so tired that tonight I can't even study French, I go to bed with my big tummy as always, without my period, as always, with my virginity intact, as always; and now it's four o'clock and the beautiful sunrise and the day's plan which is so sad and the train and the conjugation in French and the malodorous smell that emerges from the armpit of the man seated beside me enters me violently through my nostrils, there's no where else to sit and this desire to vomit stays with me until Caimanera, we've already passed Novaliche and I run to the launch and think about how the sharks would rip us to pieces if the launch were to sink; the soldier, the English, the coffee and the forty five minutes, the typewriter, the card that judges out time at eight and at five; showing the pass, again the launch, again the train, the old woman who sells plantain chips in Caimanera station, that I eat slowly during the first kilometers and now we've passed Novaliche and getting off the train at the final station, walking eleven blocks to the huge house with the old women crazy about honor and sex; the tedium pulls at my throat, I take Belladonna, today I'm too tired to study French, I don't remember if I took the Belladonna, I know that I was going to take it and I take one capsule and I lie down to sleep; it's four in the morning and I have to leave this town, the American Consul at the Naval Base told me a few months ago, with his mouth like a constipated anus and his nasal voice, that they wouldn't give me a visa unless I had five thousand dollars in the bank; I left his office in tears and I cried the whole afternoon over the typewriter, here there are no miracles and one dies from four in the morning until seven at night and then one goes to bed to rest from death and the rest is very short and once again it's four; they tell me that the American Consul is on the base and I go and see him with my insistence that I know will be useless; I see myself in the office of the contracted mouth and say, excuse me, Mister Consul, but look, I have to leave here and my miserable salary and the five thousand dollars; I'm interrupted in my imaginary dialogue by the presence of the constipated one with a captain with huge balls, always pressing against his khaki; in his brief visits to the Club, he had hardly noticed me and today I don't know what's gotten into him and hello, how are you, you're going to the USA, I hope you have a good trip and success and a joke and he laughed and I laughed without knowing what he'd said and the one with the contracted mouth thinks I'm a good friend of the captain's and come in, you won't have any problems with the visa, I wish you good luck, and I got ready to fly to the USA; the airline, the people saying that the old man is a fag and that no, that we all know that the fag is his son although they're both married and that the old man was unfaithful to the woman as fat as inflated Michelines and that he was unfaithful with another man, we all know it because we've seen him riding around in Rufo's carriage around Periquito Pérez Park but I'm always in the clouds and I thought that Rufo's horse had died a long time ago but the indifferent mouths in the town open and close to eat and to say that Rufo took the two fags for rides in his carriage because they always speak in the aggressive tone that makes fun of homosexuals, I don't open and close my mouth with everyone else, except that, look, Mister Travel Agent, my reservation from Guantánamo to San Francisco, yes, in California, yes, for July 21 and he doesn't ask anything because I'm known in the town as a strange, solitary being but I carry my strangeness with me because it's the only thing I have and I give you only the date of the 21st and I imagine you walking towards the Michelins with your hip inclined and your boney bottom, look, that one's going to San Francisco on her own, and I keep talking with my mind that doesn't collect the angles of the streets nor the edges of the sidewalks because no great miracles will happen, but very soon I'll leave this town; Caimanera's mosquitoes have stopped biting me, the stink has vanished and in the train and on the launch over and over again *USA in a Thousand Photographs*, page after page until I reach San Francisco and stay there, in these four photos until the violent stopping of the launch makes me take out, automatically, the pass from my purse; the cycle from four in the morning to seven at night began spinning around like a ferris wheel, the vertigo, I fall into time, into the strange way time passes because I feel as if I've left and still struggling with the pass and there are the plantain chips while I look and look for myself in the four fixed, absorbing photos, that speak to me until I'm in them; yes, Mister Travel Agent, my reservation was made months ago, no, there's no mistake, yes, to San Francisco, in the USA, I just came to confirm it, you can't have forgotten, how could you have forgotten when you even gave me the departure time and the flight number, well look Miss, or rather Ma'am, and he calls me Ma'am as if it were necessary to remind me that after so much Belladonna I decided to get married for a few days and there in Santiago, in the Hotel Casablanca, I had to hold onto the bars of the headboard so as not to scream and him, as if it were nothing, and once the act was over, there, in the bathroom, between the toilet and the bathtub, me bleeding to my ankles, and him shouting, I am hungry, that he wanted to go and eat; I descended the stairs as best I could, holding tightly to the railing with him in front of me, in a big hurry; a taxi lets us out at the restaurant, he chooses lobster from the little glass tank and so happy that he devoured it all, and afterwards it was always the same, that violence on top of me, inside my body and the daily litany, that it would be best to drown you at the beach or throw you from a fishing boat and on the third day I come back from the dead or were they three weeks or three months perhaps and I pulled off the divorce so that he and his violence would disappear, so that he would go and practice it with another woman or perhaps, and very probably, with another man and now I'm ready to go to the USA without my virginity and now this with the reservations, look, Mister Travel Agent, if you tell me that there's no way to get a ticket to San Francisco, tell me right now if you have a ticket to Santiago and it should be for the 21st, yes Miss, yes Ma'am, that's right, but I tell you, there is a reservation only to Santiago, because it's the July of 1957 and Cubans are traveling like crazy and Cubana de Aviación is always full like a meat pie; well, the one with the twisted rear doesn't speak like that, he expresses himself in few words and dryly, but that's what I heard and I went down the stairs and I arrived at the huge house without seeing the streets; the news fell on the huge house like a bomb, the two mourners multiplied and spread sisters made in their image and likeness throughout the house, imprinting themselves on the walls where there appeared thousands and thousands of black silhouettes with open arms, their linked hands forming a chain that covered the entire perimeter of the house on guard, and on the other side, the walking mourners that wandered through the house like flagellants paying penance because now who is going to be the walking stick of our old age and I told myself with a perverse paranoia that the mourners had pressured the Rufo's passenger with the force of our honor and the good name of our family so that I don't leave for hell because, after all, who is going to be the walking stick of our old age, because a girl is obliged to be born to look after the old ones; all of a sudden my departure day arrives, the virginal mourner has refused to speak to me for the last seven days, the elder mourner sighed through her raised lip and upon hearing: taxi, the taxi has arrived, she retreated like a snail into herself, rolled on the floor, always with the elegance that slowness gives, she tumbled into the neighbor's house, came back transformed into a lead or aluminum ball made from the metallic paper wrappings from cigarette packs and she seated herself in a silver dish inside the china cupboard never to move again; my mother, without voice or vote, fell to her knees before me sobbing, with her arms in the shape of a cross, it hurt me to leave you that way, Mamá, with those sobs that came from deep inside you because you were afraid to upset the will of the mourners with that profound fear that comes out of you for them, because of them, in them, and also, Mamá, I know, you were crying over our separation because you never know how definitive distance is and you don't know, Mamá, that my pain became silence, a fine rain that fell inside me, I turn my back on you and with steps that almost landed in the air I moved towards the door carrying the heavy suitcase and without turning back, said, look, get up, you'll hurt your knees on the mosaic; there was no time for the others to march past, the silhouettes stuck to the walls detached themselves rebelliously, protesting at not being able to parade their complaints one by one, and ended up resigning themselves to forming a chorus of laments, waving like jellyfish, contracting like jellyfish, ascending to the roof to come down again intertwined, all in a chain or in groups of twos or threes, embracing now in electric convulsions, driven away by their own groans; the walking black figures rebelled against their sisters on the flat surface because only to them belonged the right to wander with their afflicted lethargy and to punish them, they brought a terrible wind which blew away the zinc sheets from the neighboring houses, and they were transformed into willows; I went down the front steps for the last time, I looked furtively at the houses that surrounded me in Crombet Street, I entered the taxi's open mouth, I seated myself comfortably, and this silence when I closed the door; there's a delay in Santiago until yes, there's a cancellation; a delay in Havana, give us your name and if there's a cancellation, we'll call you over the loud speakers; Rancho Boyeros is a warm summer square, the travelers on the benches, in rows, they become shapes with white guayaberas, with inlayed moustaches like decals; in their hands the tickets slip and the suitcases escape on the moving platforms; I'm a sentry to waiting, I travel unnoticed past the vigilance of space, looking for hotels; everything is full, and in my eye sockets rest the dead of a deep rock-pool: the cenote; granite I've said are my eye sockets and without light chambers they invent visions and uselessly shout your name, as if recognizing you in the crowd; almost night, the loud speakers call me and now at the counter and look, there's only a first class seat, yes, for Miami, I accept that flight where they promise a glass of champagne and now the take off and a comfort so sad; I watch my land getting smaller in the distance and a vision of my grandmother appears to me, in her open coffin, her jaw, that was always submissive, rebelliously open, fallen onto her chest, yes, it's better to tie it with a white handkerchief knotted on top of the head; in that room where we shared so much, I saw her approaching the moment of her death, I heard her speak about dogs that came out of my mouth, about cotton balls that danced persistently before her eyes and that ran away like cowards before the gesture of her hands that were raised up to catch them; it's delirium, the doctor diagnosed, it's blood that doesn't run and threatens to go gangrenous in her tiny feet; and when the potties filled with blood, the doctor also diagnosed, it's a burst vein and a coagulant will accelerate the gangrene and an anticoagulant will accelerate the blood that escapes from her body; waiting for her death is an agony that stretches on and on and there's no space to be in this world, sit me up, child, I can't lie down any more, lie me down, raise me up, turn me, bend me over, when will my death come, when will it come; and now almost the hour of your death, the rebellious astonishment and the fear, where will they take me, where have they taken me, because this isn't my house nor is this my room, and at the very hour of your death, the snoring of a thousand puppies, unconsciousness, immobile muscles, my hand on your chest and a brusque movement to expel the last air that inhabits your lungs, and you stayed like that, so still, like stone, after so many years of look, child, it's day break and I've brought you a cup of coffee to help you study, and always the thoughtfulness of preparing my socks, my uniform, and to wait at the door in the afternoons, are you coming home tired, child? did you know the lesson? give me your panties and your handkerchiefs, I'll wash those; after your beloved scolding, goodness, gracious, let me be, then, come child, and now the toast and the coffee with milk for an afternoon snack that you prepare for me with such love, and my house coat in your hand and I quickly take off my uniform that you take away to look after it; we're going now, hand in hand, through time, I'm five years old and you're taking me to the 24 of February Park so near to the house in Calixto García and Donato Mármol and you secretly buy me ices and candy from the street sellers and you let me urinate in the cans we pick up in the streets, and when the black boy ran past shouting, holding his head that was bleeding, I asked, Abuela, Abuela, why is he holding his head? and you said, because they have split it, child, like a gourd, and if he lets go, half of it will fall off; we used to sit on the low walls of the park garden where you told me, so many times, the story of the man from your village, the one who threw a little goat over his shoulder and while he was walking it grew and grew and became a dead man, and tell me, Abuela, why did it grow, why did the little goat grow? and you said, these are mysteries of my village and no-one knows why it grew; it's three in the morning and now I can't cry for your open mouth nor this wax like hardness that covers you; my eyes are so open and a voice is suggesting that I rest; I moved away from the sarcophagus, I lay down in the next room in an enormous iron bed, obscenely white, that seemed like an intruder to me and to punish it, I masturbated until I fell asleep;" the silhouette returns to me when, in the window of the plane, a sprinkling of yellow and orange lights appeared, fasten your seatbelt, no smoking, place your seat in the upright position, and now, Miami airport, I collect my bags, Immigration, the green card appropriately covered in plastic that determines my condition as an immigrant, the stamp that they give me in my passport, US Department of Justice; admitted July 21, 1957; Immigration and Naturalization Service, Miami, Florida, and now in the waiting room, and now at the counter, yes, to San Francisco, if there isn't a direct flight, any plane heading west, and now the employee says that well, that they'll call me if there's a cancellation; the night advances, the cafeteria, I drink a lonely coffee, the smoke from a cigarette that hangs around me, and a whole world that has been left behind; the ladies room, several Argentine women are combing their hair, they laugh, pee, and talk about the wonders of their trip; a burst of voice breaks the tension on insomnia, my name and please come to this company and the only thing we have is a ticket to Chicago and at six in the morning Welcome to the Windy City and at all the counters, that no, that there's nothing for San Francisco, check back in a few hours; I set off towards the traffic, a bus to the center, I'm well stuck to the window through which fountains and elegant store windows pass and among the loneliness caught in the air, a feeling of freedom; my return to the airport, my name on the loud speaker, a direct flight to San Francisco, I advance towards the west and start loosing hours; Marianita has just moved to Alameda, without a phone, without being able to warn her and no-one is waiting for me at the airport, strange mouths inform me, take the bus that will leave you right outside a hotel in the very center of San Francisco and from there you can take a taxi wherever you want to go; the steep streets, the trams, an elegant hotel, we get off; loneliness becomes more acute with the coming of night, with the movement of the cars, with the unknown faces that pass before me; still lost in bewilderment, I address the doorman of the hotel, please, a taxi, where can I take a taxi, he pulls a face, you have to wait like everyone else, I will assign you a taxi when it's your turn and to go to Alameda, go to the bus station that's about five blocks from here; my turn arrives, the fat driver, who looks like a gorilla, his hair standing on end, he looks at me as if he's like to bark at me when I tell him in a voice to which I'd like to give the weight of confidence and which becomes timid, the bus station, the one that's five blocks from here; everything happens dizzily and five, ten, fifteen, twenty minutes also pass, the taxi keeps moving, and, look, the station's only five blocks from the hotel, and the bulldog gives voice, are you going to tell me how to get around San Francisco? he drives at full speed until I say, look drop me at this corner; and he says, you're not getting out until I tell you to; at the next red light I get out and desperately search for a policeman, there isn't one and the bulldog, shouting, thief, she's trying to get off without paying, and I, as soon as I have my suitcases I'll give you the fare, he throws them unto the sidewalk and leaves like a meteorite and what am I going to do on this sidewalk and where am I; the little old man in the brown suit, as if appearing from some ancient trunk, shaking his head from side to side; he approaches to me with deliberate dramatics, his accent, Hungarian, I've been watching this whole incident with the taxi, there's so much cruelty in this world, how can I help you; and I say, a bus to take me to Alameda, please, we'll take a taxi, I'd appreciate it if you could come with me, and he says, no, it's a crime to waste that money, the station is six blocks from here and faced with his attitude that didn't allow a response, I resigned myself to carrying a suitcase full of books and records while he carried the other; at the ticket window, no, there aren't any buses to Alameda out of here, he gives an address that I don't understand but which I imagine will be the station that's five blocks from the hotel; and the little old man says, oh, well that is indeed far, very far; and my enormous relief when he agrees that this time we'll take a taxi, and now at the station and the bus to Alameda is ready to leave, and the little old man says to the driver, take care of her, point her in the right direction, she's going to Alameda; I hug him so tightly, and say, look, here's five dollars to go back in the taxi, it's not payment, I could never pay you, and he stops me and no, unthinkable, you're like my daughter, like my daughter; now the movement that takes me away and his figure standing there, like a magic goblin that I learned to love so suddenly; I let myself be carried away feeling protected by that voice, look after her, point her in the right direction, by that voice that dissipates with the driver's indifference; I sat in one of the front seats to keep an eye on the driver's seat; after a stretch that seemed really long to me, I remind him with a voice to which I want to give the weight of confidence but becomes shyness, I have to get off at the exit to the tunnel, at the trailer park; he nodded his head energetically with a gesture that said to me, I already now, don't bother me any more; a few more miles and I ask again, is it much longer? and his voice like thunder, I already told you I'll let you know; we pass through a tunnel, he doesn't say anything to me, the possibility that it might be the Alameda tunnel worries me, my question is locked in fear until finally I dare to ask, wasn't that the Alameda tunnel? and he says, yes, the tunnel we just passed was the Alameda tunnel, and I don't protest, because what for, just my quiet voice, let me off at the first stop there is; the weight of the suitcases, the deserted road, a small store that's closed, the dense night and fear looms closer, there, petrified, not a policeman, not a taxi, Marianita without a phone and suddenly, a young couple in an open sports car, she's pregnant, she addresses me, I saw you get off the bus and when I got off at the next stop where my husband was waiting for me with the car, I said to him, let's go and fetch that distressed woman that was left on the road and here we are; at that moment I thought that miracles do happen, Marianita appeared at the door of the trailer, hey girl, since you didn't have a reservation we didn't know when you were coming and we won't have a phone until next week and I was saying, she's not coming today; I felt myself turn, I hugged the pregnant woman and started to cry; the temperature is 65 degrees Fahrenheit; with the maps of the city that they give out in the gas stations, one learns to orientate oneself in the streets; buses, employment agencies, what is your social security number, what experience do you have, look, I'll make a phone call, oh, so the position is still open, yes, I'll send her right over, yes, from Cuba, but with very little accent, and upon saying that she looks at me as if she's spared my life; every day, social security number, experience, your letters of recommendation are magnificent, and it's like this for three weeks and what exhaustion with those high heels and finally, the Fridden calculator company does me the favor of employing me with a miserable salary; leaving the trailer at six in the morning, the long journey in bus, the files, the numbers, the typewriter; we don't fit in the trailer, the little boy jumps on my bed until three in the morning and I move to Oakland, a beautiful boarding house where I share a room with a dried up teacher who never bathes, her face just like Azorín's and her hatred that I don't understand until I read a piece of paper that she had shredded and thrown away, on which, after much work putting the pieces together, her confession appears, that she feels guilty for not being a good Christian, because she was filled with hate by an awful envy because the men in the house noticed me, and I'm hurt by her hatred that's so useless; I wander the streets in this grey Oakland October without knowing, Chachita, that 17 years later, in October of 1974, you'd come to tell me that you had come to me to end all my sadness, that you'd come to me from other tombs, that's how you said it, Chachi, that our meetings, incomplete in so many incarnations, would be completed in the town of Westchester in which you appeared like a vision, with your wool beret and sailor's jacket that hugged you for the scent of the perfume of your nearly youthful 27 years, that jacket that hugged you like armor against the fear that entered your eyes at seeing, so stuck to my skin, the imprint of Marisol; it was the year 1957 and I let myself wander through the streets of Oakland, swallowing mist as if it were big snowflakes of solitude to end up always in a Ten-Cent store with its wooden floor and hearing myself ask in Cuban English, for a strawberry shortcake to make my life sweeter; around there, always roving about, are two women who always went arm in arm, one, with hair the color of an onion skin, lips painted almost black, greenish eyes, trousers and boots; the other, taller, with long, black, wavy hair, wears a skirt and would always allow herself to be taken by the arm, I never saw them seated in the cafeteria of the Ten-Cent Store, they were always walking about with resigned and defiant expressions, always alert, as if trying to catch the wake of the murmurs that their passing provoked, and at the same time, removed, voluptuously removed from those comments that tried to mark them in vain with blows of maliciousness; in Mrs. Avis's boarding house I met Jim, a tall, tall, very tall and thin man, and night after night, in his car carefully parked in the darkness, our attempts at tenderness become too sexual, at other times we're overcome by a kind of romance as we stroll through the rose bushes in the Rose Garden, in Golden Gate Park, in Sausalito, in Berkeley, in restaurants, at plays, and later, I allowed myself to be led to the darkness of the car to alleviate the tedium, only to alleviate the tedium of your absence, Marisol, the tedium that persists until it becomes despair; three months have passed and the sharp voices come to break the bad news; no, if we're letting you go it isn't because you're not doing your job, we just have to economize, and from there to the unemployment window and the sour voice that comes out of the extended snout, no, you're not entitled, to be able to draw unemployment you should have worked for longer, and that's that, move to the side, can't you see you're in the way? once again the exhausting search, the questioning, what's your social security number, experience, letters of recommendation, yes, a bit of an accent, we'll let you know, but they don't; I enter the theater, in the advertisement: dancers needed and the voice of the manager, a little irritated, you seem too decent, but let's see, take off your clothes or perhaps you didn't know that you would have to dance naked? I leave with my silence and now in the street, I walk leaning on my grey umbrella while I try to identify in the noise of my heels, the rhythm of life; I walk into the studio where they're asking for models, a nice young man, with a protective tone, warns me: what we're doing is taking photos of women in the nude, I don't think you'll be interested, I leave, grateful, to the church of the Protestant minister, will he make me a deaconess? will he send me as a missionary to some village in Africa? until his condescending voice reaches me, look, the work I have for you is this: fold this pile of programs, one by one, fold them like this, in quarters, and I fold and fold until a fourteen year old girl takes me to her house which is nearby and says, look, I've made you this toasted cheese sandwich and I've made another one for me; we eat without talking, we return to the church, I fold and fold until the pile disappears and again the girl, look, here's five dollars, the Reverend says that whenever you need to, you can come and fold programs and have lunch with me and I never returned because the Reverend has more than enough people to fold programs; one morning I head for the job of the day and how did you find out about this work? oh, from the paper? no, don't give me your social security number, no, it's not necessary to have experience, we're leaving in a few minutes; six sellers in each car and miles and miles until they let us loose in a little town that seemed dead to me; this is what you must do: knock on every door offering these bedspreads, and when you've sold all your bedspreads, come back to the car to get more; a little shyly I knock on the first door and I've come to show you these bedspreads and before I can finish the sentence they slam the door in my face and at each house, we don't want anything, we've got the flu, we don't allow hawkers and slam after slam until I went to sit under a bridge and I didn't show one more bedspread; before we got back to Oakland they took us to a McDonald's, they bought us a sandwich and a shake and now in the office, yes, we insist on paying you the six dollars, even if you haven't sold anything, here it is, just as we promised in the advertisement; Mrs. Avis is starting to get nervous about my unemployment even though I don't owe her anything and she always comes with the same story, look, I'm a Christian and the only thing that I want is for you to find work, abruptly she throws herself on her knees, eyes closed, she pulls me to the ground, now we have to pray, repeat after me, and I repeat, imitating the tone of unpleasant lament that ends with an invitation that seems like an order: come with me to church on Sunday; the luxury car takes us to the church, we're in the front row, the minister sermonizes for interminable hours during which, from time to time, he gives a turn to one of the faithful who rises to shout, to cry scandalously, my son was saved by the power of prayer, the stories of miracles multiply concluded always with a chorus of laments; now in the cavity of the car, the voice of Mrs. Avis adopts a confidential tone: if you convert, you'll find work immediately, moreover, it's possible that you'll find work very, but very quickly, I have a friend that sometimes comes to stay for a week or two in the house, an itinerant guest, a very influential man, soon you'll be able to meet him; several days passed and several nights during which we ate at that long table like the one in the Last Supper, a tolerable dinner, a bit of bread and my silence, until, come, come and meet my friend; before me, a paunchy old man with the head and snout of a pig, a pleasure, pleased to meet you, I may have a really great position for you, and I say, I would be very grateful, yes, sir, tomorrow at two will be fine, but don't go to any trouble, all I need is the address, and he says, not at all, it would be my pleasure to accompany you and moreover, that way I can introduce you; now in the luxury car we're crossing Oakland, the outskirts of Oakland, a road I don't recognize, miles and miles until, sir, if the job is so far, I can't take it, I don't have a car, so; the old man starts moving his pig's eyes nervously, looking from one side of the road to the other and what a coincidence, this is it, this is the place, go on alone, you don't need me to go with you, you don't need to mention my name, go, go on; the factory building seems made of granite, I address the receptionist, look, Miss, I've come because they told me that there is a vacancy; a dry look, a hand that hands me some application forms, fill these out and, if you want, send them back by mail although we don't have any vacant positions, I leave with a bye that falls on emptiness because the receptionist wasn't listening; the old man has become even more piggish during the wait and now his little eyes glow desperately, pretending to be surprised that there wasn't any work; we pass some communities that I don't know, the old man trying to stay animated and to make jokes, talking ceaselessly about some soldiers of Hitler that they called the Gustapo and have I ever heard of the Gustapo and I say yes, but that where I come from we call them the Gestapo, and the old man, that's it, that's it, the Gustapo; we enter the outskirts of Oakland leaving behind the desolation of the communities, of the factories, of the roads, the residential sections had already started when suddenly, the movement of the car ceased: this is my house and I have to go in for a few minutes; and I say, well go ahead, I'll wait for you in the car; it's just that my wife isn't here and we can be alone; well, look, sir, you stay in the house because I'm going back by taxi; his little eyes moved nervously when the car started, he stopped at a bar in the shape of a ship where, luckily, they wouldn't let us enter because I said I didn't have any ID and they severely penalized the owners of bars for not checking that their clients were old enough; stopped in another bar where they didn't ask for ID, the old man orders a drink for me, and almost at once I tell him that if he wants to stay in the bar, I'll catch a taxi, and oh, well no, I'll take you and now in the house, Mrs. Avis with the stealth of a cat and the sweetness of a good Samaritan, I imagine you've had a good time, right? her eyes shine momentarily before going dead when I answer tersely, no, there wasn't any work and the factory is far away; Mrs. Avis, restrained by her surprise, didn't dare say another word, but the next day, look, when this month is finished, I can't rent you the room any more, I can't take risks with people without work; Jim, the thin man, indignant, advises Mrs. Avis, if she goes, we all go and offers to lend me money if I ever need it; my insecurity begins to melt away, the fear of imagining myself walking the streets at night, trying to find shelter under some bridge, where do you hide when you have nowhere else to go, because Albert already said, if you don't have work, don't come around here because I can't support you; December passes, the streets fill with Christmas decorations, badly made in any factory in the East, and you know, Mochi, what happened years ago, one Christmas Day? our little Christmas tree caught fire and my only worry was the smoke, the smoke that was going to asphyxiate Papi and I ran out to fetch a bucket of water to throw at the tree and I don't remember who it was who was standing there and stopped me and shut off the electricity, just think, Mochi, if I had electrocuted myself we would never have met, and your story, Marisol, left me with a kind of minuscule terror hidden in some corner of my being; now in Oakland, in front of me, one of the Christmas cards that I had printed with my name, placed in an envelope addressed to you, piled with the other envelopes full of names and addresses that hardly interest me; I waited for your letters, Marisol, day after day, until I overwhelmed myself with the dream of your need for me, I imagined you searching for me desperately, investigating my whereabouts, I imagined you telling yourself that you would not accept this so bitter abstinence, but not one word from you and this emptiness becomes so big; I walk the streets of Oakland calculating with each breath the day on which you will have received my envelope, my address, my name which you will receive without having searched for it, and now your letter, so short, that all these months it seemed incredible to you not knowing where exactly in the world I was, and nothing more, and there's this repressed complaint that thunders within me: why didn't you look for me, Marisol, why didn't you look for me; fill out this form and how did you find out about this opening, social security number, experience, very good recommendations but it all depends on the salary you expect, we can't pay much, let's see, how much were you expecting? well, look, sir, whatever you can pay me, I need to work; ah, well if it's like that, you can start next week, and with that miserable wage I became one more employee of the Hartford

Insurance Company in California Street between Nob Hill and China Town; yes, I have no choice, Jim, but to move to San Francisco, it's impossible to pay for a daily commute and an odyssey of busses and trams; Myrtle comes with her hypocrisy and feigned friendliness and her air of superiority because she works for the phone company and because she has a whole room to herself and her forty five years of age; her attitude to men is like that of a spider that wants to devour them between her hands stiffened by arthritis and how happy I am that you've found work because you know how hard I tried in the phone company and I couldn't find you anything; and my silence, because Jim had told me, Myrtle set up a false telephone interview for you and the woman who said she was the supervisor was merely a coworker of Myrtle's and the two of them set out to interview you to have some fun; from the beginning, with her friendship so false, come, to initiate you into one of the wonders of this country, I allowed myself to be taken to a café, and she tells the waiter, bring us two chocolate shakes, and between surprise and astonishment, I suck through the straw and Myrtle asks, is it true that you've never tasted something like this? it's called a chocolate shake, I try to make my face show gratitude and each one paid for herself and then, in the car, she caught me shaking my head, and, what are you thinking about? and I didn't tell her, but where does this spider think I come from? I say goodbye to the Russian cook in her apartment in the basement, the mysterious woman and her strange relationship to Mrs. Avis, as if they dominated, feared and rejected one another mutually; the son of the Russian woman, delicate, blonde, twelve years old, about whose father nothing is ever said, studies violin; in her pleasant and welcoming apartment she introduces me to her carpenter friend who leaves us alone after a few seconds, and the Russian says, I like raw meat and my son continues with his violin lessons and how I would love to leave this house because I can't stand Mrs. Avis; and my surprise, because I always thought that the Russian woman was Mrs. Avis's spy and that she spied on the guests to report back to her everything we did; and she says that Mrs. Avis is a bad woman who was livid every time I went out with Jim and when she asked why she was angry, Mrs. Avis started shouting, because they make a very bad pairrrrrrr! the guest house in San Francisco, an elegant mansion, marble floors, marble stairs, solid, black grille, Grecian columns, 1900 Pacific

Avenue; in the pleasant room, I'm kept company by a fireplace centered between two beds; the harmony is broken by the brusque entrance of the other occupant holding her best-seller, clinging, blond hair, repulsive, blue eyes, pink skin like that of a newborn mouse and the furious activity of chewing gum; my bed right by the windows and she insists on leaving them open night after night, wide open; the cold penetrates me and my best-seller roommate ordering that the windows must not be closed but is also not ready to swap beds because she doesn't like direct cold; I speak to Mrs. Allen, tell her that I can't stay there with the gum eater and Mrs. Allen says that she's about to move, and a few days later I see her disappear with her gum and her best-seller, protected by her innate animalness; days pass and one night, late, I open my eyes and in front of the tea table, the shoes, the legs, the long coat, her elegance, black hair in a French bun, green eyes, the face of a naughty child; Mimí, my name's Mimí, I'm from St. Lucia; we don't speak further, I fall asleep with the impression that something nice had entered the room; Mimí, twenty four years old, with her insecure and restless life, itinerant, car almost always without gas, elegant clothes from I. Magnin, never having a dime; from time to time an invitation to the Beatnik quarter on North Beach, to what used to be a spaghetti factory where we drink beer while the night advances, but before leaving, she always spends a few seconds in the apartment of Pat, blonde, handsome, serene, green eyes, and comes down smiling with the money that Pat gives her, and her happy voice, let's go have a few beers; almost daily I explore China Town and walk as if looking for you, Marisol, in Cathay House Restaurant, in the stores perfumed with incense where I bought myself a Chinese dress in pale yellow cotton and some beautiful letter-writing paper, like a transparent parchment with oriental designs, delicate branches softly sad; now in my room, I inaugurate the paper with Greek letters that we use as code, today I love you more than ever, and I don't even sign my name and almost at once, an envelope with your handwriting, the most beautiful letter I've ever received was delivered, it said simply, today I love you more than ever; after the nostalgia that I seemed to feel in your words, you tell me about your boyfriend, that you had broken up with him but that you've made up; I go out to wander the streets, the fishing wharf, Little Italy, the trams, as if at each step, you might appear; I had become accustomed to thinking that

Mimí would always find a way to live off air, without stopping to think about how to solve problems, managing to forget them, to buy on account the elegant wardrobe for which she would never pay, when Mrs. Allen decided that Mimí had to leave the house immediately; while Mrs. Allen was choosing suitcases and other possessions of Mimí's as partial payment for what she owed, Mimí talked about the next art courses she was going to take at the University of San Francisco; her car full of those clothes she hadn't paid for and with her as relaxed as that day when one of the elegant stores took her to court for not paying; only once did she appear in tears, saying that she had bashed the car of a paunchy old man, and the pig insulted me and I got out of my car and started punching him in the stomach and the guy turned out to be the Consul of who knows what Latin American country and that's why he got carried away; but her tears soon dried and she never again spoke of the incident; yes, yes, when I have somewhere to stay I'll call you to give you my address; Mimí's house is far, far from Pacific Avenue, until I reach the bus stop and walk a few blocks and there's the number, Mimí smiling in the doorway, in a wink I'll make you some soup and here are some crackers, when the old lady that I'm looking after finishes eating we can sit and talk; from my seat I see the old lady's pink, scaly skull between the few hairs she has left, she eats with the difficulty of a handicapped child, and Mimí asks, have you finished? the old woman hardly answers, Mimí helps her to stand up and seats her on the sofa in the living room; the open cans of tomato soup, the crackers, and Mimí says, let's go to the recreation room; we sit down to watch a Perry Mason program, the old woman stayed almost asleep, seated stiffly on the sofa, and Mimí says, come so you can see my apartment; in the basement of the house, her apartment seemed pleasant and comfortable to me; no, here I don't have to pay, I just have to look after the old lady; and I say, try to keep this until you've finished studying, and she says, well, I've still got my car, it won't be the first time I sleep in the car, and you, who are you sharing the room with? and I say, with Aziza, the Persian, who's now madly in love and who never loved the man they married her to and from whom she was widowed and that the family of the dead man threatened her that if she marries this one they'll take away her son and Aziza sighs constantly while she writes love letters or reads to me in English books by Persian poets, and always there's her sadness, alleviated only for a few hours on the day that they invited her to a reception in honor of the Shah who was visiting San Francisco; I don't tell Mimí that I've started to write a novel so that your absence is dissolved by my handwriting, and to the rhythm of Aziza's voice and Persian poetry, I let myself think about our love, I allow myself to sway slowly, like a bed of reeds lulled to sleep by the wind, rocking back and forth between certainty and disappointment, taking shelter in the yellow Viennese light, it's true, isn't it Mochi, that ours is one of the great love affairs of history? in this enormous house on Pacific Avenue, I'm frightened by the sad and mute fear that you will disappear, that your scent on my skin will disappear; the days pass and early one morning the loud rings interrupting the silence and the voice of Mimí, I'm coming to pick you up so that you can come with me, I don't dare spend the night alone in this apartment, I'll tell you all about it; in the apartment, almost everything's been completely destroyed and her only explanation: I think that man's completely crazy and he didn't seem it when I met him today at the beach, I can't continue to live here, I think I'll head off to Lake Tahoe, and a few days later she disappeared taking along her distinctiveness and her French bun; I break the routine of work by becoming an actress in a small theater group, The Interplayers, Leon, the director, invites me to attend his night classes in a school located in the Marina, my small part in *The Drop of a Hat*, that we perform in the classrooms of the school, and later, my name among the group of extras in the program of *The Devil and Daniel Webster* and if anyone gets sick I substitute but no-one got sick and I never walked onto the stage of the small theater in China Town; day after day in policies and at night the rehearsals; in San Francisco loneliness has been sown among the vertiginous beings that pass by without touching me, the good and boring Peruvian woman, the twenty three year old Jewess, her expression of stunned surprise and her stories, my father escaped to South America, he escaped from Hitler's ovens, he is my father and my mother and witnessed my first orgasm there in Bolivia where one day I was dreaming among these convulsions that threw me to the ground but now I live alone in a house where they rent out rooms; she never mentioned her mother, not even that night that I spend with her so far from Pacific Avenue and we went to bed in her oh-so narrow bed and when it was still night a fat, slobbering, old man comes into the room and sits on

133

the edge of the bed and when I begin to get alarmed she says, no, no, it's OK, it's Tom, the manager of the house; and then, to him, not today, Tom, and the old man leaves with his clumsy gentleness and she explains, Tom likes to fondle, but he's inoffensive; the next day we don't talk any more about the old man, just that she likes chicken fat spread on black bread and about when she started to move from the waist down until the convulsions threw her violently from the bed and her father there, helping her to stand up, don't be frightened, my child, this is something natural; during our coffee break, in the fifteen minutes when we're free, she reads aloud to me the verses of Gabriela Mistral or we go to some Chinese restaurant for the accelerated lunch hour of forty five minutes; the Catholic Philippine woman with her cross on her forehead on Ash Wednesday and her lace mantilla, in charge of supervising the processing of the policies, she gives me instructions that I follow faithfully, only to later tell me, that wasn't what I explained to you, and then going to Robert, the section head, so that he can see that her supervision is invaluable and that she's able to detect errors, everyone says that she and Robert are lovers, and to counteract the rumor, she constantly talks about her Philippine husband; months without any word from you, since that letter in which you announced your marriage because I'm in love with him and I love him and when I marry I will go and live in Tope de Collantes, and my few words and my desolation while I tell you that I hope you'll be happy, and today I write you a postcard with a painting by Van Gogh, I assume that you'll already be in Tope de Collantes, despite the fact that you will have stopped loving me, I wanted some news of you, now I live in a small furnished apartment and I don't tell you, Marisol, this yearning I carry inside me; very soon, your letter that for several days I don't dare open: I decided not to get married, at the last moment I broke our engagement, regarding what you told me, that I've stopped loving you, how can you say that, seeing as for almost three years I was engaged to a man and I think that I never, really, loved him; with the year 1959 arrives the moment of my departure, my mother has emigrated to Miami, she lives with her sister Amparo, the one who used to live in New York and I remember her letter, I'm not up to paying for anyone's university career; my mother demands my presence; I say goodbye to these streets that house my sadness, Cathay House with its fried rice, its barbecued pork ribs, that napkin, damp from hot perfumed water; in front of the restaurant, on the corner of California and Grant Streets, the cathedral where one can cry privately before a small altar; the stores of China Town with their penetrating incense; in Little Italy, the Sorrento Restaurant with its grapevine leaves on the ceiling; the fishing wharf with its profusion of restaurants and those caldrons of seafood boiling on the sidewalk; the Franciscan with its glass walls where one lunches looking out over the bay; Coit Tower, the trams, the vivid orange-colored lights that survive in the fog of the Golden Gate Bridge; the rose gardens, the Rodin sculptures, the earthquakes that shook me on the sixth floor of the Hartford building, the winding dragon of the Chinese New Year, the exposition of Van Gogh in the Golden Gate Park museum, the steep streets sown with rails and the trips to Milpitas where Marianita and Albert now live, a small town in the mountains and my arrival, always late, in San Francisco, and my fear while I wait for the bus to go home, the bus stop on the depressing corner where I feel the grime of the vagabonds and drunks close by, I stay there, so tensely still in the cold that is almost a mist, a woman of about sixty years old, dressed in black, with really old-fashioned boots of black leather and a bonnet like the ones the Mennonites wear, gives voice to the fires of hell, her arms waving in this air, her gaze fixed on me, a shudder runs through me when I look into her eyes and the fury of her arms threatening, I retreat in fear of the black boots that approach, I begin turning until completing a circumference on my axis, I continue turning and leave behind the shouts that move off as they cross the street; in the routine of work this city becomes strange to me and I leave it daily in the trams, in the Hartford building, on the sidewalks where I stop to vomit from time to time, in this mist that falls and surrounds me without touching me; San Francisco, completing its cycle, has signaled my departure; Jack, the young Japanese, occupier of one of the many desks of the Hartford building, takes me to the airport; a hug, we say our goodbyes, as the flight takes off I sense my ghost wandering forever in the trams; my arrival in Miami, everything so desolate, where has the beating heart of San Francisco gone, I wander straight and insipid avenues, what part of their itinerary are the trams completing at this moment, over what part of the bridge has the oh-so beautiful fog settled; among torrential rain I go from office to office filling out papers, social security number, letters of recommendation, why do you want to work for this company, how can your experience benefit this company; the nasal and guttural voice of the Jew who looks at me over his glasses, he announces to me, I can offer you a position as assistant bookkeeper, and that's how I commence with the miserable salary, the tedium of the accounts, that such and such a company paid for the cargo of vinyl pipes and the other company also paid, and I'm setting up payments from eight to five, day by day, marking slavery on the perforated cards, desks where enormous, ferocious cockroaches wander, PVC pipes, workers with sad faces, the dirtiness of the floor and the voice of the Jew barking like Hitler in those Movietone speeches to later move off on his varicose legs, wrapped like those of the mummies, so stretched and straight as if they had stuffed one of his vinyl pipes up his anus till it reached his brain; Sarah, the bookkeeper, obese, thirty six years of age, always laughing, always in a good mood, always making excuses for the little Hitler, it's that Mister K, as he likes to be called, came from Poland as a child, he couldn't speak any English and the other children made fun of him and he swore that he would end up as someone important, an eminent physician, and that then, no one could laugh at him; and there he is, with his factories and his branches, his beach houses and his barking, and as he couldn't become a doctor, he made two children on that woman with the mongoloid face and sent them off to study Medicine; from time to time they visit the factory with their impeccably white coats and their care not to get too near poverty; the one is olive-skinned with the face of a bear and the other is extremely pale, very delicate, and he looks at us as though always about to say to us, I wash my anus with champagne; Sarah continues with her admiration of Mister K, and I say to her, Sarah, don't be so good, you're mistaken about this like all us workers were mistaken with you when submissive George took up a collection so that we could send flowers to your mother's funeral, and you, already in the funeral procession, saw those flowers on the coffin and then your desperation and your consultation with the rabbi, but my mother is an orthodox Jew and they don't allow flowers at the funeral and the rabbi had to console you, well, this resulted from an inoffensive act of ignorance on the part of your Christian friends, and you, Sarah, forgave us because you know that we love you and you continued in your benevolence until the little Hitler, with his guttural voice pushing at the hole in his throat, insulted you in front of everyone because you bought, without his permission, a little box of rubber bands for twenty cents; the humiliations add up and his capital multiplies as if a mysterious force compensated him for kicking us; fat Bill, always silent in the face of the insults, asks for my help with his overdue work and when we finish, well into the night, Mister K, with a pleasure small in its perverseness, comes up to me and says, look, this is your last check, don't come back here, if you have to work after five, even though I'm not paying you for that time, it's because you're not efficient; I saw him turn on his heels and move his small behind away, the central point of his tenseness; the *Miami Herald*, the other newspapers, job advertisements, the forms, social security number, the unemployment compensation checks that conceal a little the misery and with the unemployment checks, the warning, we will take care of finding you employment and if you do not accept this work that we find you, help will immediately be discontinued; I walk the streets, I want to return to my childhood, to those nights when Carmita's husband, good-for-nothing and a gentleman, would bring us an enormous portion of ice-cream in cardboard containers, accompanied by sponge rusks that came out of the Refectory with the name *esponrús*, later known as Montecarlo Café, also accompanied by ham and cheese sandwiches made with midnight bread, upon hearing him enter and being called by Carmita, Marianita and I jumped out of bed, to enjoy the banquet that with such affection they offered us; the tedium of the rectangular announcements in the newspapers once again awaits me, I can't manage to frighten off that tedium without being Louise, the crazy dreamer of 1900 pacific Avenue, so you're leaving? yes, for Miami; ah, well you can't leave without seeing my little bird, we climb the marble stairs to the second floor, the smell of old that takes me back in time as if we were brusquely entering the Nineteenth Century, Louise, like a great southern lady, with her Alabama accent, her long satin gown, that enormous sun hat that she would never remove, her face covered in a greasy cream, her hair burned by repeated dying, determined to stay a blonde, always talking about great deeds long past as if they were part of today's moment; she half-closes her fifty-year-old eyes like a coquettish and innocent damsel while I contemplate that museum; her voice becomes welcoming, I brought you here to give you a surprise, so that, before you go, my little bird would sing something for you; she stops before a wicker cage covered with a flannel cloth, now my baby will sing for you, poor thing, today I haven't given him his food, I see her so happy before the cage until finally she pulls on the cloth with a theatrical gesture, like a princess who, by just waving her hand, were pardoning some life, the skeleton of the cage is revealed with its wicker bars on the outside, like fleshless ribs and in the very center, on its miniscule little perch, an embalmed canary, immobile, made a thing by death and Louise says, let's see, my baby, sing for our friend; she intones a litany of affectionate words to convince the canary until I say, it's better not to force him to sing, perhaps he doesn't feel well, and Louise debating in a gesture between satisfied and resigned says, you must be cold my boy, the spread returns to cover the cage, we get ready to leave the room and now, almost at the door, how happy I am that you've got such good company, Louise; she smiles at me grateful for not counting her among us outcasts who inhabit the exile of our solitude; we descend the marble stairs and upon arriving at the round tables of the dining room, Louise separates herself from me because the well of our communication had run dry and she addressed herself to other beings who were cutting meat or finishing off their soup without any interest in listening to her, with no interest in participating in her discourse on the great ladies of the South; in the heat and rain of Miami, I continue without spreading over myself, on the inside of my skin, the craziness of dried up birds; one day in that year of 1960, Marisol appeared with a French bun and gloves of black leather, like her friend Nenita had announced to me in a sudden telephone call with a slow voice and an intimate tone a little false, look, Mari told me to call you, she's arriving on Saturday afternoon, and if you have a car, ah, a Corvair, well, look, we'll go and meet her at the airport; that night we met, Nenita suggested that I smarten myself up a little, a perm perhaps, some earrings perhaps, perhaps a bracelet, because you know that there are stones of many colors and really pretty, you should do something with yourself, I don't know what you were like before but you seem, well, pale and worn out; I don't tell Nenita about the absence, so much absence in these three years and how I looked for Marisol in the humid air of San Francisco and in that house on Camino Real by which I passed on my return from Milpitas, how many times I saw myself there with Marisol, I would appropriate the room, the dining room, huge salads that you would prepare for dinner, many lights lighted in a clear and brilliant yellow, I painted, you wrote, and we wandered through that house within the exact and powerful fact of our love, it was always the same house on Camino Real, between Milpitas and San Francisco, the one my avid eyes searched for through the bus window; in the hair salon of Jordan Marsh I beg the hairdresser, a soft wave, really soft, only to give some life to this hair that's so wilted, the hairdresser makes the face of an expert and assures me that those tongs and hot airs will give me a natural, rejuvenated wave; I left the salon curled like a chicken with ringlets, with miniscule and abundant curls, infuriatingly horrible, I left with some earrings of white and indigo blue stones, with a matching bracelet and a floral cotton dress of the same color with a wide skirt that hung gracelessly from my 92 pound body, I felt as though I were wearing a costume, with hair that wasn't mine and an enormous desire to hide myself inside an hermetically sealed sack; now in the Corvair, in shorts and a sport shirt, on the road to the airport, chain smoking, the arrival hall until they announce the Cubana de Aviación flight and Nenita rushes forward, owner of the moment, owner of Marisol's first words, of references to people and places I don't know; I stay timidly at a distance, with a desire to run so that she won't see on me this worn and fearful expression; Marisol turns to me without emotion and I go rigid, without daring to hug her, without daring to reply to her quick interrogation that sounded like polite formulas spoken from a distance, how are you? how's it going? what are you doing now? how's your mom? I say something clumsily, empty words that rolled without purpose to lose themselves in the density of the air until I hear myself say, wait here, I'll go and fetch the car; while I walked to the parking lot, I felt alone, strange, as if Marisol weren't there with her French bun, her smile that I loved so, her oh-so beautiful eyes; we arrive at my house that isn't my house, where Amparo's greed reigns in the exact number: 210 on 53 Court, South West neighborhood where for months now my mother and I pay her rent for one small bedroom for me and another that my mother shares with Amparo, Marisol will stay in a third bedroom, empty at the moment, that Amparo rents out when she can, when she finds some trustworthy tenant; I park the car in the carport, we enter, my mother appears friendly, Amparo assumes an attitude of the great hostess, showing Marisol her room for which I have already paid her and offering her later on a dinner for which I have also paid her; Marisol busies herself unpacking her cases, she bends over and feels all the compartments and pockets as if looking for something until she takes out a little, black flask of Chanel, made of something like ceramic, the kind that are for carrying in one's purse, and she shows it to me, this is for your mom, I didn't know that you lived with an aunt so I didn't bring anything for her, and for you, a tiny gift because you can't take much out of Cuba, and she hands me a little, plastic comb the color of tortoiseshell, insignificant, for which I felt no attachment; days beforehand, in the Howard Johnson's on Biscayne Boulevard, as if it were unimportant, Nenita, do you have a photo a Marisol? Nenita shows me a passport photo and I keep looking at it until, if you want it you can keep it, and I kept it in my wallet feeling her almost presence, distant and powerful at the same time; it's night, we drive around Miami in the Corvair, me at the wheel, realizing that Marisol is there by a whim of fate, that she's come to see Nenita, to try and convince her not to exile herself in Miami, and she had ended up in Amparo's house because there had been no room for her among Nenita's relatives, suddenly, Nenita's sweet voice becomes insistent: let's see, Mari, why don't you sing those two songs of Álvaro Carrillo and Frank Domínquez that are so popular in Cuba, go on, sing them, because I'm sure that they aren't well known here; I agree and again her insistence and Marisol's voice: "enjoying this love for so long, embracing you would be enough to remember, how much life I gave to you, although you carry also, a taste of me... I don't pretend, to be your possessor, I'm not anyone, I have no vanity, of my life, I give the best, I'm so poor, what else can I give... more than a thousand years will pass, many more, I don't know if there is love in eternity, but then as now, on your lips you carry, a taste of me..." the song begins to have an effect, to dissipate the strangeness between Marisol and I when Nenita's sweet voice is heard again, now the other Mari, sing the other song, and Marisol begins: "as if in a dream, without warning, you approached me, and that night, so marvelous, you kissed me, in the magic, of your smile, there was tenderness, and in the spell, of that surrender, warm sweetness, but destiny, marks a path, that tortures us, and in my arms, remained the emptiness, of your form, and since then, I look for you, to tell you, that, like a child, when you went away, I was left crying, crying, crying..." a deep silence has filled the car and a need to speak alone with Marisol, until now, the conversation had centered around the possible exile of Nenita, because I came with the idea of going into exile, but my Mami is still in Cuba and I can't leave Mami on her own; and Marisol, yes, Nenita, but you're also my only friend in Cuba, if you stay here, what will I do; the identical dialogue had been repeated several times to end with a smiling Nenita, satisfied at being indispensable; after midnight, finally alone in the Corvair, Marisol's voice, I know we have to talk, I think, Mochi, that it would be best if nothing happened between us, to begin with because we'll be together a few days and then there's a separation again, no, nothing should happen, don't you agree? and I, too timid to tell her that I feel adrift from everything, from myself, that life never lets me keep anything, that a few day's happiness could break this misery that lives inside of me; a small movement of my head that serves as a substitute for the words that I don't articulate: that's how it will be, Marisol, that's how it will be; at Amparo's house, darkness and silence, Marisol in her bedroom, perhaps already asleep, and in me a nervous anguish that doesn't fit into the small room in which so many times I've missed Marisol and now the carport and the Corvair and the road that I drive alone until sunrise takes me back to Amparo's house; my mother, in the afternoon, after coming back from the factory where for eight hours a day she embroiders cashmere sweaters, addresses me with a mixture of censure and indignation, but child, where did you go out to at those hours of the night? where did you go? and I, dully and with no desire to give explanations, I went for a drive; our voices disappear leaving my mother with a reproachful expression; that night, while my mother and Amparo sleep or watch in the darkness, I go into the bathroom with Marisol, Mochi, I asked you to come in here because it worries me to see you like this, in this desperation; we begin a slow and caressing embrace, my mouth on her neck rediscovering the curves as if time had not passed, I feel her breathless in my arms, and now her open blouse and her hand on my head guiding me to her breasts and soon, her voice, be careful, I thought I heard a sound, it would be better if you left because it seems they're awake; the morning of the proposed trip to New Orleans arrives along with the news of the approaching cyclone; now on the road, I've left behind my mother's worry, and you're going to leave like this, with this cyclone that they've reported? I take

Route 1 North, Hollywood, Dania, Fort Lauderdale, West Palm Beach, driving faster than the cyclone, running from its fury; now at night, San Agustín and a motel with two large beds, Marisol and I in one and Nenita in the other; I move closer to Marisol, her muffled voice, not tonight, because if Nenita wakes, what a disaster; I fall asleep believing that her voice included a promise; daylight sends us past Jacksonville, takes us to Tallahassee, we take a walk around the University, we stop to decide our direction, and Nenita's voice, it's impossible, completely impossible to go on to New Orleans, we'll run out of time to return to Cuba before the entrance permit expires; we change the direction of the trip which takes us to Cypress Gardens, Silver Springs, The Singing Tower and its bells that welcome us with *Dream of Love*, I detain Marisol by the arm, give me tonight, tell me that you'll give me tonight, her smile brings me a reconciliation with life, a peace in which I feel like my own master, recovering pieces of myself that for so long had been left loose, useless; it's already night when we arrive in Miami and Nenita determined to stay over to sleep in Amparo's house, I follow my road as if I had not heard her until soon, look, Nenita, here we are in front of your relatives' house, so good, we'll see you tomorrow and sleep well; Marisol and I in the intimacy of the Corvair, my hand between hers; we stop at a motel along the road, in the room, a kitchen that we won't be using, on the bedside table, a telephone from which I don't dare call my mother; day breaks too soon for us and now in Amparo's house and her acidic and taunting voice directed at my mother, what did I tell you, that you shouldn't worry so about the cyclone, that the girls would be having such a fine time and did not even bother to call, and you, here, distressing yourself over nothing; that night once again the struggle to get rid of Nenita and finally we manage to leave her at her relatives' house; in the Congress Hotel, near the airport, the night escapes us without time for sleep, as we leave, Marisol says goodbye to the room: one day we'll return; Amparo's house, my mother's reproachful silence, Marisol's absence, the wait for her letters and the fear that Amparo would open them because now, Mochi, we can't write anymore with Greek letters because if they intercept my letters in Cuba they will think that I'm writing in code to plot something against the government, I'll only put my initial and last name; her love letters begin to arrive, I know, that on my life's journey, I'll find you in each corner; and then, to relive them, allusions to our nights of love; I've been waiting in the Telephone Exchange for hours, yes, a call to Cuba, to Havana, until finally my name, the booth where they direct me, her voice that I feel so mine, and now Amparo's house, the Corvair already parked in the carport, my mother's rigid face, and her reproach that falls on me while she hands me an open letter from Marisol, look, Amparo opened this letter by mistake; I read the letter recognizing each word of Marisol's and I stay there, standing, pretending indifference before my mother's contained indignation, I try, carefully, not to move even one muscle of my face when I come to a word of love or sentences that should have remained between Marisol and I until a voice that I hardly recognize as mine, tries to explain, oh yes, the thing is that now, with all the accusations of being a counterrevolutionary, you have to use the language of love when you refer to what's happening in Cuba, it's a way of sending us news; and that's how we seal the afternoon, my mother and I, in a closed silence lacking in communication; on this April 17, 1961, the day on which the exposition of art opens in the Di Lido Hotel and in which I participate with several paintings, I hear the news about the Bay of Pigs, the desperation of not knowing how Marisol might be, the anguish of not being able to phone her for fear of committing an indiscretion that might prejudice her, news of the invasion's failure and the fact that Cuba has been transformed into a giant prison inhabited by thousands of prisoners to prevent possible counterrevolutionary outbreaks, weeks pass, a phone call, the voice of a woman I don't know, I'm only calling to give you a message, Marisol is fine, that's all, don't worry, she's fine; shortly after that Nenita and her mother arrive to swell the numbers of exiles in Miami, her mother tells me, just imagine, our neighbors denounced us because we had a group of friends in our house, there we were chatting when some militiamen arrived and arrested all of us, they locked Nenita and I up in a cell that was so full of women that we had no room to even lie down on that floor full of rats and filth, ill-treated by the militiawomen guarding us, more than a month locked up there, without any charge, without appearing in court, until one day a militiawoman opened the door with bars and ordered us to leave, during that time we survived thanks to Marisol who brought us food, taking the risk that they would put her in prison too, but I tell you, she escaped by a miracle, because the day that they arrested us she was going to come

143

to my house too and I don't know what happened that in the end she didn't go; a few weeks passed, a sudden phone call brings me Marisol's dear voice, the operator mentions an interruption, then, again her voice, tomorrow they arrive in Miami, yes, three children, my brother's children, the boy is eight, the girls five and seven years old, yes, tomorrow, by plane, a direct flight from Havana, look after them as if they were my children; another interruption and her voice is cut off; my condition as unemployed, master of time, allowed me to dream of plans for when the children arrived; Miami International Airport, arrivals hall, hours of delay until the plane arrives around six p.m.; through the doorway children begin to appear, children of all sizes, children with signs hanging from their necks to reach the middle of their chests, on which you could read their names, and the names and addresses of their parents in Cuba, I felt that my facial muscles were stretching, I felt that something inside of me was becoming darker, the signs, those signs that expressed in concrete terms a symbol: the exodus of Cuban children that resulted when the government spread the word that it would take from the parents their paternal authority; before me, that swarm of children too amazed still by the adventure of the trip to become aware of their helplessness and their solitude; I passed my gaze intensely over those signs until identifying the names, the boy, dressed in a brown suit, white shirt and a tie, told me, with his hands in his pockets, the events of the journey, his eyes, little cups of coffee, just as Marisol had described them, sparkled to accompany the liveliness of his voice; the girls appeared a little more reserved, as if wishing to identify among the crowd, some recognizable face; guided by the man who went to meet them, the children walked towards a stationwagon that would take them to that transit area known by the name of Kendall; I assured the boy that I would go and see them that night; the trip to Kendall seemed long to me, as if I were moving myself towards a far off and remote point of the earth; in the boys' block I found my small friend, he told me that the girls hadn't wanted to eat, that the eldest suffered from constipation and that his Mamá had told him to tell me; I found the girls in the dormitory of the building opposite, soon they clung to me, I took them to my car and gave them milk I'd brought in a thermos, we returned to the dormitory; two twin girls, holding hands, heard a plane pass over and started to shout with joy: Mami! Papi! they were tiny, infinitely tiny to be alone, their parents had told them that one day they would come and fetch them in a plane, a nun tried to calm them, she assured them that they would come in another plane and tried to hide her nervousness when she assured them that their parents weren't in the plane that had just passed, that they shouldn't cry anymore, that their parents would come in another plane; I took my two small friends over to their beds, the nun in charge of the dormitory told me that my presence wasn't permitted there, that the children had to adapt because it would be worse if they took to me and had to suffer another separation, I heard these phrases like a litany during the three weeks that they spent in that transit area, but I kept going because my affection made the initial brusque and terrible change less hard, the one where all the beings that had protected them, that they loved, disappeared; the boy, transformed into his sisters' absolute protector, needed, at the same time, my protection, almost every morning he called me to give me a report: Aunt, it's been two days since my older sister went to the bathroom, Aunt, the smaller one wouldn't eat today, she hasn't eaten anything, but nothing, all day, and there I would appear, with Ex-Lax, Vitaferol, milk, cereal, sandwiches, that they enjoyed in the welcoming space of the Corvair; I got, with books of trading stamps, a basketball and two dolls; on weekends they allowed me to take them out and we went to the beach; the children underwent a curious transformation in Kendall, the girls always carried the key to a canvas bag where they kept their belongings, the boy checked daily, along with other boys, the relocation lists that were posted on one of the walls of the boys' dormitory, after reading them, they argued amongst themselves, dreamed about marvelous possibilities: perhaps they would send them to a millionaires' house in Texas where there was a huge swimming pool, thousands of horses, an infinity of cowboy suits; it seemed like a crowd of small investors anticipating fabulous deals, the Stock Exchange in miniature; on one of the lists, in the third week, the three names appeared, relocated to an orphanage in Evansville, in the state of Illinois; the morning was humid, sad, at the designated time I was waiting for them in the airport, I saw them arrive from Kendall, I hugged them to me, the moment arrived when someone came to separate us; the oldest girl began crying convulsively, began to vomit, the man in charge spoke to me and as a special concession allowed me to accompany them to the plane, for them out of me came impoverished words, faltering, spoken in a low voice; I waited for the plane to take off, I walked the corridors carrying in me a strange mixture of feelings; my car, the wide avenues of the city, traffic lights and a muted weeping that went with me; a letter to Marisol with the children's address and almost by return mail, her reply, Jacinto and I have started the proceedings to leave, they've added some flights to Montego Bay, so far there is only a possibility for Jacinto and I, they won't give permission to my sister-in-law nor to my two-year-old niece, we have to leave like this, as we can, in the meantime, find for Jacinto and I work contracts that we won't use, it's just a formality, a requirement that must be met, send us too an affidavit saying that if it should be necessary you will support us there so that we won't be a public burden, have all of this ready as soon as possible and when I let you know, send all the papers to Montego Bay; a few weeks later, a letter from Marisol, we're in Montego Bay, Jacinto and I have rented a room in the house of a family, here in Montego the stench waves in the air like a flag; I send her the papers, my notarized affidavit, the job offers that Sarah, generously, wrote and signed behind Mister K's back; the luminous morning, Nenita's mother and I search among the passengers, from a distance, from the railing of the second floor, until we make out Jacinto and immediately, Marisol's firm step walking with assurance, as if she had brought with her an absolute independence; the Corvair takes us to the North West apartment chosen by Nenita's mother, a second floor, depressing stairs, a medium-sized living room where there is a type of enormous closet which hides a bed that opens like a rust monster to butts up to the wall opposite the main door; on the right, a small space that serves as a dining room, facing that you find the narrow kitchen and next to the kitchen, a fairly old bathroom, facing the bathroom, a closet for clothing; Marisol inspects the apartment with a surprising joy, with good humor, she comments that everything is just fine, because I, really, thought that it would be much worse, but no, everything is just fine, here we will manage; Nenita's mother, between satisfied and promising, yes, this will do nicely until you get on your feet and find something better, I did what I could, because Nenita is working in a window factory, and she comes home dog-tired and with her hands ruined from so much woodwork and with no time for anything, just think that she couldn't even go to the airport to wait for you, so I managed to find you this by myself, and right away, with the air of generosity that characterizes her, she gives herself over to the pleasure of feeling grateful to herself; in a moment when Marisol and I find ourselves alone, she says to me in a low voice, I have six thousand dollars here but my brother knows nothing about this, let me explain, in Cuba we were secretly able to change six thousand dollars that will be given to me here tomorrow, but Jacinto thinks that it's only one thousand five hundred, because the rest is a bit of money that Mamaíta had and nobody knows about it, not Papi, nor anyone, it's a bit of money that she put aside out of what Papi gave her for housekeeping; at her request, I agreed to put in a bank, under my name, the four thousand five hundred dollars that Jacinto doesn't know exist; now it's night, and I take Marisol to Amparo's house to see my paintings, I started painting following her departure, feverishly, desperately, sometimes all night long, driven by a desire to save something, to save myself from the uselessness of hours in the office, so as to feel that from my hands could appear explosions of color, sad beings, mysterious houses, a small world in which a place for me would open up; Marisol looked at them carefully, excellent, I think they're excellent, I wasn't expecting this, when you sent me the message that you'd started painting I never imagined that you would do so with such intensity; the Corvair, Marisol and I alone, and her voice, we have to talk, our relashionship, I think it's better that nothing happen again; I accept without asking any questions, incapable of offering her anything, incapable of deserving her, distanced now from this dream in which I imagined her in the International Airport walking towards me with that smile that I loved so, taking her afterwards to a beautiful house that I had bought and in which we would live together forever; now in her apartment I try to find a way to say goodbye, *hasta mañana*, I'll see you tomorrow, I'll come by here tomorrow, other appropriate formulas that cross my mind, and suddenly, her voice, don't go today, I want you to stay with me, you're not going, are you? we, of course, will phone your Mami so that she doesn't worry; I dial the number on the public telephone on the corner with some fear of my mother's censure; hi, just to tell you that I'm staying here tonight, with Marisol; I feel inside myself the coldness of her acerbic reply, I try to keep talking so as not to leave things like that, with her rejection on my back, but she's already hung up, her voice disappears and I leave the booth with this bitter thing that begins to take the shape of fear; we pull out the closet bed that extends itself like a tired animal and parallel to the huge bed, about a meter away, Jacinto's narrow bed; the lights off, Jacinto's steps, the creaking of springs, the sound of someone moving around in the kitchen, the refrigerator that opens, numerous bites of an infinite number of apples echo in the silence, again the creaking of the springs, moving jaws, crack, crack, crack, devouring apples, the toilet chain, the noise of the water in the toilet bowl, the repeated creaking of the springs, until Jacinto's breathing becomes rhythmic, dense; Marisol and I, half-naked, forcing ourselves to silence in a tight embrace in which we spend our energy and we can sleep; the next day, upon seeing Jacinto so close in his narrow bed, I'm amazed that the intensity of our embrace asserted itself in front of him, with the oh-so fragile shelter of darkness and the profound rhythm of his sleep; we go to the Refuge so that Marisol and Jacinto can sign up as refugees even though they entered with a residents visa, as refugees they will give them a monthly allowance and an invoice for a huge can of spam, five pounds of yellow cheese, flour, powdered egg, powdered milk, lard, peanut butter, and they will also receive medical assistance; Marisol's money is now in the bank and Jacinto has possession of the one thousand five hundred dollars, counting them constantly, piling them up, taking out the wad of notes wherever the need to count them arises; the weeks become routine, the call is repeated, tonight I'm staying at Marisol's house, the acerbic reply, the hang up, the coldness I'm left with, the darkness of the apartment, Jacinto's moving around, the random chewing in the small space, crack, crack, crack, the noise of the water in spiral, Jacinto's deep breathing, our hands squeezed together until they loosen and sleep comes to us; the atmosphere has become very close in Amparo's house, ever since she opened Marisol's letter she uses it as a weapon to fire her irony at me, trying to form an alliance with my mother against this daughter that "turned out" like this, worthy of being derided, punished, marginalized, always excluded; in my mother's voice, reproach: today they called here, one of the jobs you applied for and you weren't here because you don't even pay attention to that, to the jobs, all just to be with that woman, and that is just revolting and embarrassing; in the State employment agency, the interviewer informs me, there's an office worker's position in one of the companies that distribute edible products, they pay fifty dollars a week, if you, being able to carry out the job, do not accept it, you lose your twenty five dollars a week that you receive from unemployment insurance; the Corvair takes me to the beach to the edible products company that turned out to be a nauseating fishery in which they informed me, yes, this is also a distributor of edible products, we sell canned goods wholesale, and we provide fish and seafood to many of the hotels on the beach; a wooden panel that doesn't reach the ceiling separates the tiny rectangular office from the counters full of fish and seafood; the floors, flooded with putrefied water from the fish that they wash with hoses, in the filth on the floor, enormous, ferocious cockroaches stroll; the Jewish owner of Russian parents, tall, thick, with black, wavy hair, the attitude of a kindly bear, accepts me immediately and that's how I started this new struggle to survive the foulness, a stench that impregnated my clothes and my skin; the first day of work in that pigsty the contractions began and the doughnut and breakfast coffee threatened to gush out; I rush to the street, and vomit the first vomit of many others that will occur daily, each Monday, each Tuesday, each day till Friday, that hollow in the street, that almost hole awaiting my jet, because the toilet, the owner has already told me, is in such a condition that it can't be used; but if you leave the job voluntarily you won't be able to claim unemployment insurance and at least here I don't have to clock in, I start at eight and when I finish the day's work I can leave and between stench and stench I gain a few hours of freedom; I return to the desk, seat myself among the cockroaches, my shoes sunk among the foulness of the water, I adapt to the new habit that my coffee with this stench that collects in my stomach, will gush into the hole; several family members work in the fishery, the mother with the look of a Russian peasant, the father, Russian too, with a friendly and innocent face, both are always there, behind the counters, selling fish, the mother disappears for a few days and they tell me she has died; soon after that the rotund old man disappears without anyone explaining his absence; I miss the old people's slow bustle because I often entertained myself imagining them in their remote village to which, for a few seconds, I escaped too; the son, managing the sale of fish wholesale in a tiny office next to mine, with his face of a gentle bear that sometimes acquires an expression of importance like the leader of gangs in mafia movies; the brother-in-law with his ulcerated stomach, the doctor has recommended that I take a walk after each meal, his beautiful head and his sad gesture, on the quiet he confides to me that everything is the product of displacement in his home and in his work; and I want to say to him, David, why stay married to the bear's sister if you don't love her, David, break the bars of your tedium, run, David, you've nearly lost your wings and the money from the fish ferments in your stomach, but we continue in silence, you with your tedium and me to fill the puddle; old Goldsmith, the accountant, is retiring and as a special concession to the owners, he chose to come and teach me about the accounts, who pays, who doesn't, the exact method of balancing the books, you can't say that six and four make ten, you must say that four and six make ten, and his bad moods and his tantrums and his shouts and his neurosis; he insists on coming daily to give me instructions that I don't need, with his seventy years, the smell of a seal that he keeps between his corpulent lips, his intestines that release air noisily adding to the reek of the fish a touch of rotten cabbage; when I tell him that yes, four and six make ten and that six and four will never make ten, he starts staying away only to return suddenly, unexpectedly, to throw tantrums that pass his wind in a salvo, a whole series that escapes without one excuse me; when he's seated in the comfortable chair at his desk, the salvo doesn't become more discrete only less frequent, as if from the seat the wind falls with laziness towards the floor; his tantrums and salvos over, he leaves with his white hair and his white moustache appropriately placed under his nose; one day when his wife came to pick him up at the fishery, he lovingly chose her a fish, submissively, softly, he returned with the little package on his open hands, like an offering, and followed her with his prominent buttocks, his pants sunk into the vertical crack, moving rhythmically, like the soft spot on the head of a newborn baby and he walks openly and slowly, balancing his balls in the air; Marisol has set out to sell from door to door, clothing, portable bidets, a whole variety of goods, sometimes she works in some Cuban supermarket to introduce new products: coffee, guava paste, cookies, sodas, usually with a uniform and a little cap announcing the brand of product; between my foul-smelling work and taking Marisol to the nighttime sales and the trips to the supermarket at any hour or day of the week, I'm hardly home; Jacinto works washing plates in the hotels on the beach and to avoid transportation costs he usually comes and goes on foot and if I can I take him; when we're alone in the apartment I spend my time painting with an intense dedication, Marisol at my side, adding brushstrokes to my painting until I convince her to paint her own; in a group exhibition in a gallery on the beach, I participated with several paintings and sold one ink on poster board for a hundred dollars, we receive this small triumph like a spark of light; Marisol and Jacinto have moved into a two bedroom apartment to accommodate Teresa and the little girl who have arrived from Cuba on a direct flight from Havana; the rectangular apartment, Marisol's room looks out into the street, next is the living room, after that the kitchen-dining room, and finally, the bedroom belonging to Jacinto, Teresa and the little girl; news arrives that Doña Florida and her husband may be able to leave for Spain and Jacinto becomes very flustered by an enormous concern: but that isn't going to be possible for us, we'll have to send them in dollars the cost of the tickets because the government doesn't allow those who are to leave to buy the tickets in Cuban pesos, also, we'll have to support them in Spain until they are granted residence here; Marisol tries to calm him, well, Jacinto, I wasn't going to tell you, but I have four thousand five hundred dollars of Mamaíta's; immediately, Jacinto's angry voice saying that Marisol has betrayed him, that she must leave the apartment, that he doesn't want to see her again or me either for being her accomplice in this betrayal; Marisol rents a room on the second floor of a guest house, half a block from Jacinto's apartment and she goes almost every day to see the little girl while Jacinto is at work; the owner of the guest house is an American woman of about sixty years of age who doesn't allow people who don't live there to stay over to sleep so I stay until eleven or twelve each night in the room with the wide bed, closet, bedside table, dressing table and a used television set that Marisol bought herself; my mother knows about the selling door to door and the promotion of products in Cuban supermarkets and almost daily, when I'm about to leave Amparo's house, she makes me a bag, look, child, take this to Marisol so that she doesn't have to cook and she sends her the food she knows Marisol likes; on this second Sunday of May, 1962, still early on in the evening, the owner of the guest house knocks on the door and gives her a message, that Marisol should go at once to Jacinto's house; a tension that grows with each stair of the staircase as we descend, we hurry along the half block that separates us from Jacinto's apartment,

Teresa, crying, Marisol, your dad, Marisol, your dad died and Jacinto isn't here, he went to Evansville to see the children, Marisol leans her back against the wall as if to abandon there her weight and a visceral sob escapes her, from deep inside; in our free time, the Corvair takes us around Miami, to distract us through speed, one night, near the airport, we pass Congress Hotel and as we make associations, I hear Marisol's voice, since Papi died nothing's happened between us, I don't know how to explain it to you, it seemed to me as though he would be watching, but now I know I'm over that, you understand, don't you? Jacinto, Teresa and the little girl leave for Los Angeles with two thousand six hundred dollars of the four thousand that Marisol had, from there, when they get settled, they will send for the three children that are still in Evansville; every week I take Marisol to the Refuge to see if there's any work for her, yes, anywhere, even if there's snow and below freezing temperatures; today we wait in a room full of Cubans applying for a position to teach Spanish in a high school in Clarence, near Buffalo; doctors, pedagogues, lawyers, doctors of Philosophy and Arts keep disappearing towards the interview room until it's Marisol's turn, with her experience as a teacher of solfa and music in the El Santo school, and the same experience in an institution for the physically impaired in Havana, without having finished her doctorate in Philosophy and Arts because she never completed the doctoral thesis; I wait in the almost empty room until the door opens and her smile appears, and right away, they gave me the job, seven thousand dollars a year, vacations in the summer, at Christmas, Easter and other patriotic holidays; our separation was dry and strange, in the passing of the days in Miami, the emptiness becomes evident; my mother and I live now in an apartment in South West because Amparo, without warning us, sold her house, we found out when we arrived home from work one afternoon and saw an enormous sign: *sold*, soon after that, Amparo disappeared in the first plane that left for Puerto Rico; my mother insists: take classes with IBM, at night, after work, and that's what I do to alleviate her need to see me in a more promising position; I receive one of Marisol's sporadic letters that I collect in the post office box that I now have, I open the envelope, an autumn leaf and a pleading invitation, come, I need you by my side, right now I'm wearing a bathrobe I've just bought, with nothing underneath, if you were to move closer..., come, even if you have no work, you can look while you're here, perhaps you'll find something in a school, you'd be an excellent teacher because you know English and Spanish grammar, come, I need you by my side; I write dozens of letters of application, by hand, including a list of all the subjects I took in high school, all the ones I took in the Law School, one by one I wrote the list in each letter, Chachi, one by one I sent them off and then I waited for those replies that were always the same: we're sorry, but no, and we're sorry and we're sorry until one day a reply arrives from the president of Russell Sage College, that's in, just think, Troy, in New York state, we can offer three thousand dollars a year to teach two courses and to be the house mother of the Casa Española, and I accept, Chachi, without knowing what a house mother is, the day of my departure arrives and the saddest moment when my mother collapses against the wall and is overcome by an inconsolable sobbing, you're leaving me, I'm going to be alone, so alone; I'm telling you, Chachi, that this pain at leaving her penetrates me like a deep blow to the chest, but something deep, deep, like when the train left for Novaliche and I burst into tears because my Mamá had stayed behind in Caimanera, and to console myself, I started to eat the little lemon cookie drops that my mom had bought for me, and in Actualidades, the orange gum drops and the Betty Grable movie and the one of the invisible man that we could see because of the return of the fish, and you love me, Mamá, me and no-one else? well, yes, you more than anyone, did you hear, Santiaga, what this child said about the pluviometer? that it's a device for measuring rainfall and just think, so many times we've come to the salt flats and I never knew that it was called a pluviometer, yes, that's what your dad said, you only die once, because he knew that he was talking to me for the last time, from the day before he had said it to me, if I die, what will you do? it would be better if you stayed here, where everyone knows you, don't go wandering around out there, life is hard, these fevers, Santiaga, that my daughter gets, so small, these fevers that she gets, and Santiaga diagnoses with her Biscayan accent, that's indigestion, an upset stomach perhaps, and now her prayers that she murmurs blessing me, kneading my stomach and my mother there, looking after me, touching my forehead, placing the thermometer under my arm and her relief upon seeing, your fever is going down, child, you're better now and immediately my insistence, today I want white rice and also liver *a la*

italiana, the one where they add onion and green pepper and I spend
the day saying that is what I want and my mother's tenderness trying
to calm me, in a little while you'll be well and when you're well I will
make you liver *a la italiana* and the rice but today we have to look after
you carefully, look, even with water, the next few days you're going to
drink nothing but Vichy and San Antonio water, all these bottles for
you, it settles me a little, the bit about Vichy water and San Antonio
water, all those bottles just for me, but as soon as I get better I'm going
to eat white rice and liver *a la italiana* that I really like and I was in the
carrycot and I wanted to shout for you, Mamá, and my voice wouldn't
come out because I hadn't learned to talk yet; now the words I have
come out clumsily and they don't tell you anything about this profound
love I feel for you, about the pain of your oh-so lonely solitude, because
that's how we are, Mamá, that's how we both are, we live in our hole,
alone, barely communicating with others, but I only hear myself say,
well, as you can see, it's an opportunity, you don't want me to spend my
life in a revolting fishery, do you? I watched you cry, Mamá, holding on
to your stomach to hold onto something, as if to hold onto yourself
when I kept my distance because if I hugged you, Mamá, I would have
collapsed, because if I hugged you, Mamá, I wouldn't have been able to
leave you, my voice sounded like an echo, you see, the president of
Russell Sage says that I can't bring anyone to live with me in the Casa
Española; I begin detaching myself from South West, I free myself from
the market on the corner, from the other market, from the neighborhood
people who get together to chat at night on the sidewalk where they
gather to talk about Cuba; in bed, something cold runs down my naked
back, I feel about with my hand, and there, before my eyes, a fat, off-
white worm between my fingers, like an anticipation, perhaps, of my
death, or it will be, perhaps, confirmation of the death of the old woman
who lives across the corridor, the mother of the lonely American, or it
will be, perhaps, a symbol of the death of an era that disappears to give
birth to another; a shake in the air and the worm falls to the floor, I
watch it slowly dragging its cold, heading in the direction of the
apartment that lies on the other side of the corridor; from Miami I leave
with maps to devour roads, dark places that terrify me, repeating stops
in gas stations, diners along the road, carrying in my speed, a sadness
that has made its home in my chest because if I hugged you, Mamá, I

would have given in; in the early hours of the morning, Clarence seems a little town out of a fairy tale and now Marisol's cabin, an enormous glass wall, a lamp at the entrance, a pine tree, the figure of Marisol marking the doorway; I enter and I feel out of place, like a stranger, as if something were missing or as if something had left us; living room, bedroom, bathroom, kitchen with a counter and her voice, let's go to bed, in the morning I have to go to work; I ask permission, I almost ask permission to take a shower and get rid of the repeated urine that the journey has left me, now clean, I enter the bedroom with the desire to apologize that I always carry with me: because I arrived in the early hours of the morning, because I woke her up, because she has to sleep to be able to go to work until her voice interrupts me, come, come lie down, if it's going to happen anyway, why not now? with our embrace, Marisol's concern that everything happen without the slightest noise, without me saying her name in the moment at which the torrent of energy escapes our bodies, shhhhhhhh, shhhhhhhh, careful, the neighbors can hear us; soon it's morning, Marisol has left in her black Ford after having breakfast, standing up, a glass of milk; I stay in the cabin with its pine smell, well into the afternoon Marisol returns, she goes directly to the refrigerator, the vermouth, one glass after the other as if looking for something in each swallow, something that calms her unhappiness, because these kids aren't people, they're savages, I spend the whole day banging on the desk and shouting to control them because that's what they are, savages; but I realize, Chachi, that her unhappiness runs much deeper, much, much deeper and I can't identify how deep; the glasses of vermouth continue without her saying anything about my arrival, nothing about how nice, Mochi, that you're going to be five or six hours from here, nothing about finally we're close by because you have no idea how much I needed you; now at night, dinner prepared by Marisol, ham baked in the oven, boiled corn, a salad and a silence that I break with tell me, Marisol, are you finally going to bring your mom here, do you know when she's coming? while I think that with Doña Florida's arrival all our encounters may end, there's a long pause, I look up, Marisol's expression has become animal-like, as if she were a savage beast from which they had tried to take away a piece of raw meat, an aggressive tone comes out of her: *I* want Mamaíta to come as soon as possible, just so you know once and for all and by the way I'm going to tell you that if some man asks me out, I go, because what excuses can I give, being single and without obligations, what am I going to say to them, if I don't go out they'll think I'm abnormal; at that moment, Chachi, I felt that a distance was opening that would never again close, at that moment, Chachi, I began to ask myself, what am I doing in this house with this woman that is like a stranger to me, hardened, in her presence I feel afraid, out of balance, a feeling of almost certainty that it would be pointless to apologize for not offering her everything that I dreamed of, the beautiful house I bought for you, the security that I bring you, the happiness that I guarantee you, the sun, Marisol, the sun, Marisol, the sun that shines for you whenever you want it to and at your command; but how could this girl have made us come all the way to Havana for us to pay four thousand pesos with no furniture and no guarantees that the guests would stay, do you want me to show you any place in Havana, Mamá? no child, we'll take the first bus that leaves for Guantánamo and that way we'll save the cost of an hotel and I don't hug you, Mamá, because if I were to hug you I would collapse; with the glass of Vermouth before her, Marisol has become softer, looking for words as if to convince herself that she should resign herself to my presence or accept my presence because well, the truth is that I owe you a great deal because if it weren't for you, my exile in Miami would have been awful and also what you did for Jacinto's children, they always say that you took care of them just like we take care of them; I swear, Chachi, that her resignation became very painful for me, that the softness that she has forced on herself reaches me like a slap in the face, like shame; the Casa Española has three floors, on the first floor, three reception rooms and in the back, my rooms: a large living room with a fireplace, a small bedroom and a bathroom; on the upper floors, the bedrooms of the students; the atmosphere of the Casa Española seemed cold to me, indifferent, almost hostile; I begin my role as house mother which consists of waiting for the students until 11:00 p.m. to open the door for them as and when they arrive, on weekends to be up until 4:00 a.m. waiting for the girls and on Fridays going with them to eat at the French House, beginning the dinner with a Spanish grace and after that dying of boredom among those spoiled and insipid girls; in the same College where I teach Spanish, I study to get my B.A., on the weekends I have off, I go and see Marisol; in a few months, so soon, Doña Florida arrives and there begins what I see as a deification, because I swear, Chachi, I didn't foresee what it would be like to see my mother, so many years later, how she would begin disappearing, how she would begin unlearning what she had learned: using the phone, taking the bus, knowing something as simple as that today is Tuesday, August 29th and that the year is the same as it was yesterday and will be tomorrow, a sad year that appeared on all the checks and letters of the moment: 1995; I didn't realize, Chachi, that Marisol was turning herself inside out to fill all the holes in Doña Florida, to give her back something of all that she had lost, to protect this being who suddenly had become so fragile in a context where no-one spoke her language; Marisol melted in affection that emerged through her voice, Mamaíta, Mamaíta, we can't go out without Mamaíta, if Mamaíta doesn't want to go out, we'll stay with her, how are you, Mamaíta, how's my pretty one? Doña Florida bathed in that sweetness that I felt like lashes of a whip to the left and the right, until I'm cornered; Marisol continues complaining about the banging on the desk she has to do to control the savages and to calm her desperation, I write letters of application to different colleges and universities for her, the replies begin to arrive, we're sorry to inform you, we're sorry to inform you until one arrives from Albany with the letterhead of the College of the Patron Saint, we'd like to interview you, and the three of us show up there; in the blink of an eye, Marisol left the interview with a contract and with a choir of nuns surrounding her, calling her Doctor, because even though you haven't done your thesis, you're almost a doctor and that's what we'll call you; in the brilliance of her eyes, the taste of triumph, because I tell you, Chachita, that Marisol was born to triumph; in September of this year of 1964 Marisol and Doña Florida have installed themselves in Albany, about twenty minutes from Troy, in a pleasant apartment on 314 Northern Boulevard, with two bedrooms, a living room, dining room, kitchen and bathroom; the weekends I'm off I spend in Marisol's house, and we go to the movies or to some restaurant with Doña Florida or we stay at home watching TV in Marisol's room, she and I seated on the bed and Doña Florida in front of us, with her back to the TV, rocking herself in her rocking chair with her eyes locked onto us until Marisol almost without daring, turns to her full of affection, well, pretty Mamaíta, I'm going to bed, aren't you tired my old dear? we see Doña Florida walk away in her unhappiness and now the door's closed, I move closer to Marisol to eliminate the space in the wide bed and Marisol, alarmed, wait, we have to wait until Mamaíta falls asleep, and then, with an almost happy tone, you know, we're like a married couple that has a baby and we have to wait until the baby is asleep; and I tell you, Chachita, that I was selfish and impatient with that fear without respite because Mamaíta could, at any moment, open the door and switch on the light and you can just imagine, Mochi, what that would do to her because I'm sure that I never managed to convince her that what Nievita told her about us was a lie; Doña Florida sees me sometimes as a rival against which she defends her territory, at other times she sees me as something convenient and almost familiar, as someone who entertains her and keeps her company when Marisol has to socialize in frequent dinners with her colleagues, but mostly she sees me as an impediment to that wedding that she dreams of for Marisol and this is something that she can't forgive me, because even if Marisol were to get divorced later, it's important that she marry, and don't think, Chachi, that I didn't realize that Doña Florida believed that the eyes of the whole world were watching, focused on Marisol and that she simply wanted to present them with proof that her daughter wasn't *that*, and then I realized that there would always be a form of animosity there, mixed with familiarity and I tell you, Chachi, that sometimes, without intending to, I reacted with the same animosity towards her, because I was terrified that Marisol would decide to remove, with her wedding, the doubts of humanity, of society, of Mamaíta and of her own because, you see, Chachita, she still insists that she isn't *that*; but I also have to tell you, Chachi, that my fear was present because I knew that Marisol had already distanced herself from me, that she was ready to follow a path that had nothing to do with me and that if we were still together it was because that's what the circumstances at that moment determined, something that step by step was disappearing although sometimes it reappeared with intensity, at other times with a familiarity that seemed to have the taste of permanence that disappeared when you went away, Marisol, from that apartment 1E that I rented in number 15 River Hill; there I waited for you, in the last months of 1966, every day of 1967 in the L-shaped apartment so close to Northern Boulevard, with its windows blocked by white shades and blue stripped curtains as you had stipulated, so that the world should not see us in those moments of love that rarely occurred; I was made smaller, reduced to the solitude of that wide bed, by the uselessness of so many academic battles in which the greatest victory consisted in Russell Sage giving me a fulltime contract with the same miserable salary, and a B.A. degree in 1966 and in 1967, the degree of Master's at the State University of New York in Albany, always running against time, putting up with the pomposity and the envy of many of the professors and towards the end of the year, once again the contract from Russell Sage with the same miserable salary while Marisol continued her meteoric line, rising, in every aspect of her life; a high salary that allowed her to buy a recently built house, spacious, comfortable, with a stone fireplace and space in the back and front yard where you see a beautiful lawn, garage, a completed apartment in the basement that is rented out, a huge living room, three bedrooms, a kitchen-dining room full of windows, as if everything were given to her for the insignificant effort of wanting it; the year is 1969, I now live in the Northern Boulevard apartment that Marisol vacated and my mother has come to live with me after having gone alone, without speaking any English, to Los Angeles, to look for work, because I know, Mamá, that you didn't want to be in my way, and that's what you said to me, that it was better not to be in my way and that pain in me of knowing you were alone struggling with life, because there wasn't any work in the factory in Miami, and I don't know if it was cowardice, Mamá, perhaps selfishness, that made me think that I had the right to live my life, I never said to you, come, come without giving it a thought, I have an apartment now, I'm no longer in the degrading dormitories of Russell Sage, and I only said to you, well, by the way, Marisol and her mother are going by car to Los Angeles and from Marianita's house in Virginia, where you are now, you can come to Albany and you can go with them to California and I never told you, Mamá, the terror I felt knowing you would have to change busses so many times on your own, with your suitcases on your back, without understanding perhaps what the loudspeakers were saying; I presented the idea to Marisol making it plain that I would pay part of the gas, to contribute, Marisol agreed forcing a momentary politeness, that lasted a few hours until her voice announced to me by phone, look, we've decided that it would be more comfortable for your mom if she went by bus and along those lines, this whole series of explanations that Marisol gives with the certainty that it makes her look good and that it's all for the benefit of the other party; I'm left with a sensation of an abysm that opens inside me but I still don't say the words, come, Mamá, I have an apartment now and here's where you ought to be because I know that now you feel for me that need that I felt for you when I was little, it's true, isn't it, Mamá, that you only love me? and now her voice on the phone frequently, almost unintelligible between the sobbing and the choking, here in Los Angeles I'm going to go crazy, sometimes I feel that I'm going, that I'm going, what I've found here is work as a darner in a hospital and they bring me sheets full of blood, full of shit, I can't take any more, I've moved several times and I'm rolling, like a ball and it's pointless going to Miami because there's no work there; and again the distress and the weeping until I can't stand it any more and well, Mamá, come here; and now my mother with me in apartment 2A with 2 bedrooms, 28C Old Hickory Drive, Loudon Arms Apartments, a few steps from where Marisol lives; a few days later I go with Marisol to Kennedy Airport to meet Doña Florida who is returning from California after spending a month in Jacinto's house; the Corvair, as has happened on other occasions, won't start in a gas station and we had to spend the night in a motel and my mother acerbic, cold, on the phone and days later, when I least expect it, her indignant voice, hurt, chastising, it's just that I, I'd almost just arrived and you left me alone, out in the street, like a dog and her voice trembles and the sobs are trapped in her throat so that my guilt would be complete and there was no point in reminding her that she didn't come to the airport with us because she chose not to; and now, every so often, listen, Florida called me and she insinuated many things, all of which, according to her, were your fault and I didn't tell her what I know about her daughter because it would be better if I kept my mouth shut; and on the other side, Marisol saying, listen, your mother has said some incredible things to Mamaíta and you know that Mamaíta is incapable of saying anything offensive because Mamaíta is a little dove; and I tell my mother, don't say anything to Doña Florida, don't call her, and my mother replies that she never calls Florida, that Florida is the one who calls to suggest things and I have to answer her, don't I? and if she continues with this I'm going to tell her what Marisol's cousin told me in Los Angeles, I'm going to tell it to her straight; and I say, Marisol, my mother says that she never calls yours and I would be grateful if you could tell Doña Florida not to call here again and Marisol, as if hurt by a great injustice, well, I'll tell Mamaíta, but she, poor thing, only called to find out how you both were doing, because Mamaíta cares about you both, it's just that she, poor thing, is a kind soul; my mother found work in a factory making academic togas and Marisol comes by between classes once a week and we make love in this programmed way and afterwards we have for lunch what I buy beforehand in the local Chinese restaurant, so that my mother isn't aware of any consumption of provisions and so, so many precautions so that in the end my mother tells in a victorious voice one day, vacillating between aggressiveness and resentment, that one comes here every Tuesday, doesn't she? I know she comes here every Tuesday; and I say, trying to make it sound unimportant, no, Mamá, she works on Tuesdays, how could she come here? and I walked off knowing that I haven't convinced her and that the recrimination was still there, jabbering in those conversations that so often she has alone, given away by the gesture of her hand, by a small movement of her lips, her head, her eyebrows; 1969 has ended with the same tensions, without the hope that Doña Florida might go, even for a few days, to be with Jacinto because last time that she was there she announced herself Teresa's victim and Jacinto, furious with his wife, went to a hotel with Mamaíta and Doña Florida has already announced, wherever Marisol goes, I go too, because to California I will not go, and with that the possibility that Marisol and I could spend a vacation together, far from so many vigilant eyes, died; and you wouldn't believe, Chachi, the changes in Marisol, that it occurred to her to give speeches about the situation in Cuba on Channel 17, to the Rotary Club, in colleges and universities and that was fine because it was necessary to inform people about what was happening there, but just imagine that she took it upon herself to organize a government in exile in which she was going to be a Minister and there in Albany she made appointments, she chose the President of the future free Cuba and various ministers, she organized a protest against the participation of Cuba in Expo 67 and we went there, to the Canadian border, a group of Cubans under her command, carrying placards, repeated our steps in the same circle, when suddenly, Marisol disappears to phone several reporters and when they arrived, she rushed forward like a vulture to forestall the possibility they might interview anyone else and in response to my surprise, her powerful voice tells me that what she wants to prevent is that we might speak a load of nonsense and if you're unhappy because I didn't allow you to look bad it's because you're a handful of ungrateful losers because if all these nobodies are going to appear in the paper it's thanks to me; that's what she told me, Chachi, and she included me amongst the nobodies that thanks to her are going to appear in the paper; when Marisol bought the house we moved, my mother and I at my mother's insistence, to apartment 2B in 314 Northern Boulevard, where Marisol had lived, because this apartment seemed nicer to my mother and there we were, me in the bedroom where so often Marisol and I had slept, and my mother in the bedroom that used to belong to Doña Florida and when we took possession any traces of the women who had been there before us were erased, as if they had never been there; in this year of 1970 I hardly see Marisol because my mother became fed up with the Italian women in the factory, they insulted me, they said things, I can't take any more, and decided to retire at 62 years of age and she never ever leaves the apartment and I, debating between this doctoral thesis that I hate doing and the threat made by Russell Sage College, that without a doctorate they won't renew my contract, and I tell myself that if Marisol and I hardly see each other it's because I don't have time for anything, but on the other hand, when I call her towards eleven at night when my mother has already fallen asleep, Marisol doesn't answer and the rare times she does, then, a quick and impatient excuse, as if wanting to get rid of me, I've taken a laxative and must run, but she never said, I'll call you later, lately she leaves the phone off the hook and I can't contact her and when the worry that something strange is happening assails me, I calm myself by telling myself that if anything had happened Marisol would have told me until worry about the off-the-hook phone arises, about the bit about the laxative, about the ringing of the phone without her answering until, Marisol, what's going on? I know something's happening but I don't know what it is, Marisol presses her lips together a little, quickly shakes her head, nothing, what could be happening? but now we go out very rarely and always before we leave, she shuts herself up with Doña Florida and you know, Mamaíta, that I'll be back early, as soon as the film finishes I'll come back here, until today, April 21, 1970, I insist, we have to talk; Marisol agrees grudgingly in the face of my resolve and now in the restaurant-bar she insists on buying me a drink for the first time, and authoritatively, to the waiter, bring us two Bristol Creams, Marisol doesn't know how to start until well, I'm corresponding with a man and I didn't tell you anything because I didn't think this would last; when I hear her, I feel ashamed, weak, a kind of fear; when we're not together I think about Marisol's absences in the small hours of the night, in her desperation to return to her house, in her whispering with Doña Florida that I now recognize as messages Marisol leaves in case they call and in those words of love in English that she now uses like a habit; again I insist, we have to talk and if you don't want to go out we can talk here, Marisol looks at Doña Florida and says, Mamaíta, I'm going out but I'll be back early, if they call, tell them I'll be back early; and now in the parking lot of Valle's Restaurant, we walk in silence, the act of being seated at a booth, our order to the waiter, a steak for Marisol, a Bristol Cream for me, and now Marisol eating hungrily and my question which is placed weakly on her hunger, you're going out with a man, aren't you? and she says, yes, I'm going out, and I say, he's a lot younger than you, isn't he? and she says, well, a little younger; and I want to know his name and his profession, I want to place him geographically and Marisol swallowing those enormous pieces of meat until, during a brief pause, well, his name is David Whitehead, he's a lawyer and he lives in Schenectady, I'm surprised at the genius of that stomach that can divorce itself from this situation that to me, at least, is viscerally painful; in my bedroom, alone, it's just turned two a.m. and I search through the phone book, Whitehead, Whitehead, Schenectady, I dial the number and the voice of a young man affirms for me, yes, Whitehead, but I'm not a lawyer, I apologize, I hang up, and the next day I insist again and Marisol resigns herself to giving me a few, rushed details, his name is Tom, I met him in Macy's, in the rug department but I don't know why you want to know this information, and when I tell her that only by knowing the truth can I learn to survive it, I don't think Marisol knows what I'm talking about; I remember now the day we went to Macy's and that while I was paying for the rug that I had just given to Marisol, she was speaking to a young employee, about twenty three years old, with greasy, blonde, clinging hair, with blue eyes, with a round face and when I noticed he was so interested in Marisol, I told myself laughing, the poor thing, so insignificant, how can he imagine that Marisol will ever

163

take seriously anything that comes from him; I remember Doña Florida's insistence one day when Marisol and I were going to go out, Marisol, the rug man is coming today and you should be here for when he comes, because he's been so attentive to you, calling you so, today even, I don't know how many times he's called already, and Marisol trying to calm her with sweet words, I'm going to go out just for a bit, I'll be back almost at once, don't worry, Mamaíta, I'll be back in time; now that I know his name and his profession as a rug seller, the pain changes, but is no less deep, that dream I had about a year ago comes to mind, one of these premonitions that come to me so inexplicably, I appeared in my room in the house in Guantánamo and I don't know why Marisol and Doña Florida dominated the house that seems abandoned and lonely; I felt sad, as if my existence were weighing me down, Marisol smiled at me in satisfaction, as if she had just freed herself from something and she said to me, I'm going to get married; I laughed stupidly thinking it was a joke, an attempt to lighten with laughter that charged, annoying, atmosphere, but your voice returned to reaffirm the truth for me in a definitive tone: he's in the living room; I put on a really old dressing gown which is the one I use since I emigrated to the United States thirteen years ago and I went to the living room; I found myself face to face with a beardless boy, an adolescent almost a child who was sitting comfortably in a wicker chair as if he were the master of the house, in a rocking chair that had ceased to be mine, ours, belonging to our family; the beardless child, thin, infinitely thin, with black hair and green eyes, blue-green eyes, American, wore a T-shirt and a pair of white drill shorts, very white, like those of a tennis player's, although he was too young to be a professional player; I thought that with my maturity I could wound him verbally with caustic satire; I began to make nasty remarks to him, I called him *child* to lessen his importance, but that being who seemed so fragile, hardly reacted, he carried on rocking himself in the rocker and you appeared, Marisol, and you said to me, bored with me, no doubt you called him *child* and you shouldn't treat him like that, he's attentive to Mamá; I felt old in my old dressing gown and I said to the beardless one, I'm your girlfriend's aunt and I'm half crazy; I went dragging my ponderousness to one of the front rooms, I thought quickly that I should leave that house, I imagined myself walking through what, from that moment, would be the deserted city,

searching for my own foot steps; I imagined finding a guest house full
of solitude where everything seemed dirty and old to me; I imagined
myself in the difficult moment of not having anything to pay the rent
with; automatically I opened the purse of leaden blue Moroccan leather,
a little worn from use, and counted to nineteen dollars; at that moment
I ceased to torment myself for my lack of money; not having anything
to pay with became something of infinitely little importance and
anyway, perhaps I could continue to live there; I waited to hear you say,
this doesn't have anything to do with us, in no way will it interfere; I
heard you ask, are you suffering? the words came out of me dry, without
melodrama, I feel the pain that one feels with a burn, in the wound of
a burn, I feel a burning heat in my arms, in my chest, in my stomach,
it's a dry ice burn; I saw you incline your head and raise your eyebrows
and I understood that in any case, what you wanted was to not have on
you the weight of my pain; I decided to leave and look for a newspaper,
to read the advertisements, rooms for rent, vacant studio; what they
didn't advertise was the filth, the smell of damp, the long, lonely
hallways, the somber rooms and corners; I don't know why you went
with me, I don't know why Tom, the beardless boy took me, in his car;
now I realize that the laws of space had been broken, that my house was
the one in Guantánamo, but the town was another one, it was an
American town, modern, the sun very yellow, everything shining
yellowly; the beardless boy didn't speak nor did you give, as I expected,
the old explanation, that society, that you have to live in it, that one has
to adjust, I wasn't given even the peace of being able to fool myself
repeating to myself that you had chosen that path because it was the
only path to choose; I don't know how we found ourselves in the
Caimanera sea, in a speed boat of Tom's in which you could feel the
minute touch of the sea spray; you were at my side, on a seat in the wide,
straight bow, in front of us, was the beardless boy lying face up, with
his thighs apart; thinking that you would say that you would prefer to
remain at my side, I suggested that you sit next to the beardless boy;
with a serene delight you walked over to him, you rested your head,
your neck, between his legs, on his bulging protuberances and you
closed your eyes drawing a smile on your face; I removed my gaze and
looked at the sea, at the wake we left behind, and I felt an enormous
desire to confuse myself with it, suddenly you appeared still seated on

the floor, always leaning back against the beardless boy, always smiling, in another speed boat tied to the boat in which I found myself, following it; I understood then that it was pointless to turn my head, that you would always appear smiling, leaning back against the beardless boy, open like a frog; a salty bitterness filled my gums and I found myself half awake, in my bedroom at 314 Northern Boulevard; still half asleep, I wanted to end that tragically, but in a tragedy in which I would escape with a little dignity; I visualized myself on TV, on which it had been announced that I had won a million dollars; I appeared on the program wearing a maxi-skirt, all in black, without makeup; are you in mourning? yes, I'm in mourning for myself, I died two days ago, with the money I intend to buy time and space, to travel to the East, to search for my foot steps because perhaps I died at birth when I appeared round in a square world, when I was born square for a round existence; when I said all this I thought that perhaps you might be watching me and that possibly you would find me ridiculously tragic, or perhaps your heart would sink thinking that it was a mistake to marry the beardless boy or that, perhaps, the years would pass and you would get tired of the beardless boy who was attentive to your Mamá and that you would feel, in your moment of truth, your great need for me and that I would continue wandering, perhaps with a black dress, perhaps with a pale face, perhaps with furrows sunk around my mouth; I felt an enormous hunger in my chest, in my stomach, in my whole body, like someone who was dying of an internal hemorrhage would feel; and up to there my memory of my dream that made me call you so early in the morning to tell it to you while you interrupted me with your laughter, oh, so he's called Tom and he's a young American? well, look, I like the fact that he's young; her light tone spared me, momentarily, from fear; today I don't know how to hide this sorrow when I'm in the classroom in front of the students, when I'm in the apartment and I hear my mother saying, I know what you must be going through, this must have been a shock to you, but I remain silent because I know that it's not prudent to say anything more; one day when the sadness was too deep, I went out into the street to phone Marisol to ask her, if one day I can't hang on any more and I need to speak to someone, can I call you? and Marisol says, well, I can't promise you that because, just think, I can't tell my boyfriend, I have to leave you to be a nanny to my friend; upon leaving the booth I walk through Loudon Arms Apartments, circles and circles, I walk by 314 Northern Boulevard several times and I continue on to Old Hickory and I cover the same route until my shoes lose all notion of time, I stop before some dry, blackish branches, from a bush that clings firmly to the earth as if forming part of it, I stand in front of it for ages, as if to hypnotize it, I imagine the flames bursting from the bush and I transmit to the branches a decree that comes out of me like an order, that Marisol should feel and live the hell of this dryness, that she should feel it deeply as I feel it, and upon finishing the order I grasp with my hand the branches to seal the ritual, and now, each afternoon, the ceremony of the branches on fire and often, at night, this same route when it's time for me to cry alone; tonight there's a dinner in the Golden Fox to say goodbye to a professor from Russell Sage who's retiring, I recognize the parking lot, the Spanish architecture, the white walls like those of Córdoba, the two torches on either side of the door, the semi-darkness in the dining room, the different tables that Marisol and I have shared; the night in which everything seems strange to me advances, between the dissatisfaction of forced conversations that persists despite glasses of wine; it's after midnight and I head for Marisol's house because I know that Tom will be with her because the salary of a rug seller isn't sufficient and he works at night as part of a cleaning team in various banks and this is what I admire in him and it seems ridiculous to me that Doña Florida should tell the whole world that Tom has a doctorate and that Tom is good looking, good looking, with his blonde hair and his blue eyes and he adores me, what he feels for me is adoration, he calls me Mamaíta and he sits in front of me to look at me and to talk to me because he knows quite a bit of Spanish and he's the most intelligent person I've ever met in my life and he loves to play tennis and he has a trailer that Marisol says is a marvel and he has two enormous dogs that look like two sheep and that adore Marisol and Marisol adores them despite, as you know, the terror she's always had for dogs; I knock on the door so that Tom can stop being a ghost and becomes a reality that I can overcome; no one answers and I continue insisting with knocks that become harder and harder, perhaps they were in the middle of having sex and had to get dressed and I'm not leaving here until they open and finally Marisol comes out with a smile, come, come in; we stay standing in the living room until Tom appears with his shirt half out covering the fatness of an awkward twenty two or twenty three year old body; the brief introduction completed without a handshake, Marisol rushes to say to me, almost happy, come, let's go to the room so that I can give you what you came to collect; now in the room, Marisol is almost moved, why did you do that? all you'll achieve is suffering for nothing; and I say, no, Marisol, I have come to pull out by the roots all my jealousy because, frankly, I thought he was something else; now in the car, I'm assailed by the image of the conveniently closed door to Doña Florida's room to facilitate Marisol's intimacy, I'm assailed by the image of the study in which there's a comfortable sofa and the rug that I gave to Marisol the day she met Tom, I'm assailed by the image of Marisol and Tom on the comfortable sofa in the study, and that's why you didn't answer the phone that's next to the bed or you left it off the hook or well, I have to go now because Mamaíta doesn't feel well, or well, I have to go now because I took a laxative and I have to run; all that hurts, Marisol, it hurts deeply now, when you can't see me, because sometimes I thought, so naively, that the day that you turned forty all the possibilities of losing you would melt away because that is an age when it's too late to start again and I said to myself, I said to that woman of thirty six years that is me, that perhaps the asphyxiating circumstances in which we found ourselves would dissipate some day and then we could live in peace; I've decided to spend this summer in Spain and my mother will stay with Carmita and her husband who live in Miami as refugees; a few days before my trip, alone in my room, on my bedside table, a glass of water and the bottle of Meprobamate, I unscrew the lid, sprinkle the pills onto the palm of my left hand, I leave them there, clasped in my fist while I dial the number, they answer, I identify myself, I hear myself say, Dr. Gautier? I'm Marisol's friend, she saw you when she went to Madrid five years ago, I couldn't travel with her then because of my studies, yes, I know that you're familiar with our situation, but that's over already and I'm calling you at the precise moment I've decided to stop living or perhaps I don't really want to die, but I do want to stop feeling this profound pain that never leaves me, and his voice that's so comforting, so wise, reaches me, calming me, speaking to me like a father, would it be possible to see you? and I say yes, that I'll be in Madrid in two weeks, and he says, put those pills away, don't think that you have to live your remaining years afflicted by that pain that's so deep, get rid of that thought, convince yourself that you have to give yourself a period of two weeks before you see me, only two weeks before you reach Madrid; and now the pills entombed back in their bottle and the memory of the stories Marisol brought back from Spain, Doctor Gautier is a saver of souls, I don't know if he's a psychologist, but he's a man so wise, you know how I am about our things and I told him everything about us and I've never felt such a great peace, did you know that he even did a test to see if I was predominantly feminine? he's invented a really tiny electric apparatus, like a clitoris and he set it to vibrate in my clitoris to provoke an orgasm in me and from that lubrication he took a sample and analyzed it and he told me that I was feminine and nothing but feminine; faced with her air of relief and satisfaction, it only occurred to me to ask her, do you think, Marisol, that the bit with the vibrator was necessary? isn't it possible, Marisol, that this doctor, and Marisol wouldn't let me finish my sentence, no, no, no, I assure you that this man is a saint, he's already an elderly man, an ex-professor from the University of Havana and if you meet him one day, you'll see just what serenity his presence generates, I don't know if the vibrator thing could be only to be able to collect a sample or if it might also have the therapeutic function of calming one, but what I can tell you is that doctor Gautier has no evil intention and that I can assure you, just think that when he put that in me, what he told me was to think of you, so you can see he wasn't up to anything, but to tell you the truth, I couldn't think about you or anything else; Kennedy Airport, Iberia, 747, the castle in the air, the brusque change from night to day at a point in space, the announcement that we would be landing, land, cultivated patches, green and terracotta squares, the need to attribute symbols, the journey is a symbol of a new dawn, it's a symbol of starting again, it's the promise that in this land, destined to isolate me from pain, I will live intensely; the descent, Barajas, the hotel right next to Puerta del Sol, my first walk through Madrid, the public telephone booth, I dial the number, please, to Leonora, yes, Leonora de Vivar, I identify myself, I'm a friend of Marisol's, she met you when she came to Madrid five years ago, yes, Marisol is the friend of your cousin who now lives in the United States, the friendly voice, we arrange to meet; I remember that Marisol described her to me, Leonora is an interesting and mysterious woman just how you like them, but I'm sorry for her, what

a horrible life she leads because Doña Ramona, her mother, is an
octopus, with the story that she's a widow and that Leonora is the only
one she has in the world, she asphyxiates her, imagine that what Leonora
has is a fear of sex and I think also of practically everything in life,
there's like a terror in her because each time she leaves her mother, even
if only to go out for a little while, her mother makes her feel guilty for
abandoning her, just think that Leonora has never been kissed and
while she's no beauty, she is interesting; I keep walking, the post office
building, Cibeles fountain, one of the park stalls where I initiate myself
into the pleasure of drinking horchata and a few days later, Havana
Street, I carefully look for the odd number, I enter through the doorway,
and now in the elevator, the forth floor, the waiting room and finally,
my turn; the long medical coat, to his knees, his welcoming voice that
reaches me from his height; now seated in front of him, I imagine that
at any moment he's going to start telling me that homosexuality is an
illness that today can be cured and that at any moment he's going to
hypnotize me like he hypnotized Marisol and his voice surprises me,
while you're tied to Marisol, so committed to Marisol, you're going to
continue suffering, you have to give her up, meet another woman, meet
several women and try with all of them because you're the captain of
space; I'm left between surprise and disbelief staring at his venerable
figure, his serene voice that falls with the rhythm of a guru; slowly, I
raise my eyes to his oh-so benevolent smile, I see him take a book from
the drawer of his desk, look, child, I wrote this book, it's a study of love
between women, for me that's the only true love, so much so that if my
wife were to tell me that she loved another woman, I would have to
accept it, I would have to understand it, because a woman doesn't know
love if it's not with another woman, but this is something that society
doesn't accept yet and that's why I haven't dared publish this book, as
you can see, I wrote it, I sent it to the printers, these are the galley proofs,
but in the end I didn't dare because there are those who would set out
to destroy me as a professional, because this contains the story of
hundreds of women of every social class who have come to see me so
that I may give them some relief, women of the stage, great ladies of the
theater, writers, the wives of doctors, of lawyers, of so many respectable
Spaniards that leave their wives unsatisfied because what they need is
another woman, the story of all these women is in here, in these pages;

the pages of the book open and the voice begins to read with devotion, with a commitment that makes me think of sacred rites, of the smell of incense; he reads a long section of poetic prose, delicately directed to tell repeatedly of the love of one woman for another, different types of encounters in a beautiful nudity; I listen until the book closes, his gaze on me, allowing itself to fall, as if illuminated; so you see, child, that at no point have I mentioned the word *case*, these aren't cases, they're love stories, of the only love that can exist; I get ready to leave carrying astonishment in my eyes that have not been able to decipher the guru's enigma and his certainty that so many women who love one another maintain silence so that they aren't burned at the stake like the witches of Salem, but their steps are there, molding the streets of this earth; when I'm almost at the door, doctor Gautier stops me, I want to do an examination, and he mentions some tests that I consider unnecessary, but I give way before the serenity of his gaze, I follow him to the next room feeling a persistent desire to turn and leave through the door; on the examination table, naked, doctor Gautier examines me with the naturalness, with the almost tenderness with which you examine a child and once again his voice, I'm going to do a test, this little apparatus was designed by me to recover a specimen that I'll need for the test, it has a feminine shape so that the woman who feels its contact identifies it with what I call the soft caress, when you're in contact with it, think about a woman; I wasn't able to think of anything during what seemed to me a laboratory experiment; now dressed, once again in the intimate office where I recognize the desk, the chairs, the degrees that populate the walls, I'm ready to say my goodbyes, the guru at my side and his prophet's voice, before you leave, kneel down for a moment; I kneel thinking that prayer could be part of this strange ritual, when I feel his left hand on my head, his right hand pointing towards the ceiling and his serene voice, repeat, my child, repeat after me, I'm ready to do/ everything that doctor Gautier tells me to do/ for my own good/ to find my way/ for relief from my pain; upon finishing these phrases that taste of litany, with the echo of a prayer, now standing, I began to reconcile with him, my rebelliousness began melting away, I saw him before me with an almost patriarchal saintliness that made me approach him to kiss him on the cheek as a farewell, when I felt him stop me to indicate, as if I had erred in the ritual, no, on the hand, kiss me on the hand; in the street, the pleasant morning between sun and breeze, I let myself walk, an Italian restaurant, the menu, a plate of pasta and cheese, a lasagna served in a small steel casserole dish, a beer; the impeccably uniformed waiter moves away, I try to analyze this strange encounter with doctor Gautier and the pieces of the puzzle escape me before I can organize them; Leonora turned out to be a cautious woman, closed, with the mystery of a nun from a medieval convent; several meetings in some café in the Plaza Mayor with a Malaga wine, rushed because Mamá is alone and I have to go back; a poem that is born of me for her or that is born simply of the need to feel that the possibilities for love have not been lost for all time; an invitation to lunch in her house, the lunch carefully chosen and presented in which I enjoyed the fish baked with a sauce of tomato, onion, garlic, olive oil and after which Doña Ramona retired for her siesta; Leonora and I in the small sitting room in which almost imperceptibly, she closes the door for greater privacy, her deep emotion upon reading that first poem and in her deadpan face, a smile of almost happiness, no-one's ever written me a poem before; we stayed staring at one another until I heard Doña Ramona's steps; Leonora hurries to hide the poem between the pages of one of those books she's taken from the shelves, opens the door and sits down to converse about unimportant things and now Doña Ramona's talking about the Republic, that she was a republican and an atheist, that she still is and that she always will be; her voice of control over Leonora, who withdraws into silence; I excuse myself, I go to the bathroom, and there, the small medicine cabinet, the mirror, the tube of toothpaste of a brand unknown to me and some toothbrushes between which I try to divine Leonora's; before leaving for Morocco, a second poem and her emotion again and our looks with which we speak in the silence and my invitation, how would you feel about going out for some coffee, and Doña Ramona's voice answering for her, no, Leonora doesn't go out, I have a bad heart and I can't be left alone, it's bad enough that she has to go out to work every day, but what can we do, but that she should go out when she's not working, that would be too much; Leonora as withdrawn as an oyster, almost begging, I'm only going to go with her as far as the bus stop, I'll be right back, and before the protests of don't be long, I can't be left alone, Leonora assures her of her rapid return; the bus arrives, a hurried hug and the voice of Leonora, no-one's ever written me such a beautiful poem, and on her face, an almost happiness; the trip full of nostalgia in the Mezquita in Córdoba, the Giralda, the Alhambra, the Generalife; every so often, in the movement of the bus, a sensation of escape, and at the same time a yearning imposing itself on my fugue from myself; the bodegas in Jerez, the long table, the little cubes of cheese and the abundance of Bristol Cream that ends up befuddling me a little; Cádiz, Algeciras, the boat that crosses, bucking, the Strait of Gibraltar, and now this African land with a Spanish accent, the beautiful hotel La Muralla de Ceuta, the small bazaars, a black vase, exquisite, that I carry wrapped in silk paper, my gift for Leonora; the border that would allow us to pass to Tangier is closed, political disturbances, assassination attempts against the king; the days pass, we cross the border, accommodation in the luxurious Chellah and my loneliness and the telephone, yes, long distance, Madrid and the voice of Leonora polite and a trace of affection that became distance; back in Madrid, I dial the number, no-one answers, I head for her house with the Moroccan vase, I sit on the steps to wait for I don't know how many hours and now at ten o'clock at night, the noise of the old elevator and before me, Doña Ramona and the surprised face of Leonora, as if her mother had caught her in a moment of sin, I quickly present my excuse, I brought this suitcase full of gifts so that you can keep it safe here, because I don't want to leave it in the hotel, and upon handing her the Moroccan vase, happiness appears in her worn face, wavering between emotion and Doña Ramona's censure who lets her protests be heard as we descend the stairs, it's very late for you to be going to the bus stop, go as far as the door and come right back; when we say goodbye, we agree to meet for a bit on Saturday afternoon, only half an hour, because Mamá can't be left on her own; in the Plaza Mayor, two hurried glasses of Malaga wine, and no, I can't tomorrow because I can't leave Mamá on her own two days in a row; I resign myself to inviting both of them to the Lara theater, row 9, number 13 and Leonora by my side and Doña Ramona next to Leonora talking about Isabel Prada, the great actress that she is and how much she enjoyed *Cancionera* and now in the hotel room on San José Avenue, I write a love letter for Leonora that I give to her the next day in the Miami café, peppermint and soda for me, a tea for Leonora, her watch checking, her serious and worried face, I only came because it seemed imperative to you, because you told me on the phone that you had to see me, but I can't leave Mamá on her own; now the taxi, I watch her disappear swiftly leaving an emptiness on the sidewalk; in my hotel room I await her call that doesn't come, I dial the number and Doña Ramona's voice, cold, acerbic, no, Leonora is feeling indisposed and has already retired; in my bed, this coldness that invades me all of a sudden, so repeatedly, until day breaks; now it's morning, I search the travel agencies, there's no space left, there's nothing, we have nothing, until I find a tour of Portugal with a stop in Avila; Santa Teresa's room, the wall from the thirteenth century, a public telephone and I dial the number for Leonora's office; her far-off voice, between polite, cold and resigned, yes, I was ill, I feel better now, I'm glad that you're traveling and hope you have a good time, you mustn't feel you have to call, and now the emptiness that her voice leaves and this dryness that accompanies me; the bus on its way to Portugal, the guide tall, refined, smelling of a convent; the bus driver, with his body like that of a bull's and his eyes like that of an enormous cow; the passengers, like shadows that I can't quite make out; our arrival at the hotel Guarda, the ancient dining room, pleasant, with glass shades, the solitary room where I ask myself if Leonora could have fallen ill because of me, an urgent need to talk to her, I dial her number, I hear her voice polite and cold, I can't stop to talk because we have guests, it would be better if you didn't call again, and when faced with my insistence, we'll talk when you're back in Madrid; the vertiginous trip through Coimbra, the Monastery of the Jeromes, Estoril, Lisbon, Fátima and the shadows who leave the bus to invade the kiosks with engravings, rosaries, statues of the Virgin; I go off on the solitary path, the persistent light rain that leaves its moisture on your arms, on your face, in your hair, I go out into the open square that extends before the white sanctuary, I stop before the enormous grills protected beneath a roof of red tiles to look at the black bars where the candles are laid, now the large candle alight melting the wax and I place it there, in this meeting with compassion, Virgin of Fátima, cure this sadness that marks me; upon my arrival in Madrid, a call from Doña Ramona, come by tomorrow morning to collect your things because soon we'll be leaving for Jaca; I knock on the door, Doña Ramona takes out the suitcase without preamble, she hands it over to me coldly and declines my attempt to give her a farewell hug; that afternoon, in the Miami café, between peppermint and soda,

Leonora's voice, I had to tell Mamá, she saw that I was sick and I had to tell her; her medieval fears, the gesture of her hand sentencing me in the false air, her hurried departure, and the taxi, until it disappeared; a call from doctor Gautier, this afternoon he'll come to see me in my hotel with Chantal, a young French woman who could be his niece, graduated from the Sorbonne, married to one of the most prominent lawyers in Madrid; I go out for a walk to pass the time, I visit a painter in María Molina Street, in a shared patio, the open rectangles like enormous doorless holes, covered defenselessly by curtains, the studio at the end, brimming with paintings of Castilian landscapes in his style so personal; the artist, timid, humble, and at the same time, with an enormous inner confidence as if he knew absolutely which path was his to follow; a subterranean current connects us in the room empty of furniture, we speak for ages, we go to a cheap restaurant where we eat like kings for forty *pesetas*, a steak, French fries, a beer, and his happiness at seeing I loved the lunch; in the afternoon, at the agreed upon time, now in my room, the two rings of the telephone chastising the silence and the voice, concierge, señor Antonio López and his daughter; I recognize the name with which Doctor Gautier would identify himself, yes, tell them they can come up; a few minutes open during which I wish I could escape from there, run away as fast as I can, without stopping, feeling in me the fugue of space torn by my speed; the discrete knocks, my unsure steps towards the door, good afternoon Doctor, I mean, Don Antonio, come in, come in; before me, a thin, tall woman, about twenty three or twenty four, dark brown hair, long down to her waist, brown eyes, full lips; Doctor Gautier's voice introducing me to the young woman who has just seated herself at my side, at the foot of the bed, this is Chantal, it's as if she were my niece; I hear her faltering voice, with a light French accent, a pleasure; I incline my head imperceptibly by way of a greeting, I imagine that at any moment Doctor Gautier will leave the room and Chantal and I will speak at length, but I see him stretch out his arms towards Chantal and his voice like a rite in which one glorifies a goddess, and he addresses me: I offer you this woman, take her, she is yours; I'm lost in amazement, standing, without moving, and again the soft and suggestive voice, undress her, I offer her to you, this woman is yours; I look at the silent woman waiting for her to protest but now her slow movement, her long, fine arms, reach up to the back of her neck where she begins to lower her zipper leaving her back naked and again the persuasive voice, undress her, you undress her, I already offered her to you, this woman is yours; almost mechanically, I lower from her shoulders the open dress that slides to the floor and now her nakedness and mine pressed together in the narrow bed; after bringing to a close her intense convulsion, her prolonged and deep moan that I didn't share, she kisses my forehead, moments of quiet that balance the unease that this strange ritual has brought me, Chantal heads for the bathroom, I hear water falling from the shower; I'm dressed, seated in the bed and Doctor Gautier is standing, as if in a mystic trance, I've never seen Chantal surrender herself like that, with that passion, whenever you want we can meet again like we did today; I decline the invitation and I suggest to him, what I want is to speak with Chantal alone, we could meet in some café, I don't want to leave up in the air this strange situation in which I've hardly heard her voice, for me it's important that we communicate; Doctor Gautier, with all the calmness that characterizes him, but with absolute resolution says, no, that's not possible, all your contact with Chantal will be made through me; the stream of water ceases, Chantal appears already dressed; Doctor Gautier standing, the polite farewell, I stay seated on the bed, stupefied, verifying with my hands the perspiration, now cold, that Chantal left and this heartbreaking emptiness; my persistent attempts to contact Chantal were useless, Doctor Gautier, without exception, all contact with Chantal will be made through me and in the same manner; and I remembered him there standing at the foot of the bed, in his role as prodigious magician preparing the ritual, pulling at the strings as if we were puppets, delivering the damsel to later carry her name away behind closed teeth; the return journey, now in my apartment, 314 Northern Boulevard, in an Albany where the days have decided to become gray until the moment in which I receive an envelope franked in Santurce with a letter from Bibi that I stare at for ages, her affectionate and almost intimate letter, as if time hadn't separated us since the last time we saw each other in Santiago de Cuba, in 1957, my emigration proceedings, the visa, the guest house, my call to the Royal Hotel, yes, with Bibi, please, and now her voice and that bubbling that anticipation causes, can you come to lunch tomorrow? yes, come to the hotel, and at seeing one another, that contained happiness, so well managed by both of us; before lunch, like an unexpected gift, the chance to speak alone on the terraced roof, a journey through the languages we like to learn, a journey through our favorite painters, of those from the seventeenth century we stick, definitively, with Rembrandt, of the impressionists, with Van Gogh, and suddenly, a type of nostalgia in Bibi, do you know, this is the first time since I got married that I've been able to carry on a conversation with anyone, I'm asphyxiated in this family circle, the lunch ritual and dinner in the hotel with all the relatives, conversations about fashion, the club, the club, fashions; they call us to lunch and while we go down the stairs, Bibi's nostalgia becomes a profound sadness, and I, as if to console her, well, Bibi, when you have a child perhaps you'll feel better, perhaps you'll fill your life a little; and Bibi replies, no, that would mean that this chain would become perpetual, without salvation, without escape; she stops me briefly to say to me, you know that when I graduated from Law School I worked out there, in the mountains of Yaguajay, I went on horse back from settlement to settlement, defending country folk, I felt free, free, but when my father died of intestinal cancer, after everything he suffered, that I myself had to remove his excrement, throughout this whole painful process Ricardo behaved really well to Mamá and I, and Mamá felt like she owed a debt to him; they start serving and we approach the table to join the family circle, they treat me with cordiality between plates of roast beef, slices of fried green plantain, tomato salad; Ricardo's mother, with her Spanish accent, as if she had just arrived from Spain, and what would you like to drink? I ask for an iced tea with lemon, and she says, iced tea? do you have an upset stomach? and before my affirmation that I like tea and that I'm not ill, she remains bemused and almost hesitant while she orders, waiter, bring an iced tea with lemon; at the end of the lunch during which I forced myself to speak more than my shyness usually permits, Bibi breaks her silence to address Ricardo, it has to be now because she has to leave, no, we can't wait until you've finished here; Ricardo agrees reluctantly and Bibi comes up to me, let's go to my apartment so that you can see it, I always have to wait until Ricardo finishes and we go together, but this way we can speak for a little bit before you leave; a few minutes by tram and now in the living room of the apartment that seemed very uninteresting to me traipsed about by a noisy maid who at that moment was cleaning the corridor; fragments of nostalgia materialize, her Miss Dior perfume, everything we never mentioned on H Street, in number 661, between 19 and 21, everything we don't mention now because silence is perhaps a symbol of forgetting, or of the death of that strange flower that passed through my life as an adolescent, like a dream; as if it were an answer, I see Bibi, slowly lifting her skirt with her hand to show me the yellow petticoat I bought her on my trip to Texas, five, six years ago, and we stayed looking at one another and it wasn't necessary to say anything more; while I read her letter I've been overcome by an enormous desire to see her again and on the way, to visit a plastic surgeon to have my expression changed, to have him give me another one that isn't this one that knows pain so well; the only flight I've been able to get arrives in Puerto Rico at 3 a.m. on December 20th, I will stay in an airport hotel until daybreak and after that I'll go and see her, and her reply of November 28th, I don't see the point of booking a room in an airport hotel, did you know that the hotels in Puerto Rico are the most expensive in the world? don't worry, we'll meet you at 3:00 and we'll rest here at home, I intend taking the 20th off (that is if I have to work); today I was reading your poems again, but I don't want to write hastily, I'm only going to tell you that they're magnificent and we will discuss them, line by line; I've planned to explore the Island, counting on you to drive as I don't know it and everyone says that they loved the trip; the interest in this country is purely esthetic (nature); the colonial architecture isn't so impressive for those of us who have lived in Santiago de Cuba; but the cultural phenomenon (the progressive assimilation by America) is strange; for me it's a period of decadence, for others, of progress; any way, the subjective conditions of this social, political or cultural phenomenon are only confirmed through direct contact with the population undergoing them, a hug, Bibi; while I read her letter I ask myself if she will have changed much these past fourteen years; I leave the plane, descend the little stairs, right away the intense heat of the Island reaches me, I look for Bibi's face amongst the crowd, and her smile and I walk towards her, her spontaneous joy at seeing me, Ricardo and I shake hands, my apologies for arriving at this hour, and now in the pleasant apartment, Ricardo goes off to bed and Bibi and I sit on a small balcony, chatting while we drink a frozen orange juice, and Bibi says, look, this morning when I bought this orange juice, I thought that I was buying it for you, each time I bought something, I thought that I was buying it for you, that you were going to enjoy it too; I look at her checking that she hasn't changed, her skin so smooth, her naughty smile, her enjoyment of being with me; tell me, Bibi, how are we going to explore the Island? and Bibi says, well, I don't know, I don't think it'll be possible, anyway, it would only have been for a few hours, because Ricardo would never allow me to spend a night away from home; I keep chatting because I've been given to understand that Bibi isn't going to work until she mentions in passing that she's going to work in a few hours and I quickly suggest, well, in that case, it would be better for you to sleep a bit, and she says, tomorrow you'll meet Ricardito, he's already 13, and you'll meet Mamá, who lives with us; when I awake to daylight, Bibi has already left and Ricardo has also gone to his job as an accountant with a perfume company; before me, the beautiful and silent face of Ricardito, Bibi's words come to mind, yes, of course I love my son, but I would give anything to forget that he's Ricardo's son; before me, Doña Carmela, in whom I intuit her almost watchfulness over Bibi; towards midday, Bibi unexpectedly appears, this afternoon I don't have to teach a single class, so if you want, we can go to San Juan, and now the bus, a beautiful combination of colonial architecture and sea, the cemetery also facing the sea, with the tomb of statues that Bibi informs me, belong to the Ferrer family; we walk through the center, remnants of cobbled streets, iron bars, flamboyan trees, all perfect for daydreaming; Bibi's words while we cross a street: it's all a question of the fear one has of words, cancer, homosexuality; artists, the most refined spirits, count themselves among homosexuals, so why fear the word? why not just say it? no one can put their hand in the flame and swear that they've never ever felt it; in the Morro, in all this blue panorama, Bibi guides me to a spot, this is the corner I like most, I'll give it to you, I want to give it to you today, I've never shared it with anyone else; and now the operation and the short stay in the Río Piedras clinic, I've come out the same, but something inside me is happy that, at least, a cell adjustment is taking place that will make me a little different from the one who suffered for Marisol; in the few days I haven't seen Bibi, I've thought about her, in the conversation that became so intimate when we were in her bedroom and everything was interrupted when Doña Carmela brusquely opened the door and said, Bibi, aren't you going to take a bath, Ricardo will be here soon and you haven't even bathed, but what are you two doing with the door closed? let's go, Bibi, aren't you going to take a bath? days later, in a few hours of freedom that Bibi has, we have lunch in a Spanish restaurant in San Juan; while we wait to be served, we gaze at one another in an intimacy that becomes a caress, and Bibi's voice, do you know what? I'm curious to feel you on my body, and she pushes her breasts forward to reaffirm her words, your mouth on my body; and I don't know if you'll know, Bibi, the effect your words had on me when I heard you say, your fluids are dangerous, I, who doesn't feel or need, and you have an effect on me, your presence here makes me feel as though I've drunk four glasses of wine, I'm curious to feel you on my body; on the way home everything opens to daydreaming, it seems to us that we're crossing different corners of the earth, a parade of children marched before us when we were seated on that bench, they turned into French shoes beating the cobbles with their rain of rhythm; now in the apartment, Bibi's like an ice statue and she affirms to me, I'm a zombie, Ricardo says that in bed I'm as inert as the Sphinx, I've never felt anything sexually, in Cuba I became interested in a doctor, one of Fidel's doctors, and I even thought of leaving Ricardo, but when the doctor and I went to bed, he felt disabled, he told me that had never happened to him before, but we couldn't even get close, and we stopped seeing each other, after that I tried to poison myself, but Ricardo came back earlier than usual that day and arrived in time to take me to the hospital, one stomach pump and the zombie walked again, afterwards, here, in Puerto Rico, I met an Irishman who was a student of mine, he had an incredible aptitude for learning Spanish, sometimes we would go out for a walk, that was all, he didn't interest me sexually, but it gave me a thrill to go out with him, he was also married, a few months after I met him he left here and I haven't heard from him; and now it's December 31st, I'll spend midnight in the plane, remembering what Bibi recommended, at that time, have a glass of champagne, at that hour I, unfortunately, will be with Ricardo's family, but what I'd like to do is throw a glass of champagne into the sea so that it can go and meet you, seeing as how I can't do that, I'll pour it into the basin if necessary, what counts is the symbol; it's six p.m., the living room is full of Ricardo's friends and it occurs to me that this is my only chance, and Bibi, can you come here a moment? Bibi follows me into the bedroom that had been assigned to me, I lock the door, we look at each other and words aren't necessary, the embrace, our mouths half open for the kiss and before our lips can touch, the voice of Doña Carmela, Bibi, Bibi, open the door, why have you locked it? Bibi moves away abruptly like a frightened deer and I hurry to open and with all the calm I can pretend, oh, Doña Carmela, come in, it seems I locked the door without realizing, but come, come in, we're just finishing up my packing; Doña Carmela sits on the bed with the attitude of an on-duty policeman and Bibi, pale still from the fright, disappeared from the room; now in Albany I'm assailed by a boredom that I relieve by escaping into daydreams with Bibi, the heat that her memory causes in me I'm forced to get under control in the strangest places: in the faculty meetings, while I explain the subjunctive, at the market while I confirm that they've lowered the price of lettuces; when they notify me that I've received a literary award, I use the excuse to phone Bibi; in her restricted voice I intuit Ricardo's presence and I say goodbye without saying hardly anything; a few days later, a letter from Bibi, that my phone call had caused a confrontation between her and Ricardo, that Ricardo went mad with jealousy and made her show him all my letters and my poems, that his scenes had been so frequent that they've almost caused her a nervous breakdown but that she's told Ricardo that he couldn't blackmail her because nothing had happened between her and I and that as much as he might shout she would never give up my friendship; I end up reading the letter so many times, and the ending, know that I'm your friend, always; it causes me endless pain that Bibi should suffer because of me, and I'm also hurt by this wistfulness I feel for her as I let the months pass without writing to her; in April of 1972 I break the silence, a few brief lines, that I'm thinking of going to Puerto Rico in May to have an operation on my breasts to relieve me of the pain of what they have diagnosed in the United Sates as *cystic mastitis*, that a friend from Albany has found me accommodation with a family in Puerto Rico; and immediately, a letter from Bibi, I can't accept that you arrive in Puerto Rico and immediately check into a hospital to spend three nights making crosses on the wall, come here, do the tests, come back and stay here until the night before the operation, love, Bibi; and in another letter in May, I hope you come on the 19th after your tests, you'll be less bored than in the hospital, didn't you like the bed? when I arrive at Bibi's apartment, I stand looking at Ricardo, assessing what he's going to do until he stretches out his arm, smiles, shakes my hand and I reply to his greeting; after the operation, convalescence in the home of the family that my friend Berta had recommended to me, I still miss Bibi and today, May 31ˢᵗ, I make up my mind, La Concha Hotel, room 604, curtains and rug in shades of cobalt blue, bamboo furniture, I dial the number, the surprise in Bibi's voice, the risk, the danger, I could run into someone there that knows Ricardo, come, we'll talk; when I arrive at the apartment I'm met by Doña Carmela because Bibi has had to leave to give a class, the wait for hours until her return, a few minutes alone during which Bibi talks about risks, that she was never, nor will she ever be *that*, that why should she look for problems for a fleeting escape and once again Doña Carmela and my polite goodbye and I go directly to the hotel, to enjoy my room in solitude; in the few days that remain to me in Albany I prepare for my trip to Madrid and now on June 23ʳᵈ, walking through Cibeles, the jets of the fountain, a summer that melts away in research for my doctoral thesis, a pointless trip to Greece, and now the return and the presentation of my new thesis in a last attempt to save a job that I need and that couldn't interest me less and my thesis advisor at the University of the State of New York as useless as the previous one, requiring changes and changes and changes in material with which he isn't familiar and I see myself pushed and pulled between quarrels and jealousies between academics who have taken my small literary triumphs, my publications, as an insupportable insult and everything ends with the rejection of my thesis project and everything ends in May of 1973 with the closure of my cycle at Russell Sage because we regret to tell you that as you have not finished your doctorate, we cannot renew your contract; during this October of 1972, Marisol's wedding in a Greek church, that day I left Albany and from the road I saw the church at the moment when I knew that she was getting married; hundreds of letters of application until I found work at Briarcliff College starting September 1973 with a promotion to Assistant Professor; my mother is in Miami spending the summer with Carmita, and I, piling into enormous boxes hundreds of books and papers, so many necessary and unnecessary things that we hoard in our houses; it's eleven p.m. and loud knocks hammer on the door, I continue packing with no intention of opening when I hear Marisol's voice, it's me, open, open up, it's me; surrounded by the doorframe Marisol appears half drunk, with a strong odor of alcohol, and her voice, I would like to sleep here tonight, I was going to stay at the motel on the corner, but I said to myself, why should I pay for a motel? I prepare my mother's empty room for her and once installed Marisol decides that I should distract her with conversation, with nothing to say to her, I read her one of my short narrations, and I explain it to her and as I say goodnight, I hear her voice so deeply disillusioned, did you know that my marriage, from the beginning has been hell? I've left the house now because Mamaíta's in hospital, being operated on for a cyst on a kidney, but when she's home, I have no escape, I have to put up with leaving the room to sleep in the living room; and almost immediately, as if sorry for having told me, well, the truth is that it's not always like that, things aren't always bad, in fact, often things are good, but during the days that Mamaíta's in the hospital, I would like to sleep here; as I leave I prepare to close the door to the room and Marisol says, no, leave it open, please; in my room, with the door closed, I think that it's only been eight months since Marisol got married and it seems a century ago to me since the exact moment in which, from the road, I knew she was getting married in the Greek church; during the days that Marisol spends in the apartment, I leave everything ready so that she can prepare her breakfast before going to the hospital and at night, I have dinner ready for her and we hardly speak before going our separate ways to sleep, each to our own room; one morning, a note from Marisol, today Mamaíta gets out of hospital, so I won't be coming back, but thank you for your kindness and generosity; in the afternoon, the telephone and Marisol's voice, listen, I wanted to explain, what happened between Tom and I was nothing, it has absolutely no importance, things between a husband and wife; and she repeated, between husband and wife; in a moment of cynicism, I hear myself say, oh, Marisol, I'm glad that you're so happy, the other day when you told me about what I thought was a separation between you and Tom, I immediately made plans to take you to the East, to take you to Japan with me, yes, this summer, now, in a few days, but now everything has changed, I know that you can't leave your husband; I keep waiting for her to tell me, almost offended, that I must be crazy for thinking that she would be capable of leaving her husband but her voice becomes light, and a spontaneous happiness emerges from the receiver, well, no, I can tell Tom that I'm going to Japan with a friend, because that's no big deal, but you're going to spend all that money on me? and I, laughing so cynically to myself, say of course, Marisol, why not? and when the room is empty of sounds, I ask myself what made me say that to Marisol, because I don't intend to go with her to Japan or anywhere else and already for months now I've had my ticket to go to Argentina, but I was amused thinking about the excuses she would give me not to go, I can't leave my husband because we're husband and wife, husband and wife, husband and wife; then come the hours of sleep until harshly, at seven in the morning, the sound of the phone wakes me, Marisol's voice, so full of happiness, I'm going with you, we're going to Japan, I told Tom that a friend was paying my way and Tom said that if he couldn't pay for my trip, he has no right to forbid me to go; and I'm half asleep with this unexpected news between my hands, until, well, Marisol, I've thought about it and I think it's better that I go to Argentina because I had reserved my ticket but I didn't think that they would confirm it, but yes, they did, and Marisol, disillusioned, that's OK, I understand, that's fine; now alone, I ask myself once more what made me invent the story of a trip to Japan for Marisol; in Buenos Aires, searches and misses, everything could have been so beautiful but it becomes desolate; a few days in Mar del Plata digging up the last trace that Alfonsina left in the waters, her face immobile in the monument on the banks, the insult to her memory, Storni Restaurant, Drink Coca-Cola, and I take myself home, my intention to protest, to write to the authorities, but I don't write, no-one writes, and the years will pass and the advertisement for Coca-Cola will still be there, forming the background to Alfonsina's immobile gesture; August 15th I'm back in Albany, I travel immediately to the Westchester area, staying at the Hawthorne Circle Motor Inn looking for an apartment, trips to different nearby towns, everything costs more than I can afford to pay, until finally, the Birch Brook Manor living complex, on South Highland Avenue in the Village of Ossining, building 87, apartment B-25 full of light, one medium-sized room that will be mine and another smaller room, a tiny kitchen, medium-sized living room with an extension without any partitions that will serve as a dining room, between my bedroom and the bathroom, a hallway; the bathroom with its old tiles gives me the impression that I've already lived in it in some other European house, in another reincarnation; while Bojzak shows me the apartment I feel an inexplicable rejection of his apparently humble gestures, his clear, round eyes, that behind his frameless glasses, turn him into an owl keeping watch, his average stature, not thick nor extremely thin, his little moustaches pulling together with the ridiculous movement of his lip, as if they were protecting him from some little odor, as if it were the gesture of a virgin who, in her fifty sixth year, had just heard the sentence of her defloration; I've just told him that yes, I'll pay him the four hundred and twenty dollars deposit, that yes, I'll sign the rental agreement for at least a year, that yes, I'll obey all the regulations in the contract; we're about to leave the apartment, the bad smell expression disappears from his lip, the shyness disappears from the virgin-about-to-be-deflowered and a nervousness jumps from the eyes of the owl and with this nervousness the Hungarian jumps like a hare and anchors his shaking, off-white hands on my breasts, I shove him with an anger that would like to strike him down, and I watch him retreat in stages while I shout insults at him; from the distance at which he stops, he recovers his timid gesture, the bad smell, the threat of defloration to say, it wasn't anything, I didn't intend anything; I calm down thinking that with my shove this hypocrite with his face of embalmed saint won't try and bother me any more, Bojzak takes me to the basement of another building where there are cubicles separated by wire mesh, like chicken coops, that we can use for storing the junk we can't fit in the apartment; while I write my name on one of the planks of the cubicle, Bojzak approaches, once again with a rapid movement, his tadpole arm on my shoulder, he leans towards me as if to slobber on me, and this time, the shove was harder, to the extent of almost making him lose his balance and fall on his rear-end on the cement, a controlled, definitive voice emerges from me, look, Bojzak, I'm not going to bother to shout at you any more, I just want you to know that the next time you come near me, with the first thing that comes to hand, I'm going to crack your head in two; immediately the little moustache is pulled backwards, the bad smell gesture, the fear of the defloration sentence look, and his cowardly voice, it wasn't anything, I didn't intend anything; I return to Albany, call my mother in Miami, saying that I found an apartment, that it would be better if she came after the move, but her desperation to come, no, tomorrow I'm leaving for there, tomorrow for sure; so many things still to pack, calls to I don't know how many moving companies and none can move me, no, you should have called us at least a month in advance, until finally, Burkins and Foley Trucking and Storage, Inc., yes, that's fine, for August 30th, the move will cost you three hundred and seventy dollars; and now it's August 28th, a call from Marisol, that she wants us to go out to lunch to say goodbye, and I say that it's impossible right now, that she knows I still have so many things to sort out, and that's why when I arrived back from Buenos Aires, and she told me we should go have a farewell lunch, I told her that I was free then, but that at the last minute it would be impossible for me, and she said, at the time, no, because Tom and I are going next week to spend two days on a yacht that we're going to rent, so just imagine, I need this whole week to buy the things that we're going to use on the yacht; and I left it like that because in truth I wasn't interested in seeing her and it seemed more than sufficient that we should say goodbye by phone; but now she keeps insisting, insisting, insisting, until she says goodbye without recovering from her shock at my negative response; August 29th, Marisol again, that we have to go out to lunch and again my refusal and her amazement; August 30th the sound of the phone wakes me and the clock tells me that they've woken me at 7:30 a.m. and Marisol's voice speaking to me in English, can we go somewhere for breakfast? let's go to a Howard Johnson's and we can say goodbye over one of those delicious breakfasts that we like so much; I tell her in Spanish that I can't, and Marisol insists in English, that yes, that won't take much time; I assume that Tom must have left already and Doña Florida would be in Marisol's room with the orange juice or on some other pretext, stuck to the phone and Marisol doesn't want Doña Florida to know that she's insisting on seeing me and I feel detached from the effort Marisol makes to keep Doña Flora in perpetual complacency and I feel detached from her effort to see me at the last minute and I feel detached from the amazement in her voice upon realizing that this farewell will definitely take place at a distance, without overcoming the five miles that separate us on Shaker Road; during the few minutes that I stay lying down, face up, I could be invaded by the image of Marisol, some wistfulness, the need for some last contact, but I stay like that, with my eyes open, thinking about the boxes that I still have to fill; at about three in the afternoon the movers arrive, I watch the furniture, the boxes full of books, the enormous plastic bags, parade out, down the steps, and now the apartment's locked, and now in the car, driving away from Loudon Arms without it hurting to be separating myself from there, without one atom of nostalgia for the years that I left in the so-called three city area, Albany-Schenectady-Troy, and now on the highway, Taconic State Parkway, until traveling the 140 miles that take you to Ossining; the movers take hours to arrive, now late at night, Mister Burkins appears with a threat, instead of three hundred and seventy dollars you have to give me four hundred and seventy dollars or else I won't give you your furniture; I protest knowing that my protest is pointless, because I have no protection against this legal robbery that takes place daily, I hand him the check and he says, as if to feel better about stealing, it's that you had more boxes than I was expecting and when I ask him why he didn't tell me about this increase in Albany when he saw the boxes, he started to fold the check and stick it avariciously in his wallet, taking his silence away, down stairs, while he caresses the jacket pocket where he had placed his wallet; the first night in Ossining passed as if I had always lived there, the apartment, still in complete disorder, is clean, my mother and I came to clean it a few days ago because Mister Bojzak handed it over grimy with filth; I start classes at Briarcliff College, I'm comfortable, nobody bothers me regarding my freedom to teach, I intuit that to the majority of the professors I seem strange, inscrutable, with my ostracism and my invariable silence, but at the same time, they don't insist on breaking down the walls that I raise without intending to; during lunch in the beautiful glass dining room I share a table with the gardener, a Cuban I can listen to with ease as he talks about growing his roses; sometimes, some professor insists, come, come and sit with us, and then I can hardly eat, the sweat on my hands, the rigidity of my stomach muscles, listening to conversations about unfamiliar committees, about unfamiliar academic plans, comments about unfamiliar professors, about professors that are always unfamiliar until I can't stand the pressure any more and, with my plate still full, I excuse myself, I have to go, I have to finish preparing the next class, bye, I leave with quick steps until finally I can relax in the safety of my office; in my apartment, I seek a reconciliation with solitude, to confront the possibility of spending the rest of the years that remain to me without that woman that I've searched for in Europe, in North

Africa, in Argentina, in Puerto Rico; my coming and going has become routine; my mother knows no one in Ossining, she doesn't go out for even a moment to sit on the benches of the tiny square that forms the center of the gardens in the complex, so many times I've thought that she's also one of those beings destined for solitude because she's never been granted the miracle of a lasting friendship, she's never been granted the miracle of security in life, something on which she could have counted, something that would have been profoundly hers, when did you stop trying, Mamá, when did you stop expecting anything from life because everything became, I remember your words, salt and water in your hands and perhaps my noble mission could be this, to make you feel that you have someone to cook for, to worry about in this town buried in the Sing Sing of Ethel and Julius Rosenberg; I, for my part, feel a lack of purpose that I try to dispel with bottles and bottles of *G & D* wine, bottled in the San Joaquín valley, described on the label as *Tawny Port*, with the procedence specified: *Private Stock*; to escape my mother's censure I hide the bottles in the trunk of my car and watch for the moment to bring in each bottle and to take out of the apartment each empty bottle without my mother realizing, and of filling each glass and carrying it to my room and drinking it with the door closed; when hours pass without my mother moving from the living room, I have to make do with a Librium capsule; the drawers of my office are never without a bottle of *G & D*, and between classes and with the door closed, one glass after another, until I'm calm; at the beginning of June, Marianita comes to visit us with Bill, her new husband, she divorced Albert two year ago because, no, girl, as for Albert and his dreariness, no way, I put up with too much, it's just that sometimes I would stare at Albert and it seemed to me that what stood before me was a mummy; Marianita and Bill want my mother to spend some time with them in Virginia, where they live now, and my mother unsure, that she doesn't know, that let's see, that later, and I pressure her because I need to be alone for a bit, Mamá, if you don't go with them now when they've even brought the car, you'll never go; my mother, still unsure in the days that Marianita and Bill spend here, begins, with apathy, to pack a couple of suitcases; the moment arrives when the car is ready, running, my mother separates herself from me with grief, as if they were tearing her away from a place she didn't want to leave, and now the farewell and the distance that begins to separate us; I return to the apartment, an intimacy all my own, a reunion with other dimensions of myself, freely scattered; on the table, I recognize my mother's glasses and this sad tenderness with which I touch them, as if to retain a little of her between my hands before hurrying to send them to her, protecting them in an empty can of coffee; now at the post office, I'm moved by the sensation that my mother won't return to the apartment, that her things that remain there will go to meet her, but that she will never return to collect them, her depressed disposition during the last months come to mind and when I asked, but Mamá, what's wrong? she always responded, I don't even know myself, it's like a dread, a fear; until one day, while she was drying her hands in the bathroom, I see in her a deep sadness and tell me, Mamá, what's wrong? and she says, well, it's the same thing I've been feeling for months now, that I'm going, that I'm leaving here, all this, that for some reason I'm leaving definitively, a total separation, and she begins to cry inconsolably; I try to calm her without completely convincing her, without convincing myself with my own words, because I also felt in that moment, that the separation was definitive; and now that you're not here I can tell you, Mamá, that I was crushed by a deep sadness when I saw you like that because you became attached to me, without saying anything, like I was attached to you when I was little, wrapped in those fevers that ran from me with your care, now soon you'll be well, my child, now soon you'll be well; and I'm satisfied, Mamá, that now the bottles of Vichy water and San Antonio water, they're all for me, and don't think I've forgotten, Mamá, the longing that overcame me in the night in that house in Caimanera with its posts sunk in the sea, because I know that before I learned to speak, Mamá, even from the carrycot I, without a voice, formed your name, and afterwards, when I could say your name, I would sit on the window ledge that separated your room from mine and I called you without cease until you gave in and came to my bed so that peace would return to me under the mosquito net; now in the separation urged on you by me, I look for silence, to not see anyone, to not talk to anyone, to follow a rigorous diet, to lighten my physical being, to walk, to walk the town daily, to do exercises, and an intensive reading of the works of Anaïs Nin, the five volumes of the *Diary* published to date and her works waiting for me on the shelves: *Winter of Artifice, Seduction of the*

Minotaur, Under a Glass Bell, Collages, The Four Cornered Heart, Children of the Albatross, Ladders of Fire, A Spy in the House of Love, House of Incest, and to feel myself kept company by Anaïs's life, so full, so complete; little by little I achieve peace, a reconciliation with peace, eliminating the need for wine, that *G & D*, that with such care I hid in the trunk of the Plymouth, only the intensive reading that carried on sometimes until the next day at eight or nine in the morning, sleeping then for a few hours, eating breakfast during any part of the day, remembering lunch at three in the morning and solving it with a sandwich and a glass of cider; June 29th, I receive an invitation to the baptism of a book by a very bad poet I have no interest in hearing, but perhaps I need to end this hibernation and to pay attention to the call of the generous Elba, the Puerto Rican that I met at a CEPI prize giving, so friendly, don't forget to come, I live in the same building where they're celebrating the baptism and afterwards you'll stay with us, with my husband and I because my daughters don't live with us anymore, so there's room to spare; the invitation taped to the wall of my bedroom, reminding me, June 29, 1974, in New York city; at times I firmly decide to go and at others I firmly decide that it would be best to keep hibernating; now it's the 29th, I get ready to leave with reluctance, I take the slowest route and with the least traffic, Highway 9 South that connects to Broadway in Manhattan; I felt welcomed by Elba and that disposed me to a sociable cordiality so that, even though at times I had to force it a little, I join in the applause at the moment in which the godmother spilled the bottle of champagne between the open pages of the volume of poetry; the night melts away almost as though it were any night until suddenly, Elba turns to a young, olive-skinned woman and greets her affectionately, stand up, stand up, Laura, let me introduce you, look, here's a Cuban poet who's recently published a book of poems; I stare at this woman who seems to me to be about twenty years old, her almost withdrawal, the edge of her silence; Laura has moved away, is seated now in a chair whose back touches the wall and at her side a part-Indian man who might be her husband but I isolate her in my mind from that man, I isolate her from everyone there and in an unexpected instant I had the impression that the intensity with which I watch her, reached her; it has to be, I won't debate any more, I surprised myself walking towards you, Chachi, giving you a small label that carries my address, send me some of your poems; your agreement while you stow my label in your wallet and my abrupt return to the group where the voices with which I don't communicate are superfluous; a few minutes later, this inopportune desolation that her absence causes me; staying up late in the kitchen-dining room in Elba's apartment, it's almost four in the morning and she's frying tiny fish in an iron skillet so that hunger doesn't interrupt our conversation, which we continue until I begin to feel more distant as the light of day draws closer and my questions hang in the air, tell me, Elba, what's Laura's poetry like? where does she live? what's she like? who's she with? the months jump, and in me, a search that is now confused with solitude; I have frequent nightmares in which Marisol, Bibi, Chachita appear with different names, I write down the most recent one: Rosa María's ancient and vigilant mother appears, transparent, without substance, like the spirits; and I, woman-woman, trapped in this civil condition, clinging to Rosa, in the asphyxia of this undocumented marriage; I'm overcome by subterranean needs for the young woman, for her mysterious olive skin from the Mediterranean; a third woman about my age, insubstantial, transparent, who's law degree, so worn, has ceased to be important, will the Political Economics Exam also cease to matter? will that kiss that you insinuated to me cease to matter? Rosa looks at me severely: if you go off with that woman, don't ever come back, it's all over; the transparent jaw of the old woman closes into a wrinkled and satisfied crack, I can see her eyes shine, I see her happiness because with our undocumented divorce she'll have Rosa all to herself or for a legal marriage, presentable to society; the old woman doesn't know that I also want to liberate myself from this civil state that although non-existent, I find asphyxiating; I leave with my young lover to walk the beloved streets of that town; the transparent shadow of the other woman of my age, follows us, and from the piece of paper that she carried stretched between her hands smoke begins to emerge to form the date, 1952, and the words, POLITICAL ECONOMICS EXAM; I continue on with my lover, her olive skin so young, we walk down cobbled streets, we write down the date in our letters, 1870, we feel the light of the street lamps in this town in Spain, with the same steps we explore the city of New York in this year of 1975, but it's almost always 1870, when everything is old and provincial; Rosa's house is now made of wood, of old planks, packed with antique furniture made from wicker, I refrain from talking to her about the changes that we were going to make in 1871, in secret, murmuring so that the old woman wouldn't hear us, but nothing matters now, let the old woman stay in the labyrinths furnished with wicker; I've already won my freedom in this town and my young lover and I wander the streets, followed by the transparent shadow with which I won't go to El Vedado, the sign stretched between her hands doesn't say anything about the erotic abortions and when the shadow becomes a statue, on the sign my signature doesn't appear either: Pygmalion, now the shadow slips along to the rhythm of my steps and the sign becomes smoke to form the words, San Juan, but I don't go with her because Doña Carmela stretches out her arthritic hand and rips out the kisses she has hidden between her full lips, and she rips off her lips, and, if Doña Carmela hadn't ripped out the kisses, would she have ceased to be a statue? I'm not going to look at the sign because I'm walking among the cobbles with my lover's beauty, I want to follow this path for always, walking with her to infinity, but she stops suddenly to recognize as hers this dilapidated house, closed in the front with a door of zinc, of aluminum, like the ones the Chinese use in their restaurants in Caimanera; my lover faces me and speaks and in the moment in which we jump the barriers to return to this century, her voice emerges as a challenge: you have to stay here in Manhattan, in the studio on 79th and I have to leave for the other studio; the glass windows of the studio and the zinc door become superimposed, the cobblestones and the asphalt become superimposed, and I, between two centuries, my need is the same: to retain this woman, but I don't have a voice to call her and I watch her move away until she disappears; I return to the aluminum door as if looking for an answer, there are no indications on this wrinkled, metal board, I decide to stay in this century in which I once was, I refuse to cross through the glass, to walk the asphalt, I move away with the will power of my canvas shoes that fill with the dust from between the cobbles; the woman-shadow follows me and materializes, she's the same, as if at any moment, she were to fill her breasts with ice, she approaches me, we speak very little, she wants to know, she insists in knowing if I want to continue wandering eternally and I remind her so belatedly, that what I need is a kiss; her voice gives me details and the address of an old Spanish restaurant rooted in the town, where there is a spacious bathroom in which we can kiss, we're among the black and white floor tiles, like the ones that my bathrooms have had in other reincarnations; we've closed the door, we've shot the bolt; I still have in my eyes the vision of the waiter with the long, white napkin asleep on his arm, his apron, the tables with the white, not very clean, tablecloths, and a curtain of wooden reeds that I liked to pass through, as if, upon opening it with your hands, you were going to uncover some mystery; we continue in the spacious bathroom, oh-so spacious with the old bathtub and the floor tiles, mostly white; the materialized shadow approaches me and from close up I notice her profound sadness, something that frightens me a little; the hour of this belated kiss has arrived, of this long kiss that will extend into the walls, into the grout between the floor tiles, I suck her lips to collect her bitter taste, of saltpeter; I hug her with a light movement, inviting her to leave, I want to rid myself of this kiss without surrender, I see her solidify, petrify, the statue moving with slow steps, crosses through the door, disappears; the air in the street seems pleasant to me, the freedom to walk without a destination, but your voice reaches me again, Chachi, like a wound, the torment of your sentence: you have to stay here and I have to leave for the other studio; I throw my voice in to the deep hole in my chest so as not to call you, so as not to shout out your name while your Mediterranean eyes move away from me; I have to return, I return, I slip through the narrow angle of time, through the wide angle of time to establish a dialogue, to continue a dialogue and I tell myself, you see, this earth becomes too small to separate us; I'm in New York, between glass windows, asphalt and the advancing years to return to this century of ours, to our favorite village, the one of the Sing Sing of Ethel and Julius Rosenberg; I begin waking up and I tell myself firmly that I've heard you say: this is all part of growing up, to learn not to leave when I want to stay by your side, to learn that sacrifice is something so sterile, to learn that it isn't our turn to live on a desolate earth; or perhaps you didn't say it, Chachi, because of so many things that you already know, because of so many truths that today I save to dream a little more, to dream that space has opened so that we can travel it, our hands entwined, without this tiredness that overtakes me so suddenly